I0693027

Safe Journey Trilogy

An Adventure in Sydney Australia

Hugo Vaes

Safe Journey Trilogy – An Adventure in Sydney Australia

Hugo Vaes

Facebook.com/authorhugovaes

Copyright © 2015, 2015 Hugo Vaes

Published by: epubli GmbH, Berlin, Prinzessinnenstrasse 20

10969 Berlin

Germany

Phone: +49(0)30 617 890 200

 Email: contact@epubli.co.uk

www.epubli.co.uk

Printed by CreateSpace, An Amazon.com Company

Available from Amazon.com, epubli GmbH and other book stores

Available on Kindle and other devices

ISBN is: 978-3-7375-7643-7

This is a work of fiction but based on a true story. Names and characters, events are either the products of the author's imagination or used in a fictitious manner. Any resemblance to actual persons, living or dead, or actual events is purely coincidental.

Print on demand in Germany by epubli GmbH.

Printed by CreateSpace

DEDICATION

In memory of my dear mother and grand mother who I miss and dedicate this work in their honour.

Table of Content:

Prologue

In a small and dark apartment somewhere in North Sydney a young Dutch girl was fighting for her life when she had a row with a man whom she thought was her friend. The fight started with some serious threats but she thought he wouldn't have the guts but then suddenly he became violent.

"Give me what I want and I will let you go!" "I can't. You know that if I would give you whatever you want from me I can never leave this country and I want to go home. I have enough of you and your country."

Suddenly she felt his hand hitting her face hard and she went down. He grabbed her by her long hair and punched her hard in her face. She tried to defend herself but he knocked her down to the ground. Vaguely she could hear him laughing while she wanted to cry.

"Get up, bitch! Get up or I will kick you!"

She laid still on the floor and felt his boots hitting her body. He grabbed her by her hair again and noticed she was bleeding. In panic he let her go and saw her head hitting hard the old wooden oak floor.

A rush of panic hit him and he didn't know what to do. Was she dead or did she pretend to be dead so he would stop hitting her. He went to far and it made him sick. He never hit a woman that hard. The only woman who got some beatings was his wife when he had some fights over money and drugs. This was different and he felt very guilty. He was afraid one of his neighbours might had called the police as they made a lot of noise earlier in the evening.

He looked around and checked if he didn't leave to many clear marks behind in the dark apartment. He never checked her pulse as he thought she was dead. She looked dead and in his eyes he pretended he killed her. He had to leave and run away as far as he could without leaving any traces. He was from that moment a marked man. The police would start searching for him and see him for a sick murderer. He would probably end up in jail where other prisoners would punish him for killing a young and innocent Dutch backpacker who came to Australia for travelling and some adventure. He was the last person who saw her alive and he was responsible for her death.

Very quietly he left the apartment and ran away from the apartment block till he found a phone box. There was one number he remembered and dialled. All he hoped now that the person on the other side of the line was willing to help him as he had helped him before many times. He just wondered how many of his old friends would help a murderer when he's on the run.

"I need your help. I think I might have killed her."

"Where are you? Is there anyone in your neighbourhood?"

"No, I can't see but I am not sure." "Did someone hear a thing before you ran away?"

"I don't know but I fear the cops are searching for me."

"Keep a very low profile and don't shop up near the place."

"Where can I go?"

"Take a long break and leave the country. They

can't follow you if you're away and don't act suspicious. They will look for clear signals if they will cross your path. Try to be honest but deny you have anything to do with whatever happened tonight. Stay cool and stay away."

He hung up and looked in the darkness for a cab. With a bit of luck, he found a cab driver who brought him all the way from North Sydney to Eastern suburbs of Sydney. In Bondi the cab driver dumped him on the big parade and drove away.

One week later he said goodbye to his wife and left a successful hostel and business life and went on sailing on the Pacific Ocean for three long months on a big yacht with a couple of friends whom he knew from his childhood. He hoped the sailing trip would clear away all his problems but when he returned months later in Sydney his whole life had changed for ever.

01 Introduction to new friends

"Julia! Julia! Where are you? Can you please come to reception?" She heard her name while she was busy with cleaning a filthy looking kitchen that hadn't been cleaned properly for at least a few years. The usual cleaner had the night off and when he was on he did a lousy job. The chef was already leaving town while she was left behind in the dining room and kitchen dealing with the mess what was left behind by a bunch of lousy backpackers and overseas students. None of them had any manners and didn't care much about others.

Although she was part of the backpacker's gang she wasn't as bad as they were. At least she got a job and did her best in keeping the place clean and tidy while others were still looking for work or just had a great time.

"Julia! Julia! Can you hurry up! I have someone who wants to meet you!"

Julia sighed when she heard her name again. She inspected the kitchen what looked better after an hour of cleaning. It still looked awful but not as bad as it used to be. At least she did her best in cleaning it properly. She wondered how it would be the next couple of days when the other cleaner had to deal with all the mess.

Julia donned her working apron pulled up her dirty pants and straightened her t-shirt before she showed her face in the reception. All she knew it was Robby her Aussie friend and room mate who was alone at the reception desk who helped her with this job. Without Robby she wouldn't be working for this guesthouse in between Bondi and Tamarama Beach at the eastern suburbs of Sydney.

"Julia. At last you show up." He shouted with joy. "What took you so long?"

"Have you any idea how filthy that kitchen is? It is just a wonder that they haven't inspected this facility and I can tell you without me they would close it down."

"That shouldn't be your concern, Julia." Robby replied. "There are so many businesses and they can't inspect all of them. I don't think they will come soon so take it easy. I know what you mean."

Robby did. Before he started to run the reception desk in the evening he used to be doing her job while Julia was still a free person. She took over his job when the normal receptionist on a Sunday ran away from his work without a reason and never showed up again. He disappeared without a trace and left behind a big gap and trouble.

"Robby, what is so special to meet me while I still have lots of work to do?"

"I want to introduce you to an old friend. He owns a motel in Surrey Hills and we know each other for many years. He helped me when I was desperate and I helped him when he started his own little guesthouse in Clovelly. I learned him all the tricks of the business to make him a successful manager."

Robby pointed to a man who sat quiet on the two man's comfortable coach opposite the reception desk in the reception area of the lobby. He was smoking a cigarette what was against the building regulations but he didn't care. He didn't show much respect towards this form of hospitality what he had wasted a couple of years of his time by running one in Clovelly.

Konrad stood up and inspected Julia. She was tall, quite thin but not too thin. He paid close attention to her clothes what looked messy but then he remembered the job she was doing. No wonder her clothes looked so messy after he heard her complaining about the filth of the kitchen. He looked at her face and her smile. She looked friendly, she showed a nice smile but she looked at him with not much interest. She was trying to read his mind while he did his best in reading hers. She was different than the usual kind of backpacker he had seen before. She was totally different. She was clearly no backpacker but a traveller. He had seen them before but she did her best not to show she was wealthy.

"Hi, I'm sorry that I was a bit rude. I'm Julia."
"Good evening, Julia. Where're you from?"
"Holland. And you?"

She spotted his slight German accent. The longer she stared at him she more could see he was half German, half Austrian with some Polish blood. His grey hair was cut very short, he wore an old dark leather jacket and dark grey pants. He looked smart but not too smart. He wasn't wearing a tie and a jacket but his shirt looked smart enough. He looked more like a manager than Robby who was dressed in a polo shirt and some old jeans that had seen better days. Robby had long blonde curly hair tight back in a ponytail. He looked compare to Konrad shabby and wasn't very representative towards customers.

"So, you are Robby's new friend, am I right?"

"We share a room and he helped me with this job, yes."

"But are you his new friend?"

"Sort of. We share a few common things but yeah, I am his friend."

She took a seat next of him and ran her hand through her short bristles. Her dark hair was cut very short but it had been much shorter a while ago. She didn't look feminine and did her best not to be feminine. She was that kind of girl who liked to be a tomboy.

"So, what did bring you all the way from Holland to Australia?"

"I always wanted to make a long journey and Australia is one of those countries I wanted to go so here I am."

"How long have you been here in Australia? When did you arrive? What's your next destination after Sydney? Have you seen anything yet of the country?"

"Not that long if you want to know and yes, I haven't seen much of the country but I hope will. That's my big plan anyway. All I can say on my first week I went for a day to the Blue Mountains. I arrived here in December 1999 two weeks before Christmas Time and celebrated the New Millennium in the city with thousands of others where I watched the best fireworks show in the world."

"Yes, that was a quite a good show. So have you seen much of Australia yet?"

"No, I haven't been to Melbourne although I was about to go when Robby asked me to stay a bit longer for a while and as you can see I am still here. I hope one day to leave this place and do a bit of travelling through the big country."

"Yes, you should go and travel like all the others. So my question to you and please don't see it as an insult but are you are a backpacker like many of the other young folks that arrive and stay in these kind of places?"

She nodded and saw how his expression in his face changed. He wasn't keen to hear from her that she was like them a backpacker. That meant she wasn't rich and only took this kind of job so she could travel. He had seen them before when he owned his own little hostel in Clovelly.

"Tell me, Julia. Are you one of those cheap shit backpackers?"

"No, Konrad, she isn't a cheap shit backpacker." Robby shouted while he did his best to defend her from the sudden attack from his friend.

"Don't call her that. She has more class than the ones you want her to refer too."

"It's ok, Robby." She replied. "I travel with a backpack and yes I am a backpacker but I am not cheap shit if that is what you think most of them are. I do have money and I am not a poor backpacker but a quite well financed traveller. Besides many of them work hard and save as much as they can so they can travel for quite some time in Southeast Asia. I just want to do the same thing what they all do."

Konrad wasn't impressed with her explanation but didn't continue in offending her. He would see and meet her again so he would have enough time to learn her better.

"Anyway, Robby. It's good to see you again. It has been a while ago. I hope I can come often to have some time with you."

"Good evening, Konrad. Hope to see you soon again. I should be around most of the evenings. At least I am here every Sunday and Monday evening."

Konrad stood up and left the Bondi Lodge guesthouse while Robby and Julia both looked at him. Julia returned back to the kitchen where she finished her work while Robby continued with his work at the reception.

An hour later Julia reappeared again in the lobby with two mugs of coffee and took a seat opposite of her new friend Robby. She hardly knew the guy but she thought she could trust him and didn't mind to share a room with a man she hardly knew.

"What was this all about? Why is he so rude when he heard I am a backpacker? Doesn't he like them and what have they ever done to him if I may ask? How do you look at them? What is your opinion?"

Robby took a cigarette and offered Julia one. She was a social smoker and only smoked occasionally when people offered her cigarettes. She bought a big pack of cigarettes on the airport together with a big bottle of The Glenlivet Scotch whisky so she could share it with others. She was after all a very social person.

"I know my friend for a long time and we were both hostel owners but he didn't like his clientele while I had a very good time with them. I had once the best hostel in Sydney but nowadays this is where I work and live. I lost so much. I will tell you my story later when we have more time. You will love it and you wished you were here a few years ago when I was still running my hostel."

Julia thought of her flight to Australia and how she came with the crazy idea why she wanted to travel to Australia. She could have travelled for some months in Europe but it was close to home and she wanted to make this once in her lifetime crazy long trip so she could tell others how much she loved to travel.

Australia was always a big journey for so many people. Her friends were jealous as she made the trip but she learned most about long distance travelling through an aunty and her elderly sister who had been here before. She told so many interesting stories that it intrigued Julia to make her own long journey to the East.

02 First meeting

"I can't stay any longer in that place. I can't work for him any longer. He's treating me like a slave although he pays me well but still he treats me like an animal. He has no respect for me."

"Stay a bit longer till it right to leave. You just cannot walk away from him now. Not now he will suspect you immediately."

"Whatever we plan now we will see us as his prime suspects and he will hunt us down. If we are smart what we are we can make his life miserable so, he will become a suspect instead of being a victim. He knows he's not following the law and if we can have him caught with his pants down he can't hunt us as he's a suspect too."

In a dark little Italian restaurant on the Campbell Parade in Bondi Beach Paul Shackle told his associate Valery Tubbs that he couldn't stay any longer in the motel he was working. The place was a very busy motel with fussy guests who paid top dollar for their stay. The place was reasonable cheap for a motel. It provided some extra services where the customer paid cash in US dollars as soon as they checked in. No one actually knew what those services were but they paid them.

Paul took a sip of his wine and looked at Val who tried to eat a bit. She wasn't very hungry and ate a little bit. The food wasn't bad but she wasn't hungry at all. She hardly eats daily and drunk more alcohol than she should do.

"How's the hostel?"

"Oh, that place is a complete dump. I don't know how much longer I can keep it open. I have hardly any guests and the ones that stay don't want to pay. I might close it down sooner or later."

"Is it worth any money?"

Valery looked around and observed some other customers in the restaurant. It was busy and the staff all foreigners were working hard for their wages and their tips. The busy restaurant reminded her to the good old times when her ex used to run the hostel on his own. He helped lots of stranded backpackers to jobs in the area as he knew so many restaurants and knew the owners always needed staff. He was that kind of guy who helped others while no one helped him when he needed help when he returned from a sailing trip. Not even his wife helped him and did her best to dump him hard.

"I don't care. How much does he have by now?"

"I don't know but it must be at least half a million US dollars, that's almost a million bucks. You still are thinking of changing ownership?"

She nodded and stood up. She headed towards the toilets while Paul ordered another bottle of red wine. He looked for a moment to the table and saw the 5 empty wine bottles next of the two plates of food what was hardly touched by both of them. It was more a drinking party than a meal they both had.

"Sorry about that." She said when she returned to her table.

"No, it's ok. So you're still in?"

"Yes, I can use that money like you but I don't care what would happen to him. He didn't earn it so he has no rights to claim he earned it fair what he never did. So if he wants to create a fuss we should do something that can stop him from hunting us down."

"What would you suggest?"

Paul was in. He was ready to screw his employer and wanted to hurt him as hard as he could. He believed by taking a box full of money what his employer kept in a closet back in his house he could hurt him hard. he knew that money was his kind of pension funds but he didn't pay a single buck as tax so he was breaking the law.

"First of all I will have to run away from him and find refuge in the wine valley. I know a few good places where I can stay for some time. From there I can create a plan and call you for another meeting. Only then we can arrange a date and tell you how we should succeed my plan. It should work and he will be furious but we have to be very smart. We have to find a way so he won't be able to follow us and stop him from following his own path. He will try to run his own investigation as he has no trust in our police force. You should hear him talking while he trains with them every Saturday. That guy has no respect to anyone and he doesn't care. For that reason, I like to punish him hard."

"That we shall and will do."

"I guess we have a deal then. You should go back to that place and pretend to be a good worker so he would suspect you. Just do your job but nothing else. And please take it easy on the booze and drugs. If we want to succeed we have to be sober otherwise we can never do it."

"No, problem. I can take it easy but I still have to pretend to be a drinker and a drug user. Otherwise he will suspect me."

"Use only when he's close on your lip. Just take it easy. That's all. Call me when you think we should execute our plan."

They broke up their dinner meeting. Paul left before Valery while she paid for the food and the wine they both consumed. He took a taxi back to the motel where he lived while she walked back to her old hostel that she used to run with her ex whom she threw out a few years ago. From that moment the place was no longer a success and the place was falling to pieces and looked more like a dump than a successful hostel.

03 Going to Australia

The long and big adventurous journey to Southeast Asia and Australia started for Julia Meier on a cold damp and windy December morning in1999. Together with lots of other passengers on the cold damp and windy platform of The Hague Holland Spoor she was waiting for the Intercity train from Flushing to Amsterdam Central that would lead her to the International Airport Amsterdam Schiphol.

It was early in the morning around seven in the morning when she stood there with her big heavy backpack on her back and her small day bag hanging on front of her while she stood there waiting on the platform. Some people were watching at her when they saw the heavy load she was carrying. Better her then me they thought.

The night before she met some old friends in the hotel where she stayed the last couple of days before it was time to hit the roads. The night was cool and she went too late to bed while she remembered herself she had to get up early to catch her train and her flight to Sydney Australia from Schiphol Amsterdam International Airport.

She was still a bit intoxicated while she stood there a bit clumsy with her cup of coffee and a little snack in a paper bag waiting for a train that would bring her to the airport.

In the far distance she noticed some yellow and blue coming towards her. It was the Intercity from Flushing Zealand to Amsterdam Central where the train would terminate. It was the train she was waiting for together with so many others and waited patiently when it stopped on the right platform. She stood near the open doors and was one of the first passengers who boarded the train. She found a quiet place where she could dump her luggage and could sit till she would arrive at the airport. It would be her last train trip in Holland for the next couple of years so she wanted to enjoy the short trip from The Hague to the airport. For the next couple of years, she would be surrounded by warm weather and plenty of other young backpackers who had the same idea as her.

The big plan of going to Australia started a couple of years earlier when she worked in the heat of Majorca where she tried to earn some money in the hard world of time sharing. It wasn't really her cup of tea but it was a job and as the job add said it was easy money as long as you worked very hard.

She didn't like the job but she did it as she felt committed to the contract she signed and worked for at least three months in the blistering heat of the Mediterranean sun on the Spanish holiday island Majorca. It was a test case for her. If she could succeed here she could succeed anywhere else. Living far away from friends and family was hard but if she wanted to go to Australia and Southeast Asia she had to learn to live on her own in another country.

Julia passed the tests but it wasn't easy for her. She did the job twice and was more successful the second time. She used her time well during the second trip to Majorca. After a period of four months working for a time share company she found work in a small grill bar where she worked first as a kitchen hand but later on as a cook. It was her profession and she loved what she was doing. She saved money and made her future travel plans. If she worked hard enough she could finally go to Australia.

Luck came sooner but there was a sinister side of her luck. Her dear grandmother who looked after her when her mother died suddenly when she was only 15 years old passed away after she gave up life and starved herself to death. She was heart broken when she learned the news far away from her family.

No one in the family actually knew how wealthy grandma was. She lived a good life even when she had a very hard and bitter period in time during the Japanese occupation of Dutch East Indies. For five long hard years had she lived with her family in a camp and she had seen horrors she never could tell to her beloved ones. No one knew what she had seen and had experienced. Her mom was there as a young child and grew up in that hard period. She told as much as she could remember about the Japs and how bad they were to the Europeans and the locals.

Grandma married a man who earned his money in Indonesia when he worked for the Dutch Paket Maatschappij. After the war and when Indonesia became an independent country the company became PELNI and used for many years the old ships built and used by the Dutch.

When Julia returned back from her stay in the Baleares Majorca she was suddenly a wealthy young woman. Now she could travel to Australia as she had enough money for such a long trip.

Before she left Holland she found a job in Amsterdam lived for a while with her sister before she moved to a small place just outside the capital of The Netherlands where she stayed till two weeks before she would leave the country. She started to plan her long trip and made a long list of items of what she might need for her long journey.

The last two weeks she lived in The Hague where she arranged all her travel gear her visa for Australia and her travel money. Dressed in one of her new travel pants and shoes she waited for the intercity train coming from Flushing, Zeeland where she lived for many years with final destination Amsterdam Central.

She was no ordinary poor backpacker but had the looks of a flash packer a well funded traveller. Thanks to the heritage of her late grandmother she finally could make a journey to Australia what she always wanted to make but never had the right funding. She worked hard and saved a lot but her main travel plan was for many years constant out of reach. The limit was high but she saw it as a challenge what she now finally got achieved.

The train appeared and people made space for the passengers on board who wanted to leave the train. She managed to find a space for her big backpack and herself before others filled the train. She drank a coffee and had a pecan nut cake while she waited for her train on the platform.

"Where are you going?"

"To Australia and Southeast Asia."

Julia smiled when a young student took a seat opposite of her. She was in a cheerful mood as she would finally go to the land of her dream; Australia.

"Wow, that's a long trip. How long will you stay away?"

"Around two years if God's willing."

"That's very long. What will you do in Australia? Do you have that working holiday visa?"

Julia shook her head. That was the only thing she

couldn't get but still she was allowed to enter Australia on a double six months' visa but she wasn't allowed to do any work or study whatever she could study.

"No, the Embassy gave me the wrong visa. I asked specific for that working holiday visa and I have enough money to fund myself for this long trip but the person who signs and stamps the visa's thought I don't need it. A bit annoying but what can I do. At least I can still travel for twelve months in the country."

"Planning to find work and work without that visa?"

"No, unless I find someone who can help me. The future will tell."

She liked the guy opposite of her. He reminded her of her ex. It was hard to break up a long and serious relation but in the end it was the only way. If she still would be with her lover she wouldn't be in a train going to the airport where she was about to catch a flight all the way to Australia. She might be with some luck travelling to Asia but her boyfriend would always be in her neighbourhood. She wouldn't be able to do things on her own.

"What do your family think of your travel plan?"

"I have some good support from both my father and my sister. She went a couple of years ago to Australia and had an amazing time. She met her husband during her long trip and now they are a happy couple with a baby."

The young guy left Julia when the train stopped at Leiden Central. It stayed for fifteen minutes before it went further to the next destination; the international airport Schiphol Amsterdam. She got out and headed towards the Departure floor.

A month before she left Holland she booked and planned her big trip. In Alkmaar she paid a visit to a specialised travel organisation Australian Backpackers where she booked a special travel deal. They offered her a big list of options and of airlines she could travel with but in the end she decided she would fly with Cathay Pacific. It was a cheap option and perfect matched for single travellers like herself. Some of staff members of Australian Backpackers had done the same and had flown with Cathay Pacific.

Julia had one slight problem but that didn't seem to be a big deal for the travel agency. Not every traveller would be able to receive their flight tickets to their destination so it was no problem for Australian Backpackers to send Julia's flight tickets to the airport where she could have collected with the help desk of Cathay Pacific. Many others used this service and it was free of charge.

Julia wondered a bit on the airport when she found the service desk of Cathay Pacific and the check in counters. There were a few other passengers queueing up while she walked to the service desk. Two members of staff greeted her and were ready to help her.

"Good morning. I come her to collect my flight tickets. They are under the name Meier, Julia Meier."

"No problem. let me have a quick look and see if your tickets are with us. Your flight is today?"

Julia showed the member of staff a printed copy of her flight and her booking. The staff member read it and checked a small stack on the desk. Weird, it should have been there but there was nothing. She checked again but still couldn't find it. Her colleague helped her but couldn't find them either. They checked the flight manifest and found Julia's name on it. She was due to check in but no package was there waiting for her.

"I'm so sorry but your tickets aren't here. Are you sure they weren't sent to your address?"

"No, I don't live there anymore and have no longer access to that address and I asked Australian Backpackers to send it to the airport. They said that was fine. They offered that service to many others and no one ever complained. I assume that they made a mistake."

The colleague overheard Julia and searched straight for the phone number of the specialised agency. She got through and discovered that they made a dreadful mistake and would send it by courier to the airport before Julia could board her flight.

"Good news. It's still there in Alkmaar. They will send it to the airport. Why don't you check in and when you board your flight one of us will give you your tickets so you won't miss the other flights. Otherwise when you land in Hong Kong pay a visit to our Customer Service Desk and they will be ready to help you. We have all the details in a computer so you can contact us in

Hong Kong or in Sydney your final destination."

Julia was pleased with the good news and went together with the staff member to the check in counter. She put her big backpack on the band and showed the flight attendant her passport and her printed booking. A couple of minutes later she got her passport and documents back together with two boarding passes. There was no need for her to check in again in Hong Kong although she was permitted to enjoy a 12-hour layover in the old British colony what was a country on it's own.

The flight to Hong Kong was a long one but luckily for her she had no one next of her so she was able to stretch her legs during the long flight. She slept nearly eight hours' rough but it could have been worse if it was a fully booked flight. She wouldn't be able then to sleep comfortable.

In Hong Kong she had a long layover what came handy. Australian Backpackers were so kind to book a guesthouse for her so she could sleep a couple of hours more in a normal bed and was able to have a shower before she would enjoy another long flight from Hong Kong to Sydney, Australia her final destination.

In Alkmaar the staff explained to her that most of their customers preferred to have a long stopover as they all suffered a nasty jet lag. In Hong Kong, Singapore and Kuala Lumpur Australian Backpackers knew a couple of good guesthouses and booked a day for their customers when they booked a flight with either Cathay Pacific, Singapore Airlines and Malaysia Airlines. The stay in the guesthouse was for free as it was in the price included. It was just a form of good service.

The guesthouse wasn't easy to find and run by an old Chinese who couldn't speak English. He knew about her booking but he wasn't very helpful to her.

Julia was at least glad she could sleep for a few hours and had a shower. The room was small and hot. As soon as she opened the little window she could hear a cacophony of sounds that came from the tower block. A quiet room in a guesthouse in Kowloon was impossible but the bed was good and so was the shower.

Before she went back to the airport she made a long walk through Kowloon and saw the busy and crazy streets of this part of Hong Kong. She came to the waterside close to the Peninsula

Hotel where she could see the rich part of Hong Kong Hong Kong Island.

She took a few photos before she caught a bus back to the airport where she was fast through the check in and waited to get boarded for her next flight to Sydney, Australia.

04 Robby's nightmare

Before Robby went off for a long sailing trip to the Pacific Ocean he had to end up a relationship he had with a young Dutch girl. She was a simple young but quite poor girl who lived with him in a rented apartment in the north of Sydney in Hornsby. Robby rented the place out while she signed for the whole thing. He used her till she had no more money and hell broke out when she tried to do difficult. She wanted to leave and go back to Holland but Robby didn't want her to leave. He wanted to keep the place as his when he would be back. He had a hard feeling that his wife was up to something. Their marriage was at an end and his hostel was no longer his. She took control of the business after a range of complaints from young female backpackers. Robby was a bit too popular and thought he could do whatever he liked with them but this series of complaints made it impossible for him to function as the only manager of the hostel. Valery was ready to take over the place and it was time for some big changes.

In a small apartment in the north of Sydney a fight broke out between Robby and his former girlfriend Suzie. When they met everything months earlier everything was hunky dory but after a couple of months later she wanted to leave him. Robby didn't want to hear it from her and demanded her to stay in the apartment. She refused and found time to buy a flight ticket back to The Netherlands when he got really angry. That moment he showed her his real face. He had enough of her and wanted to get rid of her but she didn't want to leave the way he asked her. She refused to do whatever he told her to do and for that reason the fight ended in a dirty fight where there was only one winner.

He looked at her while she laid down on the floor with her face facing down on the filthy floor. Blood was everywhere and he inspected his own clothes and hands before he could walk away from her out of the apartment. He wasn't sure if she was still alive. he couldn't hear her breathing but then he didn't care. He walked away from her and left her alone in the filth and couldn't be bothered if she was still alive or dead. The only thing what mattered him were his fingerprints and other marks that might be left behind in the building. If the cops would show up and she was dead, they would call in forensics to check for prints and other specific marks what could point to his presence. He had to make sure they weren't there.

The only thing he could do was cleaning the place and to check if he didn't leave any mark behind. He couldn't have it if the police would find his DNA. He didn't want to find his name ending up in the big computer system of the Australian Police Databank

Robby walked out of the building with rubber gloves on his hands. He was so scary to leave marks but he had to hide them when people passed him on the pavement. Luckily it was dark and late at night when he searched for a public phone where he could call someone he could trust. There were only a few people in Sydney whom he trusted.

It took a while before he found a phone box that was still working. He remembered a phone number and dialled it.

"Konrad, I need your help. I think I killed her."

"What? Who did you kill? What's going on? Where are you?"

"In Hornsby. I had a fight with my girlfriend you

know the dumb blonde one. We argued about money what she didn't want to give me although she promised me she would pay me for all the services that I have done for her. She suddenly attacked me so I had to hit her and hit her so hard in her face and stomach that she fell over. She went down and never got up again. there's a lot of blood and I am afraid the police might find some DNA of me so I think I am screwed."

He could hear Konrad thinking while he looked around. He was sweating and he was afraid for being caught. A police car drove by but the coppers didn't see his sweaty face what he kept covered from them.

"Call the cops explain what happened and that you found her in your apartment. Say it was an accident but don't give them to much information. Don't give them your name or number. Let them find out who did it and don't ever do it again. Stay away from Hornsby and never ever talk about it with others. I will see what I can do for you but it won't be much. One other thing uses a public phone and don't hang around. Maybe someone might have heard what might have happened so stay away from the crime scene and keep a low profile. I suggest leave town for a while before you should show up again. By that time, they might have forgotten what you have done and don't talk to anyone about what you just did. Don't call me again. I will see what I can do but don't expect I can solve your problem. If you're lucky you can escape prison but in future, it might haunt you. Stay away from women and never ever tell them what you did."

Robby nodded and hung up. He took a taxi back to Bondi and planned a long sailing trip to the Pacific Ocean. He was an experienced sailor and was able to sail a huge boat on his own. He knew several sailors whom could help him with a yacht while he could escape the craziness of Sydney and of a crime he just committed.

It took him a week to sort out a boat and replacement for his hostel. His wife would take over the business with some help from a group of young Israeli backpackers who stayed for some time already in his hostel. he told them his plans and left for three long months Australia. What he didn't know was the plan to throw him out and to bar him from his own hostel. As soon as he was out on the sea they turned their back on him and screwed him hard together with Valery.

Valery his wife saw a good reason to end their marriage. She had enough of all the bullshit he was telling their guests and how great he was. She sold his flat and froze his accounts and cut his credit cards in half. She changed the locks of the hostel and wiped his name off the business and made sure he wouldn't get his business back forever.

When she sold his flat she had to get rid of a lot of collectible toys what he was investing his money. Just before he showed up again after three months of sailing she sacked the Israelis and threw them out of her hostel. She changed all the accounts and transferred all the available funds to her own account and made sure there wasn't a buck left for him.

Robby found out he was skint and homeless when he reappeared in Sydney after three months. He tried to get some money from an ATM when the machine ate his card and didn't give him any money. He tried all his cards and got constant the same treatment.

He tried to call a few guys he knew but none of them answered his call and left him alone on the streets of Sydney. He tried to call Konrad and

even he didn't help him while he had helped his
friend when he started running a hostel in the east
of Sydney in Clovelly. None of his friends
wanted to help him what made him angry and
very frustrated.

05 Loosing it all

Robby had the worst night in his life. After three long months on the Pacific Ocean he had a wonderful sailing break what he so desperately needed. The long break did him good but not on all counts. As soon as he arrived back in Sydney he couldn't use his credit cards and got stranded in his own city with no money. None of his friends were able to help him and left him alone.

Konrad was too busy with his own career and spent more time in his motel and had no time for Robby. He helped his friend a lot in the past but there were moments Robby had to sort out his own problems before he would ask for help.

In the end it was his young friend and fellow collector Anton who offered Robby some help. He knocked on his door when he looked like a homeless guy what he now technical was. He didn't want to live on the streets and he wanted his friends to help him. Why couldn't they help him while he always stood up for them. Life wasn't fair and none of his old friends shouldn't treat him like dirt. He didn't deserve this treatment.

Through the little help he received from his friend Anton he moved to a friend's hostel where he could stay while he managed in finding some work. The money wasn't great but at least he earned a few bucks so he could pay for his bed. He was off the streets and was ready to meet his his ex.

It was three months after he got back from the sea when he paid his wife an unwelcome visit to his old hostel. She was now in charge and hadn't spent a buck in maintenance. The place looked wrecked and was in a very bad condition. Lots of windows were cracked floors had holes and the place was slowly falling to bits.

"Robby, what are you doing here?"

"To take over what I left behind." He replied when he found access to his old office. He tried to open the safe in the office but noticed the code was changed.

"You don't belong her anymore. This is now my place and there is no space for you. Please get out or I will call the cops."

"Val, I am sorry I left you so long but I needed that break. You know I promised you I would come back so we can run it again like we did in the past."

"Forget the past. You are no longer welcome and I don't want to see you again in my life. About our relationship that's over. I am no longer your wife."

"No, don't divorce me."

He cried like a baby but she ignored him. A hailstorm broke out that night while he was in his old hostel. The guys who ran it while he was away were around but didn't speak to him. Valery didn't want them to see her ex and threatened them to throw out if they tried to make contact with him. She wanted to punish her ex for all the years they had been together.

"Robby, I learned a lot while you were away. I know you steal from our guests. I found some records in the safe and I will use it against you. I know your good friendship with that German fellow."

"You mean Konrad? What has he got to do with me?"

"Quite a lot. I know about your little scheme. It's

over. I froze your accounts and cut your cards in half. Don't try to reopen your account. It's blocked and don't try to talk with the banks. I can report you to the Authorities for fraud and theft so that will destroy your future."

"You wouldn't dare."

Val walked to her little office and came back with a thick folder full with files that shouldn't be left behind. She had all the evidence she needed to prove to the courts what her ex was doing to his own guests. She had him right there by his balls and he couldn't do a thing.

Robby was furious but he couldn't be angry at her. She was right. He did some bad things while he ran his hostel but none of his guests ever complained. He continued till the day he left Australia for a period of three months on a yacht in the Pacific Ocean. Now he had nothing and he couldn't have access to his money that was blocked.

"What about my apartment? What have you done with my house?"

"I sold it and threw away the rubbish inside." She said without a smile on her face. She looked serious. "Oh, I met that fellow you did business when you bought all those toys. I gave it all to him so he can sell it to other crazy fanatics. I told him not to sell anything to you. If I were you I would leave Sydney and never come back. You are no longer welcome in this city. Forget Bondi. I still have a seat in the Council and I will make your life miserable if you try to disobey me."

She shouted and suddenly she turned her back on him. He left the little office and swore he would take revenge when he would ever get a chance. Their friendship and relation was over.

Robby walked out and got hit by hail as big as golf balls. He didn't see a hole on the corner of his old hostel and Jacques Avenue and fell hard on his back. He damaged his back and tried to call for help. No one came to help him. For a couple of hours, he got soaked by the hailstorm till it was over.

By some luck of faith, he found temporary refuge at Noah's Guesthouse where he could stay for a couple of days to recover. The owners knew Robby and did their best to help him. Robby was very bitter after the treatment his ex gave him when he paid her a visit. She had done her best to destroy his life and career. He had to start all over again what was hard for him. He wondered if he would ever get back to the life and career he loved so much. He liked the work and life in guesthouses and had a long and successful career. He managed to get his own hostel as one of the best hostels in Australia in one of the travel guides from Lonely Planet. His ex did her best to destroy his career and his old hostel. She was wasting money instead of earning money.

Robby had to start looking for work so he could earn enough money to pay off some debts he had with old friends. None of them wanted to help him. He lost through that sailing trip everything he owned and had to rebuild his life again.

He remembered the previous owner of the Bondi Lodge. When he still owned his own hostel he helped the old owner with some maintenance jobs when someone else could run the desk for him. It was in the time when he had enough trustful guests who didn't want to screw him while he screwed everyone. He was a crook and a thief but also a very handy guy who didn't mind to help others so maybe one day they would help him.

The Bondi Lodge changed of ownership and now

two men took over from Mr Michael Lenski, who used to own and run the place for 25 years. Now it was in the hands of two inexperienced owners who thought they could run it.

All the old staff stayed and some new faces appeared. Although they had no one for maintenance the name Robby Henson appeared regular on their desk and he was asked when he showed up one day to do some odd jobs to keep the place running. It was for Robby a way to get back to normal work and back to hostel business. Within a short period of time he would be back where he loved to be; the reception of the hostel being the face of the hostel.

06 First time in Sydney Australia

Julia arrived early in the morning in Sydney after a long and a bit delayed flight from Hong Kong where she had a long layover of at least 12 hours.

Again she had no one next of her so she could sleep on board the almost empty Boeing 747-300 from Cathay Pacific. She arrived rested in Sydney where she followed other passengers on arrival.

The first hurdle she had to take was immigrations. At least she had a double six months' visa sticker in her passport so she was able to stay a long time in the country before she would have to leave for at least a week before she could return and could continue her journey in Australia. She had already flight tickets for New Zealand but that wouldn't mean she would go there. Time would tell but for now she focused herself on her first day of arrival at the airport of Sydney, the oldest city of Australia.

"Good morning. What's your purpose of your stay in Australia?"

The immigration officer checked her passport and noticed the special visa she had. It was not a working holiday visa although she was still in the right age category. Strange that the Embassy in the Netherlands didn't give her that visa.

"Travelling." Julia replied.

"Are you planning to do some work?"

"No, I don't. As you can see I don't have the right visa so I won't be able to search for work but I have enough money on me."

"Please, don't try. If we find out, you have been doing some work we can detain you and bar you from this country."

The immigration officer was clear and very strict.

Julia nodded and waited till he stamped her passport and gave it back.

"You should have applied for a working holiday visa. Normally they give it to every young student who wants to work and travel here in Australia."

"Believe me I did but the embassy in The Hague made the mistake and they couldn't change it."

She received her passport after the officer stamped it and wished her a nice pleasant stay in Australia. From immigrations she had to look for the luggage band to retrieve her big backpack before she could pass the other hurdle; customs. Every passenger had to go through customs where they checked every bag the new arrivals were carrying. No new arrival could ignore them. They just waved at everyone and took now and then their time when someone carried a backpack or too much luggage.

"G'day, Sheila. Could you please put your luggage on the table and open them for us so we can inspect them?"

She smiled put her bags on the table and opened them. One of the inspectors from customs took his time while the other paid close attention to the little form she had to fill in on board the flight due to arrival.

"Sorry, Sheila. How much money do you bring in to Australia? You should know if it is more than ten thousand you have to report this to us customs for clearance or you will be charged. Let me remind you that if you ignore the charges can be higher than if you just play ball."

Julia nodded and showed him what she carried. The officer was only interested in the cash money and not in the traveller's cheques. He waived them and counted her money. He used a calculator and checked with the current rate how much Aussie dollar she had with her. Just within the limits but very close.

"You're lucky. A few dollars more and we had to charge you. You can go. Have a nice stay in Australia. Open an account for your own safety. Most backpackers do open an account but I guess you are with one of the few major travel organisations, don't you?"

Julia nodded and repacked her bags, she hid her money safe in a special pocket in her travel pants under the suspicious eye of the customs officer and was cleared to go.

Australian Backpackers was part of a bigger travel organisation Travellers Contact Point that had several offices in London, Sydney, Melbourne, Brisbane, Adelaide and Perth. They even had a few offices in New Zealand as plenty of their customers made journeys to New Zealand. Many of the young backpackers went there for work and travelling. They were the lucky ones with the special working holiday visa for New Zealand. Julia applied for that visa together for the working holiday visa in The Hague but she wasn't lucky to get any of them.

The headquarters of Travellers Contact Point (TCP) was in downtown Sydney. They were based on the seventh floor of one of the major bookstores in Australia; Dymocks and the building the bookstore was named; Dymocks Building. TCP was a major player and many new young backpackers used their services. TCP provided lots of services including pick up from the airport to the hotels from where they could go anywhere they liked. The first two nights were paid and were in some decent hotels spread out over the city.

Pete was waiting for two girls and was there since early in the morning. He was part of TCP and his job was picking up new arrivals although he didn't pick them up every day. There were days that someone else did his job while he could enjoy some time with his girlfriend.

It was still to early for him while he sat alone at a table that contained several empty coffee cups and some leftover crumbs of a muffin. Now and then he looked at the arrivals door but he saw no girl he was supposed to pick up. He had no idea who Julia was and how she looked like. All he knew she flew from Hong Kong to Sydney and her flight had a delay of just more than an hour. He received that news a bit too late when he was already on his way to the airport. It didn't matter. He loved to hang out on the airport and had so his coffee and breakfast.

Julia finally walked through the doors of arrivals and looked around. She paid attention to all the guys with names on boards but none of them had her name. There was just a moment that she saw a sign with JULIA printed on it but it was a different woman. She was fifteen years older had much longer hair than she had and looked quite fancy. She was at least wealthier than Julia and didn't carry a backpack.

Pete noticed the man with the sign and moved a bit from his chair. He saw Julia or at least he saw a girl with a grown out long bob and she carried a backpack on a trolley. He stood up and walked towards her.

"G'day, mate. You must me Julia. Julia Maier?"

"Yes, I am." She replied and showed Pete a big smile. "And it is Meier but I forgive your pronunciation."

"Just wait till the other showed up so I can bring you both to your hotel. Do you want a coffee or something else to drink?"

"No, thanks. I am fine."

Pete had to pick up two girls. Julia was the first and a few minutes later a young girl with very short curly hair showed up and walked straight towards them. It was Emily who arrived from a flight of Bali Indonesia. Her long big journey started in Indonesia before she travelled to Australia.

"Hi, you must be my pick up from Travellers

Contact Point, am I right?"

"Yes, I'm Pete and I am here on behalf of TCP. Welcome in Australia, Sheila's." he showed a big smile and noticed how the two girls met each other.

"Hi, I'm Julia from the Netherlands."

"Hi, nice to meet you. I'm Emm. Emily from London, England."

Pete liked the way how they got on together. He did his best to introduce them to each other so new friendships would start immediately on the arrival. Although they looked different they had a few things in common. They were both young backpackers and used both TCP and they liked each other. He liked it when people made friendship straight on arrival.

"Emily, do you want something to drink or do you want to go straight to your hotel? Julia said no but perhaps you want a coffee or a tea?"

"No, thanks. I'm fine."

"Right, let's go then, girls. Just follow me so I can bring you to the Y in the Park, your temporary home for the next couple of days. I have some welcome packs that you should read when you are there. If you have any questions, please pay a visit to our office in George Street. We are on the seventh floor of the Dymocks' Building. It's a big bookstore but there are offices from the second till the eight floor. We have the seventh all for ourselves and we would like to see you when you have time."

He took them to an old rusty and full with stickers covered minivan. He helped them with their bags and drove away towards the city. Julia sat in the back while Emily sat next of Pete. He smiled constant when he looked at them. He liked them and had a feeling they both would have a great time in Australia.

"Do you carry lots of cash on you?"

They both nodded. He grabbed two folders that laid on top of the passenger's site of the dashboard. He gave one folder to Emily who gave another to Julia. "My advice is open an account as soon as possible. You are using our address if I am right so you can use that when you open an account with any bank here in Sydney. I would advice open an account with the

Commonwealth Bank of Australia. Nearly every backpacker has an account with them and they offer the best service and have interesting packages for you guys. It's up to you but there are other good banks so look around and open an account. Commonwealth Bank is by far the easiest bank but First National are a good second one. There's a branch near the Y in the Park and many new arrivals have used them to open an account. Just show enough ID if you have it on you. With in a week you will receive your bank card so you can use it when you want to do some shopping. We have some interesting shops and malls. You will have a great time here in Sydney."

He drove them all the way to the oldest part of Sydney; The Rocks. It was there where the ships of the First Fleet arrived and started the penalty colony of Australia. At Dawes Point they had a nice view of the skyline of the city. In the distance they could see the most famous opera house designed by a Danish architect Jorn Utzon; the Sydney Opera House. When they looked up they stood underneath the famous Goat Hanger bridge; The Harbour Bridge.

 "We offer every new arrival a free day trip on

the Parramatta River so you can see our lovely city. With TCP you can book trips in the country, city trips and we can even help you with cheap flights to Southeast Asia. We have doctors so if you think you would need some jabs for the countries you want to visit pay a visit to our docs get some consultation before you fly."

Emily and Julia looked inside their welcome pack. There was a lot of information so she would be busy with reading for the next few days. First she wanted to rest. Julia felt a bit tired. She suffered jet lag and was not in the mood for partying. Emily didn't suffer any jet lag. She came from Bali where she spent two weeks on the beach before she would be reconnected with her boyfriend. He was already in Sydney and she hoped to see him as soon as possible.

"Right. I guess you both want to go to your hotel. Get in so I can bring you to the Y in the Park. There should be a bed ready for you. We reserve some beds for our guests and we offer discount rates if you plan to stay longer. Just say you are with us."

From Dawes Point he drove into George Street; the main street of Sydney. From The Rocks they landed in the CBD of the city. They passed Dymocks and the office of TCP. Pete pointed to the old building before he passed it. They both looked at it and memorised it. At Liverpool Street he turned left and pointed to a big park on the left. He looked at Emily.

"Like you we have our own Hyde Park. It's open every day and a good place to chill out. We have plenty of parks but this one leads into the Botanical Gardens and the Domain. Do visit when you can. There are some old historic buildings you should go if you are interested in our history."

From Liverpool Street he turned right into Wentworth Avenue and stopped in front of a big hotel; the Y in the Park. It was a YWCA part of the YMCA hotels anywhere in the world. They got out. Pete helped them again with their heavy backpacks and carried them into the lobby of the hotel. He walked to the reception and helped them with check in.

An hour later Julia laid finally on her bed and slept for a couple of hours before she spoke again with Emily. She was constant on the phone next of the lift and talked with her boyfriend. She wanted to see him and wanted to introduce Julia to him and his best mate. She didn't know if she had a boyfriend back home or were single. All she tried to arrange was a good night together with her friends and a couple of beers to welcome her in Australia.

At five in the afternoon Julia woke up and had a shower. She changed her clothes and met up with Emily downstairs. Emily was dressed to kill in a short tight skirt and a tank top. Her short curls were styled with lots of gel and she wore make up something Julia hardly used. She wasn't so girly although she had a few dresses with her.

"Do you fancy a beer and meet my boyfriend?"

"Huh, I don't know. I just woke up and still suffer jet lag."

"Oh, you get over. Just come and have some fun. They are not far away from here. There's a sports bar on George Street and they are there. Just come, please."

Julia sighed but in the end she joined her new friend and had a wonderful evening together with Emily and her friends. The bar was near the hotel and she passed the nearest branch of

Commonwealth Bank. George Street was the main street in Sydney and lots of things were to be found. There were bars, restaurants, shops and other businesses she would see visit and deal with. There were three cinemas next of each other. It was the most important street in the city.

07 Konrad the motel owner

Konrad never thought he would run his own motel in a city like Sydney. His parents weren't wealthy but he learned to work hard to achieve his goals in life. He went after five years of National Service to the university where he studied hospitality management. He found work in some five star hotels in Vienna Austria where he lived for some time. From one top hotel he moved to other top hotels were he learned the tricks of the job.

He was in his Thirties when he met his first future wife. She was an Aussie and liked him. He was in for some adventure and played along with her. Soon enough they got married and they moved to her home country Australia. Life was hard for Konrad. His English was not so good then but he worked hard and learned the language in a short period.

Robby was one of the first persons who became a friend. He was the owner of a successful hostel/ guesthouse in Bondi and helped him with running his own hostel in Clovelly. Although they were competitors they were good friends. When Robby's hostel was full he referred guests to Konrad's hostel and reverse.

Konrad's wife got pregnant what he didn't mind but she wasted her child with crap talk about Konrad's past. She didn't like Germany nor Austria and talked regular negative about the two countries. The relationship suffered but he stayed with her till he got what he aimed for.

When she asked him to move to Australia and to

have an easy life on the eastern suburbs of Sydney she promised him Australian citizenship what he could get after five years.

Five years long he ran a hostel in Clovelly what did well but not as good as Robby's. He was a smart guy and found different ways to make money from his cheap guests. He didn't mind they were not all wealthy but Konrad disliked the backpackers in his house.

Robby learned Konrad a trick to make easy and fast money without getting caught. The scheme was simple and easy. He learned over the years that most of his guests actually didn't pay much attention to the bills they had to pay for staying in a simple hostel. All they wanted was a cheap bed and to stay as long as possible. It was the simple trick of hidden costs that didn't exist but were easy to claim.

"It's very simple, Konrad. Just create a simple cost and you will see they will pay it. Even they don't see what it is they are stupid enough to waste a few extra bucks on nothing."

"Did someone ever discover what you were doing?"

"No, and even if someone would find out I would throw him out and blacklist him. When you are long in the business and know more hostels you can play a dirty game with these fuckers. I had to do it a few times and warned some other guesthouses for them. They never returned to Sydney and they couldn't prove a thing that I did something wrong."

Robby was very convinced in his new successful business. He made lots of money and invented regular new fake costs and hid the money in a special safe together with a notebook where he kept all his notes. His wife knew nothing and had no idea he was stealing money from his guests. They didn't notice and paid whatever they had to pay.

"Konrad, I can make you a rich man if you try this in your own hostel. Don't tell your wife. Just keep it to yourself."

"You know, Robby. I will divorce her as soon as I have my Australian passport and citizenship. Till then I shall be a good husband and a ruthless hostel owner. I shall charge them for everything and keep the money for myself. Hopefully I can earn some good bucks so I can start my own motel. I found an old motel in Surrey Hills and hope to get the funding so I can run that instead of this crap business."

Konrad found a partner who was willing to fund him and to help him with running a motel in Surrey Hills. His ex wife had no interest in him and didn't want any share of the old hostel he put up for sale. He used the money as start up capital for a motel together with the money his new partner lent him. A couple of years later his motel was a big success and he earned more money than Robby with his hostel. His new customers had more money to spare and were better and friendlier. That they were gay it never bothered him. At least these were guests that didn't mind to pay for things and soon found out they were actually easier and better to skim. He created a new scheme and made a fortune while his partner knew nothing.

Konrad had years of experience when he worked for some years in Europe. He learned all the tricks in the job in Switzerland, Austria and Germany where he worked for only five star hotels and studied hard to be a manager. he met through his work lots of rich gays and heard them talking about Australia. He heard of a small motel where they always stayed but the place needed proper management.

As soon as he got all the money to buy the property he cleaned the place and threw out all the poor folks who shouldn't live in his motel. He borrowed money from a few banks and earned the money back after he redecorated the place and gave it a modern and fresh look. The old clientele changed to the ones he remembered from the days he was working and studying in Germany.

The prices went up but to his big surprise none of his guests ever complained about the price they had to pay. They got what they wanted. Clean and spacious rooms with Pay on Demand films and most of all; privacy. They could do whatever they liked to do in their rooms as long as they didn't take drugs or smoked inside. He kept a blind eye on alcohol but smoking inside his building was not allowed except in his office.

Konrad managed to get his motel filled every night and had an occupancy rate of 75 to 85 %. The place made money and through that it was time to earn more through a sophisticated scheme what he had learned from Robby.

He remembered how Robby made a few hundred

bucks a night while he could make more. He had to be careful but he found a way to increase his revenue without writing it down in the books for his wife and the authorities. The new revenue would be his pension funds and he would keep it for the first months safe in a locked box in his office. He later removed it when he got caught by his only in-house employee who saw he was stealing money from his guests.

Konrad learned from that moment that he had made a big mistake by employing Paul for his front desk reception. The kid threatened him so he had to pay him lots of money to keep his mouth shut and made a deal. He would employ him even when his working holiday visa expired and sponsored him till the day he would leave. Till then Paul would be his only employee what a top salary and a room and all the amenities he would find in every room.

08 First couple of weeks in Australia

Julia stayed the first couple of weeks since her arrival in the Y in the Park. She moved room after her free nights were over and got herself a better more private nice single room just a few floors higher. The hotel was busy due to the coming festivities but what she discovered during her stay that a lot of the people inside the hotel weren't normal guests but women with all kinds of problems. On her new floor she met a few women who ran away from their marriage and lived with their kids in this YWCA hotel. Broken families were a common thing and the YWCA was for them a shelter. Here they were safe. The husbands had no access to the place and the security was protecting them from ex husbands with very loose hands. There was a police station not far away and the police was aware of these situations. Luckily for Julia nothing happened during her stay in the hotel.

Straight from day one Julia and Emily went out every evening for drinks in a sports bar named after a well known TV series from the Eighties and Nineties 'Cheers' not so far away from the hotel in George Street. She and her friends were pleased she showed up every time. Although she didn't want to drink too much she joined them constant with every round but handled the booze quite well. The beer in the bar wasn't so bad and she only drank beer and no other funny stuff.

Emily was a bit of a weirdo. She was cool and lovely but also crazy. The day after their arrival in Sydney she went to a barbershop and had her head shaved. She wanted to be special and by shaving her head she would stick out in a busy crowd. She didn't mind. She hardly knew anyone in Sydney so she could do all the crazy things she wouldn't do back home. She had several piercings on her body and her face and she wanted to get some big tattoos. She was even thinking of getting a tattoo on her shaved head.

Julia followed Emily's new hairstyle two days later one day before she would go to the Blue Mountains. The hot and sunny weather and being so far away from all her friends and family it was time to do some crazy stuff. She loved Emily. She was a good friend and had lots of fun with her and her friends in the pub every night.

The night before she went for her dramatic haircut she talked about it with Emily while the boys were playing pool.

"I might cut my hair off. I don't know why but I want a radical change in my life."

"You should do it. It feels so smooth and my boyfriend hopes I keep it this way. I save myself a lot of money now I am bald."

Julia took a big sip of her beer. It was a Tooheys and tasted fresh and cool.

"Do you know any barber or hair salon in the area?"

"There's a big barbershop further in the street. They are very cheap and they do cut women. It will cost you a lousy six bucks but think about it how much would it have cost you if you would have it done back home?"

"I don't know. Never thought about shaving my

head but you inspire me to give it a go. What do I have to loose except for my long hair?"

Emily laughed. She understood Julia's concern. Her friends and family wouldn't understand why she would do such radical thing and hardly anyone saw some beauty in it. Now she was completely bald she didn't mind what other thought of her. The job was done and she was now completely bald and loved the feeling of having no more hair on her head.

"You have done it before haven't you?"

"Yes, this is not my first time. The first time was at uni a few years ago. Since then I keep my hair short and cut it when I feel it needs a cut." "

How often did you cut it?"

"Not regular but say every three to four months but then my barber cuts a lot off. As you may know and remember my short hair on the day of arrival I go very short; as short as possible and this look was the next step for me. You should ask if they can shave you smooth. It's such a wonderful feeling. Here touch it. See what I mean?"

Julia touched her head and noticed how smooth Emily was. She looked like a small skinhead very punk. Now and then people in the bar looked at her but never a nasty stare.

Julia walked along George Street on her way to Glebe. Every day she made a nice walk through the city. Now and then she took some photos but most of the times she just looked around. She loved Sydney.

Emily mentioned her about a big barbershop. Julia passed a big barbershop and saw the notice board on the pavement. MEN $5 WOMEN $6. An old man sat in front of the shop on an old wooden chair and noticed her interest in his business. She looked inside while she checked again the price list. Emily had her head shaved for only six bucks so they were quite cheap.

"G'day, Sheila. Can I help you?"

"I don't know yet."

She looked up and smiled to the old man. He got up and held the door open. He pointed to a few chairs. The barbers were glad to have a customer when she looked with great interest inside their business.

"You want a haircut, don't you?"

"I might, yes." She replied.

"Get inside. One of my barbers will deal with that hair on top of your head. We had yesterday a POME and she went very radical. Maybe you are interested in her new look."

Julia laughed and knew he was referring to Emily. Yes, she was now bald and she mentioned to Julia that she should shave her head. She wasn't so sure about this dramatic and radical look. Still she wanted a new look and didn't mind to go very short so she walked inside and took a seat in the chair near the big window.

"G'day, Sheila. How can I cut your hair?" An Aussie barber with a mullet approached her and caped her before she could change her mind. She looked in the big mirror while he combed her long hair.

"Just cut it off. I want to start fresh here in Australia with a complete new look."

"All off or just a little bit on top?" "I leave that to you." Julia replied.

Her Aussie barber with the mullet gave her a very short crew cut and cut most of her hair off at the sides and back only on top she remained a bit more hair. he used some different clippers and cut the sides and back close to her skin leaving nothing but stubbles. At least she didn't look as bald as Emily though she lost a lot of hair.

"Satisfied with your new look?"

"It's perfect. Just the way I want it."

He removed the cape and let her go. She paid the old man who smiled when he saw Julia's new hairstyle. She looked like a boy so short was her hair but she didn't mind. The new look matched with her clothes and her brave appearance. She was a lone traveller and didn't want to look too girly.

The next day when she went for a day trip to the Blue Mountains she received mixed remarks about her new look. Most of the guys liked her but the girls in the group weren't impressed with her new tomboy look. Only one Japanese stayed near her but she couldn't speak much English so she couldn't have a nice conversation.

Her tour guide picked her up early in the

morning. She just finished her breakfast and was ready to go. They drove though Sydney crossing Glebe and drove over the ANZAC Bridge. He told them why it was called and it was a remembrance of the First World War when Aussie and Kiwi troops fought together in the southeast of Europe in Turkey.

Julia had seen the ANZAC Memorial in Hyde Park. She went to see the Hyde Park Barracks where new arrivals stayed in the 19th Century and early 20th Century. It had been a prison. It was one of the buildings created by the first settlers of the new nation. It was then a penal colony but some lucky ones joined the long trip and started a new life.

The tour guide promised the group some long walks. He stopped the minivan when they went for a long walk of a few hours to see a waterfall three rocks sticking out from a cliff what were known as the Three Sisters. He told them a few stories of the rock formation. Julia listened and took most of the time the lead with the walks. She loved to be in the countryside and although it was very hot and sunny it was a bit cooler where the guide took them. She stopped suddenly when a lizard blocked her path. They all gathered and took photos of the creature. Julia smiled while the guide asked them to be quiet and just walk with some distance from the poor creature.

After the first walk they went to see some kangaroos. There was a park where they could see them and be close with these native land mammals.   The afternoon he drove them further into the Blue Mountains and took them near Katoomba. There they walked again till they reached the scenic railway. They had a barbecue lunch between the two walks. The second walk was lighter and shorter. From the scenic railway they ended in Katoomba where they had a final drink in a pub. The view from the little train was amazing. The train was used for moving the ores they dug out of the mines near the little mining city.

Julia was too tired to go out when she got back to the Y in the Park. Emily missed her presence but she respected her decision. The day trip was an awesome trip but it would be one of the few trips she would have in Australia. Not knowing then that she would stay and life for a whole year in Sydney.

09 Second Meeting

Paul saw Valery some months later again in a small Italian restaurant in Bondi near her place and the house of his employer. The table was filled with a couple of wine bottles all empty except for one. They both drank their share and had a discussion about Paul's employer.

"I say we have to move fast. He knows I am onto something. He suspects me and keeps a close eye on me whenever I am in the motel."

"What do you know, Paul? How much money does he have right now?"

"I would say close to a million. It can be more but it can also be less so I have my doubts about the right amount he collected from his guests. Lately we had a very good long weekend full house. As a matter of facts the motel was full for the last couple of weeks so he made a nice fortune only from those last couple of weeks."

Mardi Grass was again a big success for the city. It attracted lots of tourists, all kinds from all over the world to see and experience the big Gay Society in and around New South Wales. Sydney was the place and Darlinghurst/ Paddington was the scenery. It was even used for a film.

Paul suddenly looked Val in her eyes. His eyes were troubled and there were some things that were bothering his minds. He had to say it to her.

"Val, I can't stay much longer in his motel. I have this feeling that I should go soon. I have to run away and never to come back."

"Right, do you know where you will stay if you would run away from him?"

"Oh yes, I know a couple of farmers up in the Hunter's Valley. They know some of the dealers where I get my drugs from. They told me if I needed ever a safe place to hide the farms in the valley are the best place. Cops don't come there. They are not welcome. IT's a different society and the farmers protect each other. They don't like city slickers like Konrad. He is no match for them. He might be a glass a combat warrior but he is no match to these bunch of farmers."

"Where does he keep his money? Does he keep it in a safe like Robby used to do in his hostel? Is it in a safe in the motel or does he have a safe in his house?"

 "For all I know he has a little safe in the motel but he only uses that for the money he receives from his guests who didn't pay him by card. Most payments for staying in his motel are done by card. I saw a while ago a metal case what can be locked and it was open. It was filled with US dollars. I caught him a short while ago when he was skimming a couple of guests. He was counting big bank notes after he ripped of these poor guys. I saw he put the skimmed money in a special metal case what he keeps in a cupboard what is always locked. There is a locked cupboard in his office where I don't have access and if he guards the office with his dog so I can't enter that space. He knows I am afraid of his dog and don't try to hurt the dog. If we want to steal it from the office or his house, he will find out who stole his money. Don't underestimate him. He's not stupid but very smart and patient but also very ruthless. There will be blood in the end so we have to be smarter than him."

"Mention the name Robby. He would suspect my ex and it would keep me for a while of my back. He knows that Robby needs money and he's desperate. He will do an attempt in stealing money sooner or later. He's so obsessed with big wads of money. It makes him horny. It's like sex that's how he sees money."

Paul took a big sip of his wine topped up his glass while he shook his head. He had seen Robby and a weird looking girl near him during a Saturday on Mardi Grass weekend. They all looked as if they weren't so desperate in need for money.

"Your ex has a new fling. I don't know much about her all I know she's bald and looks wealthy."

"He likes European women. He dated a Dutch girl a while ago as if I didn't know it. He lived for some time with her and sucked her completely empty. So he has a new victim. I wonder how long it will take for him to suck her empty."

"Konrad offered her a job in the motel but as far as I know she rejected his offer. I wonder why. What does she know about him or Robby?"

"Don't worry about her. We can use her. I have to find out where she lives what she does and if I can talk to her. See if she can help us."

Valery was thinking out loud while she looked around. Paul filled up her glass but didn't order a new bottle. There was business to be done and he wanted to leave as soon as possible.

They both agreed to steal the case hide it somewhere safe and split the loot. the money would be more than enough to build up a new life anywhere in the world as long as it wasn't in Australia.

"Your ex works for a hostel in between Bondi and Tamarama Beach. It's called the Bondi Lodge. Maybe you have heard of that name?"

"I think so." Val replied. "I remember there was a house for overseas students ran by an old guy I forgot his name but all I know my ex knew him. He did some favours for the old guy. Robby knows nearly all the hostels in this part of Sydney but also on the north shore and in Glebe. He made a name and lots of the other hostel owners still try to stay in touch with him even now he's back in that place you just mentioned. I have to see it for myself. See if he recognises me."

"Val, I will be from Monday gone but we stay in touch. I have made my decision and I'll need space to think of a perfect plan how to get access to his money. We should meet somewhere else next time so we won't be so close from him. I call you when we should meet before we can strike. Till then if you don't hear from me I will be somewhere in the Valley on a farm setting up all the important preparations for the job. We might need a third person to do the job but not your ex Robby or his new fling."

"Oh, that is new to me. So he's seeing another woman, huh? What can you tell about her? What do you know?"

"Not much I'm afraid. All I know she was there when Konrad invited Robby and her to watch the parade on Oxford Street. She's new in town and she's from Europe. I forgot to ask her where she's from but I would say somewhere north in Europe where they speak English. Her English is otherwise very good."

"Good for her. About your move to the Valley. I am not sure if that would be wise idea still I'm glad you know a couple of guys in the Valley."

She thought it over and created a little picture in her mind. She could see him enjoying the good life surrounded by lots of good wine and smoking the best dope in the world while she would be sweating under the smoke of Konrad, who would go soon to her place after they succeeded the action. She could deal with him. She knew Konrad's weakness and she wasn't afraid of him. "Ok, it's a deal, contact me when you want to do it. I will see if I can find some extra help and I will see how we can get access to his house if he keeps it there. I wonder what he will do if one of his household is willing to help us. He can't kill his wife nor her sister. He's not stupid but he will go crazy when he ever finds out that one of them helped us."

"He will and he will probably throw his wife and sister out of his house. It is his house not hers so they don't have much rights. He will go after us before the police will start an investigation. If he does he will do his best to find us and he might probably want to kill us. The best thing we should do straight after our job is go to the police or just call them and report them that he wants to take revenge on us. We have to stop him as soon as possible before he will start causing trouble. That will be the only way to stop a monster like him when he turns evil and start to think he's John Wayne. Why on earth did they give him a gun license. The man is a smoking gun. You can't trust him that's for sure."

"Will he go after us?"

"Oh, yeah. At least he will search for me and he will try to kill me. That's why I will stay on a farm where I am safe. He won't go there. He might look for me but the farmers don't like people like Konrad so they will stop him. If he wants to do something stupid, he will pay a severe price. He won't go far with his guns. They have more firepower even it's actually forbidden but they have the rights to protect their property."

Valery paid this time the bill while Paul left before her. He took a bus back to Oxford Street where he took another bus to the motel. Konrad wasn't around, and so was his dog. That meant for him the metal case was now no longer in the motel but at home. His place was a fortress and it would be difficult to get inside.

10 Work opportunities

March was a month that changed Julia's life. She wasn't looking for work but didn't mind in helping others. If an opportunity would show up she would take it. Why not, there were plenty of travellers in the country working without a visa and still managed not to get caught. The system was in some areas easy to beat and the authorities didn't have the manpower to control everyone.

Julia's luck started on a Sunday when the receptionist of the day didn't do his job and even ran away. She came from her room when she saw young Kenny at the desk. He was behaving weird and didn't pay any attention to phones and people. He was drawing weird stuff on some paper when she walked down the stairs.

"Hi, Kenny. You ok?"

No reply. He didn't even look up. He kept on drawing when suddenly he stood up and walked out the door. She followed him and saw him when he stopped a cab and got in. In the background she could hear the phone and wondered what her new friend Robby would think. He wasn't so impressed with the staff of the hostel. If it was him he would sack them all although there were a few who knew a bit in what they were doing but the rest including the managers weren't capable in doing their job. He would run it alone and maybe use Julia as he saw enough potential in her. She didn't mind to do some work but if it wasn't possible she would still be happy and content.

Kenny never came back but the phone kept on ringing. Robby was very busy in the kitchen with the preparations of the Sunday dinner. He had lots of work to do while the ringing phone kept annoying him. Why couldn't someone pick up that phone. He sighed. He knew why. He never liked Kenny. The managers should never employ someone with a drug habit on reception. The kid had no experience and wasn't suitable for the job. Robby was convinced he was a much better person for the job but the managers preferred to have him in the kitchen wasting his time with cleaning up and helping the chefs.

Julia walked back inside and started looking for Robby. She knew he would deal with the situation as none of the other staff that lived in the hostel came to reception to pick up the phone. She passed the kitchen and saw him at work with creating a creamy potato salad.

"Hi, Robby. I was looking for you."

"Who's on reception?"

She could see in his face he was not in a good mood. The phone was annoying him as no one was there to pick it up. He didn't like young Kenny as he was always high on drugs and never did his job properly. Unfortunately for Robby the managers trusted him while Robby had better credentials than the young lad who had no work experience what so ever. Robby could at least say he had many years of experience in this kind of business what none of the other receptionists could say about running a hostel.

"Eh, I saw Kenny at the desk but he walked away suddenly."

"What do you mean he walked away suddenly?"

"Well, he was first at reception doing some art work while the phone kept on ringing. He didn't pay any attention to whatever happened so he never picked up and then without saying a thing he got up walked out the door and stopped in the street a cab and got in. All I asked him if he was ok. Please don't ask me where he did go as I have no idea what went on in his mind. All I can say he's no longer on the desk. No one is actually."

"I noticed that." He said with a loud sigh. "Right, I can't be doing this and running the reception. Could you please do me a favour and do the barbecue for today. I will have a chat tomorrow with the managers and see if I can get you a job here in the Lodge. We need proper staff and you would be my first choice."

Julia smiled and walked inside the kitchen. She put on an apron and started with marinating the steaks. She took a few oven trays and did the chicken legs added some salt and pepper and some herbs plus oil before they went inside the burning hot oven. She made some more salads while Robby went to the reception and remained the rest of the day at the desk.

The Sunday Barbecue was a big success. The guests loved the food what tasted better than what the usual chefs produced. Julia filled a plate special for Robby who had no time to go down the courtyard to get his dinner. He thanked her and told her to have a plate for herself. Unfortunately, the food went faster than she would have expected. Not a single thing got left behind. They ate it all without throwing it away.

From one job came a second. Cooking food was no deal for Julia but cleaning a filthy kitchen was a must. The working space was absolute filthy and shouldn't be open. She had worked before in the food industry and understood the importance of a clean and spotless kitchen. Unfortunately, the kitchen of the Bondi Lodge was following that principal. If some health inspector would show up suddenly he had all the authority to close down the kitchen and even the whole hostel.

Robby knew about the kitchen. he mentioned it a few times to the daily chef. He blamed the morning chef for the mess as he never cleaned his mess properly. He didn't and couldn't care. He was a lousy chef who wasn't actually qualified to be a chef. None of them were but the daily chef had some qualifications from his native country Germany.

Julia was opposite the Bondi Lodge in a small coffee bar when the managers had a big meeting on Monday morning. Robby was around and complained to them about the lack of responsibility as none of them was on call. There was no list of phone numbers so he couldn't report it that Sunday and even if he could the owners of the hostel showed not much interest in his behaviour.

"Thank you for your concern, Robby but this is our business. We do appreciate your concern and your actions. If you can see your friend tell her, we would like to have a word with her. Maybe we can offer her a position in the hostel but it's up to her. She can take your shifts while you can run the desk. We need someone who can deal with the reception in the evening when the day receptionist finishes his daily duties. That's all we can offer you for the moment."

"No managers job? I can proof to you that I can do a much better job than anyone else. Don't forget I ran my own hostel for many years and I never failed."

"We know your reputation, Robby but sorry. We have already two great managers with experience and they know what they are doing. If you have suggestions, you can talk to them. We appreciate your concern in the management team but for the moment there's no vacancy available. Please show the other receptionists how they should do their job and please keep everyone happy. If you know where your friend is can you, please ask her to come to the hostel so we can have a chat with her. She might be interested in the offer we have for her."

Robby nodded and accepted the new offer reluctantly. He got more hours and could work if he wanted nearly every day. They promised him 20 hours but he could work more. All he had to was writing all his hours down on a piece of paper and then gave it to the company accountant Felicity who did all the payments for all the staff members and the accounts for the hostel and the managers. They just signed all the pay cheques once a fortnight when it was payday.

"Do you pay me the hour rate that your receptionists get or do I still get paid the same rate as my previous hours?"

"We keep your hourly rate the same as it was before. In future we can have a look but for the moment we pay you fair for all the hours you have worked."

Julia was drinking a latte and had some simple breakfast in Barlevento. It was a tiny little coffee bar ran by a Puerto Rican woman Camilla. She was small but beautiful and was around while a few other girls did most of the work. Camilla lived upstairs of her place.

Robby walked in and took a seat next of Julia. He ordered the same as what she was drinking and searched in his pockets for his cigarettes. Julia offered him a cigarette from her own pack and joined him outside.

"They want you. They want to offer you my old position if you are still interested. They will pay you every fortnight and you will receive a pay cheque that you can cash in at the First National Bank here in Bondi."

"What about you? What did they offer you?"

She could read in his eyes he wasn't pleased with the deal but still he accepted the new offer. It was better than nothing and at least he got a job got paid and was now able to pay off his old debts.

"For the moment I will do the evenings till they find someone else. If I want to take a day off or better said a night off I have to ask who is available to do my shift."

"Congratulations." Julia said and gave him a big hug. "Well done. You got the position you wanted so desperately. Stick to it and maybe one day a better opportunity will come up."

"The kitchen manager wasn't around but when he shows up he will have a little word with you. I guess he wants to offer you some more shifts. Perhaps you can do the Sunday dinner. You made a perfect dinner last night."

"I know. Nothing was thrown away what I noticed what these students like to do. They loved my food and everyone was happy."

"Did you eat actually?"

"No, but that's ok. I am used to that. I am not upset and can live with it. That's the life of a professional chef, you cook for other and forget to eat for yourself."

Julia was surprised with the good news. She had done an amazing job but she never thought of getting regular work as she didn't have the right visa to work in the country. She wondered what they would say or do if they would find out she only had a tourist visa and not the working holiday visa.

"Robby, I have to tell you something. You are the only person I know and I hope I can trust you. I don't have a working visa so if they want to offer me a position I have to refuse it."

"No, you don't. I ran a hostel for years and I helped lots of desperate backpackers with work even when they didn't have a working visa. Get a sponsorship and you will be safe. Just trust me."

Robby knew the mazes in the law and made use of it. It was quite normal in the world of hospitality. He had years of experience under his belly. Sometimes you had to lie to get what you wanted.

Robby went back to the Lodge and had a chat with the managers. They created a position for Julia as they needed a new kitchen hand and the present one Matthew didn't want to work more hours. He was pleased with his five days' work and didn't want to work more shifts.

In the afternoon the kitchen manager/ chef showed up after he had to cook food for a sister hostel on the north shore of Sydney; Kirribilli.

One of the staff members had to do his work. She had to cook set up and clean the kitchen before he would be back. At least there was food ready so all she had to do was heat it up and serve it to the guests.

"Julia. Nice to meet you. I heard so much good news about your job you did for all of us yesterday. Thank you for doing our Sunday dinner. I couldn't be around so I am glad you managed to run the kitchen on your own even without a kitchen hand."

"No, problem. I love cooking and Robby couldn't be at two places so I offered my services to help him out. Without me I guess it would have been a bit of a disaster."

"A complete kitchen nightmare, I would say. You just saved the hostel from embarrassments I don't know what would have happened if you weren't available for that day. It would be one of the worst disasters I have seen in this hostel."

"Glad I avoided a real disaster. Robby was very clear in what he wanted to serve so I just followed up and gave the food some more flavour. I guess the people were glad to eat my food and finished everything."

"So you have no leftovers? What a surprise. Normally we always have some leftovers so we have to create something special with that. With veggies no problem I would make a frittata and with meat I guess a simple mixed stew."

The managers agreed with Julia. She offered her services on the right moment when no one else wanted to help and assist Robby with his work. He proved he was the right person for the reception. He mentioned it before when he asked for a more regular job within the hostel. He knew the business and was willing to do whatever was available.

"Julia, what do you do this Wednesday? Are you free to help me with a dinner in our hostel in Kirribilli?"

"Sure, what time do I have to show up?" "I will pick you up from here and we can go together. I can show you a bit more of my city. Have you gear ready. Maybe I will use you for more shifts. Let me first see how good you are."

Robby heard the good news and smiled to her. He knew she wanted to be active and didn't want to sit down constant on her arse. She wanted to work even without a working visa. He was the right person to help her and did what he had promised her when she helped him with his job.

Julia was waiting on Wednesday late in the morning for Terry the chef. He was a bit late as he had to come all the way from a different part of Sydney. The morning he had been doing the breakfast in one of the two homesteads where many of the overseas students lived. The home stay was in Petersham and he had to take a few buses to get to Bondi.

"Sorry I am a bit late. I had to clean the kitchen as no one wants to keep that place clean. Another problem for me, you see."

Julia nodded and it reminded her how much effort she put into her own work when she cleaned for hours the filthy kitchen on Sunday. On Monday morning the morning chef made it filthy again and had no regrets of his bad cooking job. He couldn't work in a proper kitchen but the evening chef was impressed with Julia's work. He liked her as she wasn't so lazy and wanted to help him with whatever he could use her for.

Terry and Julia took a bus towards Circular Quay

where they took the ferry to Kirribilli. It was a beautiful sunny day and a perfect day to travel by ferry. She saw the Harbour Bridge on the left side while on the other side the Opera House looked amazing by the sun that shined on the building. It was warm and they both stood outside. It wasn't so busy on the ferry and within fifteen minutes they were on the other side of the Parramatta River.

"Every time I go to Kirribilli I always take the ferry. It's a good way to see the city and I love the view on the water of the city skyline. It is so cool to live here."

"It's beautiful. There are still moments I can't believe I am in Sydney but when I see the Bridge and the Opera House I know I am right there. You can't fake them, can you?"

It was just a short walk from the little pier to the street where the sister hostel of the Bondi Lodge was. Glenferrie Lodge was just like the Bondi Lodge a busy hostel for both backpackers and overseas students. Most of the guests were backpackers while in Bondi most of them were students. There was a group of Kiwis and some European backpackers at the moment and Terry wanted to introduce them to her. He thought they would like to meet Julia.

"How often do you work here?"

"Most of the times. This is really my kitchen but I have a few chefs who do some cooking for me when I can't be around. At the moment I run short in staff as two of my chefs left the country and won't come back. I need someone I can rely on and don't mind to work a couple of shifts when I have to be on two places at once."

"Ok, I don't mind to work some more. Although I don't need the money I don't mind to work more shifts for you. I love cooking and I can deal with the stress in the kitchen. I will not disappoint you."

"That's what Robby told me. He likes you and it seems he knows you well. Good to have some good friends."

Julia met Glenda who was in a way the manager of the Glenferrie Lodge. She was a fifty-five-year-old grand mother who lived in the lodge. She had her room near the reception so she was always around. She and Lydia a Dutch rep of TCP were the main women in the lodge while they had company from Lenny the fat guy who worked for both hostels. Julia knew Lenny as he was the person who checked her in when she moved from the Y in the Park in December a week before Christmas to the Bondi Lodge.

"G'day, Julia. Nice to meet you. It's a pleasure to see a girl in the kitchen and not a mate. Hope you will like our little place. It's different compare to the hostel in Bondi."

"Yes, thanks for being here. Hope I will like it here and the guests will love my food."

Terry took her to his big kitchen. It was compare with the Bondi Lodge very clean and spacious. it had more tools pots and a big oven that was always on. Even the walking fridge was bigger with more food. Terry used most of the kitchen budget for his own kitchen before Claus the German chef of the Bondi Lodge while the other chefs had a tiny budget but didn't do much cooking than the two chefs.

"I was thinking of a pork roast served with some veggies tatters and a chicken casserole. What do you think?"

"Sounds good for me." She said while she started

with peeling carrots and chopping potatoes in cubes so they could be roasted in the oven. "What about vegetarians? Do you cook for them too?"

"I leave that to you. If you can cook something fancy, I give you green light. There aren't many but I guess we can cook always more veggies and do less meat but most of the guests love to eat meat."

Julia was no vegetarian but now and then she didn't mind to eat only vegetables. Robby was a meat eater. She remembered when she served him a plate full of her food that Sunday. He ate everything but he left a few veggies on the plate but none of the the meat.

Together they cooked for two hours. Terry did most of the work but Julia was able in creating a few dishes on her own and a desert what was not her speciality. Terry liked what he saw. She was good had the skills and kept her space constant clean. She was truly a professional.

At 4.30 pm he left her in the kitchen and took a cab to Petersham where he had to work again. The chef of that place refused to work for him and demanded a contract from the managers. They promised lots of new staff members they would receive a contract and paid for all the hours they claimed. Unfortunately, not all of them got paid for the right amount of time and even when they got paid lots of the cheques bounced back from the bank when they tried to cash them.

Julia wasn't worried about money. She had enough on an account back home in Holland and only she and her father had access to that account. She stayed in touch with her folks back home and wrote regular a big letter to them. She missed her family but she didn't suffer homesickness. This was a journey she wanted to do and couldn't fail. Her big sister made such a trip before and she enjoyed the time being far away from everyone. Now it was Julia's turn.

Julia kept on working till ten in the evening. She cleaned the kitchen before she closed the door turned off the lights and headed to the reception. Glenda was at the desk with a coffee on the reception desk. She finished her daily reports and took the keys from Julia. She didn't need to check the state of the kitchen. She had seen her at work and was convinced that everything was in order. Terry wouldn't have to worry early in the morning.

"How did it go?"

"Fine. Better than I actually expected. I love this kitchen and this place."

"Thank you. Move your stuff and live here with us. We like people like you. You fit perfect in our society here in Kirribilli. You will love it."

Julia nodded but she didn't want to leave Bondi. She liked the small beach and she would certainly miss the regular coastal walk from Bondi to Coogee beach. She walked nearly every day. The view was amazing.

"I love to but I do like Bondi too. I don't want to leave Bondi if you know what I mean?"

Just before Christmas time she had to make a choice with hostel she would stay during the festivities. She had the options of two hostels; Bondi Lodge and Glenferrie Lodge. After a short debate with one of the staff members of Travellers Contact Point she chooses for Bondi and that where she still was. It was hard for her to leave even when she almost booked a bus to Melbourne when Robby changed her life by asking her for some favours. Thanks to him she was still in Sydney.

11 Working at two places

Time went fast when Julia got more hours with both the two Lodges. Terry was glad to have a staff member that never protested when there was work. She worked more shifts in Kirribilli when he had to be for a couple of days in the other two places. Julia was capable in cooking on her own and didn't need a kitchen hand to keep the place tidy.

Robby was working nearly every day in the evening at reception. He didn't mind and did what he was good at. Through him all the guests paid their bills on time. He chased people up when they were due to pay rent and threatened them. Most guests feared him. He created a nasty reputation but the managers appreciated his work.

The first two cheques she received didn't bounce back when she cashed her fortnight pay. She paid a visit to the small branch of First National Bank in Hall Street in Bondi. The cashier took the cheque and recognised the signature from

Veronica the Company Accountant of the Lodge. She was a former banker and worked for that branch before the managers of the Lodge asked her to start working for them. Her new job was different than her previous but she didn't mind the change. They paid her well and she had full control in all what came in and went out.

Julia received a call from Terry on a Tuesday morning when he promised her some more shifts. He had to be for the rest of the week in Ashford and couldn't deal with two places at once. If she was able to run his shifts.

"Sure, I can do it. When do I start?"

"Come early tomorrow morning. I will ask Glenda to book a room for you and the keys of the dining room and kitchen. Stay there till Friday evening. I might need you for the Saturday but I think I can handle that day. I will let you know. I will call you tomorrow when you are in Kirribilli."

"Cool. I will be there."

She went that day to the city before she came back in the evening. Robby was alone at the reception desk and was glad to see her again.

"Julia. Where have you been. I received a call from Terry. He wants you for the rest of the week in Kirribilli."

"I know. He called this morning. He will call me back when I am there."

Julia checked to see the desk if there were any messages for her. None of the messages was for her. Robby passed only an old message but that reminded her that she would need a cab early in the morning to reach Kirribilli before 5am.

"Robby, can you book me a taxi for tomorrow morning. I need to be in Kirribilli before 5 am."

"No worries, Julia. For you always."

He liked Julia. He was in love with her but she wasn't with him. He was a nice guy but not a man she wanted to spend her time with constant. He was friendly and very kind but there were some dark shadows and she just wondered what he had to hide for her.

The next morning, she woke up very early. It was still dark but Robby was already downstairs at the reception desk. He never slept much but he was quite awake when she slowly walked softly down the stairs.

"Good morning, Julia. Your taxi is waiting for you outside. See you in a couple of days."

"Thank you, Robby. See if you can get a Saturday off so we can do something together."

She walked out of the Lodge and found her taxi straight in front of her. She got in and drove to Kirribilli. This time she saw Sydney from the Harbour Bridge and not from the ferry. The ride was smooth and within half an hour she was there in Kirribilli. She paid her cab driver and walked to Glenferrie Lodge. Glenda stood in the lobby when she entered the lodge.

"Welcome back, Julia. I got you a nice room opposite the kitchen where you can keep your stuff and can get changed. Here are the keys of the kitchen, the dining room and your room. There's a towel and if you need more just ask. Lydia and I will make sure you will have a great time with us."

Julia walked to the kitchen opened the door and turned on the lights. The stove was always on so that didn't need to be turned on. She checked her room and changed into her new chef's outfit. In her working clothes she went back to the kitchen and started with the main preparations for the breakfast.

She grilled a tray load of sausages, in a cooking pot she heated up baked beans she fried bacon on the grill and cleaned it afterwards before she started frying eggs. In the meantime, she boiled some more eggs

In the dining room she turned on the lights and set everything ready for breakfast. The little fridge was already filled with milk. She placed a few trays with mugs, plates and cutlery ready and put all the dried stuff out.

There was a heating element where they kept all the cooked food and she turned it on. Slowly she brought in the beans in a special tray, the boiled eggs, the grilled bacon following by the fried eggs and sausages. She put out six loafs of bread and kept another four ready for refill. The guests in Kirribilli ate like their fellow guests in Bondi a lot of toast in the morning.

The last thing she did was turning on the dishwasher. She fried more eggs but didn't cook more eggs or bacon and sausages. She made a small breakfast for herself and waited till the first guests appeared for their breakfast.

During breakfast Julia checked what Terry prepared for her. He understood she could cook but this was his kitchen and he was a professional like her. He didn't want to overload her with lots of work and cooked for the coming days many different meals she could use and still cook vegetarian meals as he wasn't good in that.

Halfway the breakfast she collected tray loads of dirty plates and cups and fried some more eggs. She put more bread out and refilled the little fridge. By the end of the breakfast she cleaned the dining room the kitchen and started with some preps for the night. At Eleven in the morning she closed the kitchen and returned to her room. For a couple of hours, she took a nap and started with the afternoon just after two.

Only Lydia and Glenda had access to the kitchen and could help themselves with whatever they needed. Julia took a few trays out of the fridge and made sure there was enough variety for the guests. She checked the vegetables and took out what she would need for the day. She used one bag of peeled potatoes and cut them in halves.

They ended in a tray dressed with oil herbs and salt before she placed them in the oven.

There was a big rice cooker what Terry claimed as the biggest cooker. It was a simple machine and did the job. She filled it with rice and water and a pinch of salt. Terry used oil but she left it out. She turned it on and left it doing its job while she concentrated on the big pile of vegetables.

At four she took a break and checked the dining area. She cleaned some tables turned on the heating system of the elements and put plates and cutlery out. In the kitchen she cooked her vegetables and made her special vegetarian dish. Between five and six she put the food in special trays and put them in the heating element in the dining room. At six the guests of Glenferrie Lodge showed up and filled their plates with her food.

She had to refill the trays till she had nothing. In the meantime, she started with doing the dishes and ate her own plate. Lydia showed up and touched Julia's very short bristles. There wasn't much hair left on her head after she had it cut the day before.

"Wow, like your new look. You look great, gal."

Lydia gave Julia a warm hug while Julia stared at Lydia's mob of hair. She had dark curly hair and she wasn't thin neither she was thick.

"How's business at the desk?" Lydia was the evening receptionist while Glenda was around in case she needed a break or wanted to check some things.

"Quiet right now. People are happy that you are here. They love your food."

Lydia had some of Julia's vegetarian option and loved it. Her food just tasted much better less oily than Terries. He wasn't a bad cook but he used too much salt and oil.

"Well, you have me for two more days before I go back to Bondi."

"Please, stay. I like you here and I know in your heart you like it here. The guys are nice and some like you."

Julia laughed and nodded. "I know. There are a few cuties among them. I wish we had them in Bondi."

"How are the guests there?"

"A bunch of arseholes. Most of them are students. We have a lot of Brazilians. Nice folks but in a group they all behave bad. There is one who is particular rough and thinks he's cool what he isn't. He is just a big fat arse but I can't say it to the rest of the staff. The German chef agrees with me so does Robby but none of the others are with me."

Lydia nodded and started to think. She heard a name that she heard through Glenda who knew him well. Glenda was long enough in the business and knew a lot of hostels and their owners.

"You say you know Robby, Robby Henson, am I right?"

"Yep, that's him. Why?"

"You should talk with Glenda. She knows him. She knows half Sydney if you ask me. She's long enough here and she's doing this job for decades."

"Hmm, I will when I think I want to know more."

"Don't fall for him. He's an easy going person

119

and he tricked other girls before but then he shows his real face. I heard some nasty stories about him. Be careful with him. Don't lent him money because he won't pay you back. He can promise you the world but you will never get get whatever he promised you."

Lydia left Julia alone in the kitchen and returned back to her desk at reception. Julia went to the dining room and started with cleaning the mess that was left behind by some guests. The mess was less than in Bondi but still some of the guests needed some lessons in behaviour.

At nine thirty she called her shift a day. She closed the kitchen and returned to her room. She changed her clothes and went to bed. She set her alarm clock and woke up before it went off. Another day started and was just a repeat of the previous day.

12 Third Meeting

Valery was alone in her empty hostel. There were still a couple of guys who paid peanuts for their stay and she hardly saw them. Now and then one showed up and paid for them all what wasn't much. She couldn't and didn't care. The phone rang and she picked up.

"Val, it's me. Can we talk?"

"Sure, I am alone so we can talk to each other."

She heard Paul's voice and sounded from a distance. He made a sudden move not long ago and found refuge at a farm. The farmers knew him and they were his drugs providers. They had a successful business in weed that they grew in a barn on their land far away from the cops. The police had no access on their land and even if they would show up they wouldn't cooperate with any investigation.

"Are you safe?"

"Couldn't be better, Val. I'm fine."

"Right, are you drinking and taking drugs?"

"No, not for the moment but when you mention it I feel I need to drink some wine and smoke a big joint. You should try the weed. It's pure quality. It's the best ever."

 "You can smoke as much as you want after we done the job not before."

Paul understood. The drugs and booze could wait. The loot was enough to make them instant rich. Still they had to perform the act what would put them in a danger ground. Their victim was not a person they wanted to meet after. He would go after them and he might kill them if he could catch them.

"We have to do it fast. I can't stay forever on a farm. For the moment I am safe but not for that long. Bare in mind that he knows I am gone and I will go after his precious trophy. That metal case is worth a fortune and he shouldn't keep it all for himself."

"No, but we have to be careful. I know he talks a lot lately with my ex. I can't use him for the job and so goes for that girl. She's very close with him. I spoke with the sister and she hates him. She wants to go back to Korea what her sister his wife doesn't want. She wants her sister to stay put and just do whatever he tells her to do."

"Can we trust his wife?"

"No, not really but I have more trust in the sister. I will have another chat with her and see if she wants to cooperate. We have to look it from there. We can only do it if she's on the team but I don't want to pay her for her services. She will be on her own and he might kill her if he knows she helped us."

Paul thought for a short moment and replied. "Do it. We need her and I need another pair of strong arms. What about your new boyfriend? Can we trust him?"

Valery was seeing another guy lately who was from Auckland New Zealand. He was big strong but not as bright as she was. Still she liked him and he loved to hang around in her quiet hostel. He had a room in the place and now and then they slept together. The relationship was still fresh but it would be a good test for all of them if he would join them on the job.

"Ask your lover if he's interested in a job. He will get a share but it will be less than what we both take."

"Don't worry. He will help you and will accept your offer. I will talk with him when I see him. See you soon, Paul."

She hung up and checked the building. There was no one around but still she had the feeling someone was listening to her private conversation.

Later in the afternoon she walked to Hall Street where she did her shopping. In the groceries she met the sister who was nervous when Val approached her. She still had her doubts if it was wise to get involved in something she didn't want to be.

"Can you help us next week Wednesday. I know you stay alone in the house with the dog so that is when we plan. Can you take the dog out for say at least fifteen minutes and leave one window open?"

"He will kill me if he finds out what you are up to."

"We can deal with his threats. We can report him to the cops for stealing money from his guests. I know it and so does he. He won't call the cops but that is what you should do after we got what we are after."

"You put my life at risk. Where can I go?"

"Back to your country. We will contact your sister and she will hear the truth before he can hurt you. All you should do is book a flight as soon as possible to Korea and stay put. He won't go after you. He will try to find me and my partner but he won't catch us. Call the cops. That will slow him down and he can't break the law. He knows what's inside and knows he stole that money from his own guests. I know my ex did the same and he's out without a proper job and money. I want the same happen to your brother in law. He will be a loose canon who will loose in the end everything. It's time for punishment."

The sister in law sighed. She was trapped. She wanted to go back home to Korea. She didn't like Australia. The people weren't as friendly as she hoped but she didn't have much money. Her sister had money but she got married with a monster. She didn't like him and feared him. He was such a brute at home and never treated her and her sis with any respect. They were just objects to him nothing else.

"Ok, I do it. I want to go back to Korea. Punish him as hard as you can but promise me that I will not have to suffer. I have enough of being here and want to leave as soon as possible."

"Do you have your passport with you or does he keep your passport so you can't leave?"

"No, I have it with me, always. He treats me as if I am illegal in this country."

"Whatever we will do go to the police and report the crime. We can deal with that. We better be in the hands of the police who will not kill us than in the hands of him. He will certainly kill us if he gets a chance."

"If you want to revenge your brother in law report that whatever he's missing that wasn't claimed properly and he stole it from his guests. I bet you your sister will throw him out of the motel and if she can out of the house. Maybe you two together can go back to Korea. He will not harm you. He will be hurt but what I know about him he has some sense of respect although it's not much but he doesn't like to hurt a woman."

"You don't know him. I do and I want to leave. I will help you. Call me on this mobile number. He doesn't know this number so I will be safe and I will use this phone to call the cops soon after you're gone. I won't call before unless someone else in the street sees what you're doing. Be careful. It's a nice neighbourhood but people observe each other."

Valery left and called Paul an hour later on his mobile. He was waiting for a call from her. He wanted to get his hands on his employer's metal case and spent whatever was inside. It would be more than enough and it would ruin his ex employer's life.

"Paul, it's me. It's a go. Let me repeat; it's a go." She spoke him a short message onto his voice mail and hoped he would understand.

Her new toy boy showed up and was in for some fun. He entered the empty place with a bottle of wine and two glasses and a little plastic bag with some smokes. He took a seat in the old comfortable sofa and rolled a big joint for both of them. He started with the big joint and passed it over to her.

"Where have you been? I need to ask you a favour, please?"

"Sure, baby. Enjoy this joint and have a drink."

He filled the two glasses and gave one to Val. She took the wine and enjoyed the joint. The drugs calmed her busy brains and she was quite relaxed.

"There's a job coming up and I need a strong man who can help me to lift up something very heavy."

"How heavy, baby?"

"I don't know but say around 30/ 50 kg. It's a big metal box and it is kept in a place where we have no access but soon we hope we will have."

"Ok, I'm in. I don't know what you want me to do but I will do it. How much will I get?"

She kissed her boyfriend and smiled. She took another puff on the joint and drank her red wine. She was in good spirits that evening.

"I can't tell you right now but it would be roughly a couple of grand's."

"A few thousand bucks? Wow. I do it." Charley Dobbs agreed with the assignment for the job and agreed with the payment. He was a simple and easy going Kiwi who did everything she asked him and took whatever payment she had in mind. He was the easiest guy she ever met and was actually much better in bed than her ex.

13 The problem of Konrad

Robby wasn't pleased with the regular visits from his good old friend Konrad. First he didn't mind but then came a moment when he got enough. He couldn't concentrate on his work and he smoked all his cigarettes without offering him some cigarettes back.

Konrad didn't like the people in the Bondi Lodge. He disliked students and was particular rude to the few backpackers who stayed for some nights in the Lodge. In his eyes they were just a bunch of cheap shit folk with hardly any manners all dressed like hippies and constant smoking weed. Robby knew better.

"Robby, where's Julia?"

"Why do you want to know where she is?"

Konrad searched in his pockets of his old suede leather jacket for his cigarettes. He saw Robbie's pack and stole one. Robby only sighed when he took a fag out and lit it in the reception area. "Could you please stop with smoking in the hostel?"

"Oh, I am sorry." He said and only laughed.

"Why are you here, Konrad? Don't you have work to do in your own motel?"

"Why do you want to work for this shit people? How much do they pay you and are you sure the cheques they give you don't bounce back from the bank?"

"How do you know about bouncing back?"

"I bank with the same branch and I hear from my

accountant."

"Well, you're wrong. All my cheques were cleared and even Julia doesn't have any problems either. She will be here soon I hope."

"Where is she actually?"

"Working for the other hostel on the north shore. She says she likes it there. It's more a backpacker's hostel than a student home."

"That was a big mistake from the managers when they took over this place. It was then already crap but now it's even worse. Look at the place. How can a student learn English if they are only surrounded by shit people who hardly or don't speak English?"

"Thank you very much, Konrad. You know I would have run this place much better if I could have more control and more power. Now they only trust me for doing evening and night shifts so the others can sleep and do nothing in daytime."

"Is this place making money or is it a sinking ship what it was then?"

"It does but not much. I would stop straight away with the students and let in tourists' backpackers. This place needs more backpackers and no shitty students who do nothing."

Konrad shook his head. He looked around and disagreed with Robby's plan. The building was ok but if he would run it he would change a lot starting with that pathetic kitchen. He would stop with giving free food away what no one actually liked and spend the time better on a proper chef who could cook. He wouldn't eat here anyway and made no attempt to have some food. He saw the crowd and that was enough for him.

"Throw everything out and start all over again. Clean this place up and only invite people with money in this place. No more cheap shit backpackers and no more students they don't have money as they are full of crap. Oh and stop with your free food. Let people pay for a meal or otherwise let them cook their own food."

"Why was my hostel so successful when I ran it alone?"

"Because they liked you."

Robby was for a very short moment silent but

then he gave Konrad his opinion. "Exactly, it was not that they liked me. I have to say there were folks who didn't like me but they never stayed long but my hostel was successful because I understood them. I knew what they wanted and offered them services that no other hostel could or did provide. For that simple reason I was the most successful hostel in Bondi and Sydney."

"But you lost it. How come you lost your hostel?"

Robby didn't answer. Konrad tried to read his mind but Robby was a hard and cool guy. He wasn't always easy to understand or to be read. He was quite misleading.

"So, how's your ex doing? I just wonder why she doesn't want to sell it. She doesn't invest any money in the property and every time I pass it on my way to work or home it looks so pathetic. None of my properties looked so pathetic as your old hostel."

"Don't mention it, Konrad. I should never have made that deal with those crooks and her who promised me they would look after my baby and see what they have done to it. Now it's as good as dead. There's hardly a soul to be found in what was then the best hostel in Sydney."

Konrad knew the story and wanted to talk about other things. He had something on his mind and he wanted to talk with someone he could trust. He knew Robby better than anyone else but it was still hard for him to trust the guy ever the long years of their friendship.

"I have a serious problem and I only think it will be worse by the day."

"Oh, what happened?"

Konrad wanted to answer when they heard a car stopping in front of the hostel. A door opened and a woman with extreme short hair got out and headed towards the door of the reception of the Bondi Lodge. Robby looked up to see who it was. "Evening, Robby, Konrad. Sorry I am a bit late."

They both looked up when they saw Julia standing in front of them in the lobby of the lodge. She looked stunning in a tight stretch dress and it was a rare moment she wore even make up. "Where do you come from? Where have you been?"

"I just come back from Kirribilli." She replied and put her bag behind the reception. "I had to work for three long days in Kirribilli and after my three days I treated myself on a good night of jazz and some fun."

Robby looked at her hair what was already shorter than before. He wasn't so keen on her extreme hairstyle but the dress made up. She looked sexy what she normally didn't and she even used make up what she normally didn't use.

"So how was Kirribilli?" Konrad asked who liked her outfit.

"Good. It was interesting and I hope I can have more of these shifts. It was very cool."

"Glad you liked it." He replied and even smiled to her. "Now you are here I can say what I wanted to say earlier. I have a serious problem and it might effect you both."

Julia and Robby looked up and listened to what he had to say. "As you may know I have an employee who lives in my motel. You both saw him at Mardi Grass."

"Was that the one who looked so stoned? He

looks like a druggie forgive me if I say so."

"That's the one. Yes, he was always stoned but the last couple of weeks he suddenly stopped taking drugs and drinking alcohol. Now he even stopped appearing and he's gone. Don't ask me where he is I have no idea but I feel he will be back sooner or later."

Robby wanted to say but Konrad shook his head. "No, Robby. I know what you want to say so I will say it. As you both may know I have a successful motel in Surrey Hills and I make lots of money. My occupancy rate is around 80 % what is high for a hotel/ motel. Normally it's around 75% so I am a few percent higher. I keep something in my house what I don't like to keep in my hostel anymore as he still has the keys of the place so I think he might want to break the door open of my office and tries to steal what I normally would keep inside my office in a locked cupboard. There will be his problem. It's no longer there as I moved it to my house where I keep it save in a locked cupboard in my own room. So, if he thinks he can steal it he will need the keys of my house including my room door but I doubt if he got a key of my place. They can't be duplicated and even if he managed to duplicate them I will change my locks soon so he won't get into the place where he wants to steal what is so special to me."

"What does he want to steal from you what is so special to you?" Julia asked.

"Money of course." Konrad replied. "If there's one thing he's always short of it is money. He wastes money like water. I don't know where he spent it on but every time it's payday he's completely skint and I pay him more than he should have. My wife cooks for him and even cleans his room regular. We both know he drinks and now and then he takes drugs in the room but then I could always rely on him. Nowadays I can't and I have a feeling he wants to rob me. He will do it but I don't know when."

"Can you stop him?"

"If I know where he lives yes otherwise no, I don't." Robby listened with great interest in his friend's story and he was already thinking what would upset his friend the most. He knew him better than anyone else and knew what he was while his ex staff member was still working for him. He learned him a dirty trick what made him rich in a period of time. Now he was about to loose what he collected over the years.

"How much do you made so far?"

"I can't tell you, Robby but it's more than what you ever made in total."

Robby whistled and felt a bit jealous. He wished he could set up a new scheme in this hostel but the owners and managers would miss out and slowly they would see he was skimming their business. He would loose his job and been thrown out of the hostel and prosecuted for fraud and skimming innocent travellers and students.

"I hope this is only a theory and nothing will happen but if it does you will know I will go after him and the ones who would be behind it to help him. I will find them and end their miserable life so they would be able to do it again."

"And what would you do if someone called the cops who will start an investigation?" Julia asked while she looked at Konrad. She tried to read his mind. "What would you do then?"

"Ah, Miss Julia thinks I will stop when they will show up and investigate my lost case, yes?"

He looked at her and shook his head. Robby saw the expression in Konrad's troubled face. He knew what he wanted to say.

"Don't trust them, Julia. They might look very respectable but we had a big cock up case a few years ago that made international headlines. Maybe you have read it in the papers of a stupid French dope head who threatened the local Bondi Police Force on the beach with a little knife. Our shit heads were so scared they shot and killed the little fuck up but some smart arse filmed it and put it on the net. The local police made international headlines but the coppers remained their jobs and weren't prosecuted as they handled according the law."

"Hmm, I haven't heard that story. Must have happened while I was working in Spain. I didn't read much newspapers then."

"You should check it out. The French government was furious and still demands an excuse for the whole thing."

"Yes, I will when I have time."

"You should. Don't rely to much on them. They will disappoint you when you truly need them. I have seen it happen before and I hope it will not happen again."

Konrad looked for a very short moment in the direction of Robby who didn't follow him. He only nodded when Konrad mentioned about disappointments from the cops and others. Konrad showed a thin smile but then he made a sudden move and went back home. Robby sighed when he was finally gone. He knew his friend well but what he told them wasn't all good news. Bad news was brewing and would soon happen.

14 Ordinary hostel problems

Terry kept his promises to give Julia more shifts.
He was glad she liked to work on her own in
Kirribilli. He knew he had now and then some
help from Lydia and even Glenda didn't mind to
help Julia when she had time. The two women
loved Julia and some of the long resident guests
loved her. They asked him often when she would
be back but he couldn't promise them.

In the Bondi Lodge Robby showed the other staff
members that he was an expert and knew more
about running hostels than the managers. He
showed his arrogance to his colleagues and to
some of the guests. He didn't like the big group
of Brazilians who didn't learn much English.
Instead they were wasting their time with table
tennis and going out every night. None of the
guys actually attended school while their parents
paid for the school fees and their stays in the
lodge. In Robby's eyes it was just a waste of

money.

There was another thing what Robby did and what his colleagues didn't do but were supposed to do. He collected money from every guest that stayed longer than their planned stay. Of all the receptionist Lenny, the fat guy was the worst receptionist and never took payments and if he did he always screwed up. He was a lousy receptionist and made a mess at the desk while he was working.

Robby disliked him and always complained to Julia when Lenny was just gone when they both were in the lodge. "Why can't he clean the desk before he leaves?"

"You should ask him." Julia replied. "If you only complain but never say what's your concern he will never do what he should do."

"Easy to say for you. You don't have to deal with his mess."

"True, but I have my own problems too. Take for instance Jockey and the mess he makes in the kitchen. He's a pig and he never cleans his space properly. I just wonder where he learned to work and why the staff just takes his shit."

"Don't ask me. I did your job before and I know what you're talking about."

"Right, Terry should have a clear word with him. He's the boss of the kitchen and as a manager he should tell his staff how they should work and if he doesn't want to clean his mess he should leave."

Robby smiled while Julia complained about her chef and colleague. Normally she wouldn't complain but now she was doing the job for a while she thought she was entitled to say things what others didn't dare.

"Oh, Terry called and asked if you don't mind to go tomorrow and the rest of the week again to Kirribilli. He said he had to be somewhere else so you have to deal with the breakfast and dinner."

"No big deal. Can you arrange a cab for me for tomorrow morning? I will get up very early and want to be in Kirribilli by four thirty if that's possible. Thank you."

Julia went the next morning very early to Glenferrie Lodge where Glenda was waiting for her. She gave Julia again the same room and helped her a bit with the morning set up. Lydia joined when Julia was busy with frying eggs and made her a special breakfast. She knew Lydia was a vegetarian and didn't want her eggs from the grill so she used a frying pan for her eggs instead.

The long-term residents were glad she was back. They preferred her food instead of Terry's. He wasn't a bad cook but he used too much oil and salt and her food had more flavour and colour. With Julia the food had more balance and looked better. Still she had to change the pre cooked food that he made the day before and added more herbs and spices whenever she could to make it her dish.

15 The burglary

While Julia left the Bondi Lodge very early in the
morning for three days' work in Kirribilli Paul
got up at four and drove his old rusty red Toyota
Land Cruiser to a pump station just outside
Sydney. Valery was waiting there with her new
lover whom was asked to help with some heavy
lifting. He did a lot of body building so he was
used in lifting heavy weights. They suspected the
metal case would weight more than they could
lift up but then again they had no clue. Paul had
no idea how much was inside that case. There
could be a dummy case with a tracker what he
hoped Konrad wouldn't have but he wasn't so
sure. The man was very tricky so he had to be
careful.

"Good morning, Val. Did she take the bite?"

"Yes, she did. I saw her last night and she promised me she will co operate. We have to be very patient and hope for the best."

"Get in and prepare yourself for a coming nightmare. Did you explain to her that she should call the cops when we are gone?"

"She knows what to do and will call them as soon we are gone. Let's hope no one else will call them while we are busy. I don't want to get caught and face him before we have done the job. I want to see his face when he will miss thousands of dollars kept in a case in his house without reporting it to the tax office."

"Don't be surprised if he pays you an unwelcome visit to your hostel after this event. Be prepared and don't say a thing. Just let him guess. Without any proof he can't do much. He's just a loose canon but be careful. He might harm you."

"If he tries I will call the cops. That will keep him of my back."

Paul shook his head while he drove the car all the way to Bondi. It was a perfect day. The sun was about to rise and it promised to be a warm sunny day. He parked his old battered car far away from Konrad's house but still in the street. Valery got out and found a bench where she pretended to read a newspaper and looked around.

Konrad left his house just before eight in the morning. He walked firm out of the door of his house and didn't pay much attention to the old Toyota. He noticed the car but no alarm bells started to ring in his head. Instead he got into his car started the engine and drove towards the beach. He saw Valery but he wasn't sure it was her. At least it was a woman reading the paper on a bench. He saw another face who came from nowhere. It was a face he had seen the night before.

His mind was spinning while he drove all the way to Surrey Hills where he got into Crown Street. He stopped in front of a motel and got out. He opened the door of the reception and went straight to his office. He turned on all the lights and prepared himself for a long day in office.

Konrad's wife left the house half an hour later and she took a bus to work. She never travelled together with her husband and worked half the day while he stayed as long as he could. He checked his computer in the office and checked his booking lists. No one to check in for the moment and no check outs. It would be an easy day for him in the office.

The sister in law stayed alone in the house together with Konrad's dog. He had an eight-year-old shepherd dog to protect both his motel as his house. He had a sophisticated alarm system in both his house and motel. He expected he would be robbed but had no idea when. He was aware that his ex employee would make an attempt to steal his metal case with cash dollars. He alone knew that Konrad was skimming his own guests and none of them had an idea how much he had stolen from them.

She opened a window before she went out with the dog. He didn't want to go with her but she kept the big strong dog on a lease. The dog followed her while she walked towards Val. They nodded when they saw each other and continued her walk. Valery got up and walked to the car. It was time for action.

Paul and Val's lover got out and followed her. She noticed the open window and got in with some help from the others. They all got through the window and started to look around. Only Paul and Val had been before in the house but not her lover. He looked around and was ready to steal whatever he could get his hands on. He noticed Konrad's laptop computer and wanted to take it with them but Valery waved to him. "Leave it. We don't need it."

"Damn, I swear that's a very expensive laptop and you don't know what's on it's hard drive."

"Our mission is to steal one thing and not his laptop. Follow me."

Paul opened Konrad's bedroom and searched quickly under the bed and in the big cupboard. He found the metal case and tried to get it out it's hiding place. The case was too heavy for him. Luckily his mate showed up pulled it out of the cupboard and carried it to the open window. He made a mistake by throwing the case outside the window straight into the garden and jumped out of the window. The others followed him and all three ran back to the car with the heavy case in his hands.

The sister in law was on her way back and saw they got what they were after. She tried to tame the dog who got wild. It started to bark loud and was hard to get under control. It knew it had failed its job and would be punished. Konrad would go mental if he would find out what actually happened that Wednesday morning.

Paul got back on the wheel and drove away from Bondi. He never looked back but he paid close attention to his mirrors. He kept the speed just under the limit as he couldn't afford to get caught. He left Bondi and headed towards the city where he went to the Harbour Bridge. They all looked with open mouth to the view while he drove his car towards the north shore. In Hornsby he stopped and filled the tank with gasoline before they drove further.

With a full tank they drove all the way to Cessnock where Paul dropped them off at one of the two hiding places he found months before. Valery and her lover took another old car and drove back to Sydney to the pump station where she kept her own car. She got out while her lover dumped the car next of other old cars. They drove back to Bondi without saying a word. The only thing she did was praying to God in her mind. She asked him for guidance and safety. Sooner or later the bomb would burst and she would be in lots of trouble.

Konrad didn't expect the burglary on his house so soon. He believed that his ex employee had his eyes on his metal case what he no longer kept in his motel but at home. No one wouldn't dare to break in his house and even if they did he would find out.

It was a peaceful morning for him. No one checked out but also no one checked in. The motel was only for 48 % occupied what was less than he wanted but he couldn't force people to stay somewhere else. His wife was busy with cleaning all the rooms while he checked the balance on his desktop computer in the office. It wasn't a good month for him but the month was young. The numbers could still go up but he doubted they would go up.

His sister in law called around noon and ended his lovely nice day. The phone call was the last thing he wanted to hear but she should have called him earlier but she was too much afraid of what could happen to her. Konrad wasn't an easy guy. He didn't want her in his house and asked his wife often how she would stay. She insisted she could stay as long as she wanted unless

Konrad had a clear reason why she should leave. She made him clear she would leave too if he would throw her out.

"Konrad, I need your help. Your dog goes mental the whole morning and won't stop barking. What should I do?"

"Does he want to listen to you? No? Yell at him. He might keep his mouth shut."

There was a moment of silence. He could hear noises and sounds that shouldn't be there but it was obvious that were the sounds of the cops who were in his house.

"Who's there with you?"

"It's the police. Someone in the street called the cops after they had seen some strange actions around the house."

"Can you be a bit more specific?"

"I don't know what happened that morning but I have the feeling you were burgled this morning while you went to work. I saw a car speeding away but can't give you a clear prescription of the persons."

Konrad felt furious but he remained calm. He saw his wife who looked only once at him but she kept her mouth shut. Very wise of her. He wanted to insult her together with that sister in law he couldn't stand. The sis had no right to be in his house but she insisted that her sister could live as long as she lived in the house. 'What was that?"

"That was your stupid sister who will leave the house immediately. I don't want her any longer in my house. If she doesn't leave by tonight you too can leave. Goodbye."

He stood up and left his desk. He closed his office and went straight to his car and checked his Walther P99 that he kept underneath his seat. It was loaded and ready to use. Konrad started the engine of his big four-wheel drive and drove back to Bondi. As soon as he reached his street he saw several police cars parked near his house leaving him no space to park his car in front of his house. He searched for a space that he found and parked it. He walked back to his house and got stopped by two coppers.

"Sorry, sir. Crime scene. You can't enter it."

"I live there. That's my house and I want to get

in."

He snapped at them but they still refused to let him through. A senior officer appeared and saw Konrad. He had seen him before at the Gun Club where they were both members. Konrad was a special member and paid top dollar to practise his gun with the elite troops and police officers. No normal citizen was actually allowed to be a member but Konrad got his membership as he used to be a special armed force trooper.

"Let him through. He owes this house and I want to chat with him."

Konrad thanked the officer and walked through. He stopped when he noticed the open window. He never left any windows open and certainly not when he kept special valuables inside his house. He wondered what got missing but he didn't have to think long. He knew exactly what got missing; his metal money case.

"Good morning, sir. We received a call from your sister in law who noticed a burglary earlier this morning. She has reasons to believe that you know what they were after."

"Yes, I do, officer." Konrad said while he

inspected his house together with the officer and a dozen coppers. "It sounds weird but I had a feeling this was about to happen but I didn't expect it so soon."

"So you know what's missing?"

"Oh, yes and I know who's behind this burglary."

The officers stopped and all looked at him. A few got their little notebook out and were ready to write down whatever name he would announce.

"Off the record, sir. You should have a chat with the owner of the old Lamrock hostel. It's a few streets away from here and it's nowadays run by one Valery. She's a member of the Council so she might not there but she knows my house and knows a lot of me."

"We will have a chat with her and check her out. Any more names for us? She described she saw a guy who carried a big case that he pushed inside an old rusty red 4-wheel drive brand unknown."

Konrad started to think what he saw earlier that morning. He remembered he saw an old Toyota not far away from his house almost on the same spot where he parked his car. He saw Valery reading a paper and pretended she didn't see him but he recognised her. Then there was Robby who showed up suddenly so he suspected him but he would deny everything. He knew Robby too well and he would start some drama. He had to pay him a visit later on in the day when he was back for work. His shift started at six.

"By the look in your face I can see you saw things that shouldn't be there, am I right?"

Konrad didn't want to help the police but this was now an investigation so he couldn't ignore them. They could take him to their office where they could ask him more questions if they wanted. "Yes, you are. I saw that car but I wasn't sure. Then there's Valery whom I saw sitting on a bench reading a paper while I passed her. I wonder if she had seen me. Must have be as she was looking now and then around her as if she was observing the area."

He stopped suddenly and walked straight to his room. He saw his laptop computer was still there. He would have suspected the perpetrators would have taken his laptop as it was worth a lot of money plus he kept all the numbers of every bank note that he kept in the case that was no longer in his room in a special file so could trace it. "I know why you're here, officers and I will not stop you from doing your work but I say I will catch them before you and will teach them an important lesson."

"Whatever you want to do, sir. You can't break the law. If you try to break the law, we will prosecute you and you will end up in jail. I know you are very upset and like anyone else you want to investigate it alone. Leave it to us and will shall find them and trial them at court. They will not go unpunished."

The senior officer followed Konrad who needed only one minute to see what went missing in his room. He saw the empty spot at the bottom of his cupboard where the metal case used to be.

"I kept for some time a metal case in my cupboard. What's inside is none of your business but it's very valuable to me. The burglars know me and knew exactly what I was keeping in my house. They knew they had no access to my house unless my stupid sister in law helped them. That's the only explanation how they could enter my house without setting off my alarm that was kept off. She will pay her price and can start packing her bags. She's no longer welcome in my house."

"That's a lot of assumption, sir." One of the coppers said while he took notes.

"Yes, they are but then again why are you here? I didn't call you so someone else called you to report this matter. Find out who called you and start from there. She must be linked with the burglars. She must have met one of them and made a special deal."

"We will and you will hear from us. We might ask you to come to the station to sign our investigation report and will give you a copy. In the meantime, we would like to have a look around in your room so we search for finger prints."

Konrad had to let them do their job and looked from a distance how forensics took fingerprints from his cupboard door and a few other places in the room. They all looked at his little bullet factory where he made his own bullets for his match gun. "I hope you have a licence for this. If not, we will have to take it and report you."

"No need, officer. I do have a licence for all my guns I own and for my own little bullet factory. You can speak with judge Reynolds. He signed all my licenses so you can charge me on that but you won't win your case."

The senior detective sighed and knew who judge Reynolds was. The man was powerful and dealt with many cases about gun ownerships. "Yes, I know him and no we won't charge you. Aren't you a member of our special gun club?"

"Yes, I am. I taught some of your new boys how to shoot. I'm a pro and have years of experience with guns."

It was clear they were dealing with an ex military with years of practise with weapons and shooting. They were both members of the same club where ordinary citizens weren't allowed but Konrad was an exception.

For four long hours the police stayed in his house and took their time. Konrad couldn't smoke a cigarette while they wondered around and took samples of whatever that looked suspicious. A ton of photos were shot before the forensics were finished with their job. they packed up and left the premises followed by most of the coppers. Only the senior detective remained and he kept a close eye on Konrad. He didn't trust him and had some difficulties with the story he told them.

"Sir, if you don't mind but this case is different than any other burglaries. I know you're a busy man and you don't have much time for us for that reason we would like you to come to the station where we can talk further about this burglary in my office."

"Why should I go with you to the station? What's wrong with my case and this burglary?"

"Because you know more than you want to reveal to us. I can read body language and it's clear you have something to hide who you don't want to reveal. Fine if you don't want to but I have just a feeling that you weren't always following our laws and that you were hiding things from the authorities who might be interested in what it was and how much. You see I am not that stupid and most of the burglaries have one thing in common. The thieves are always searching for money and other high valuables. That made it so strange that they left the laptop untouched but had interest in one heavy case that you were keeping in your office."

"What would you do if I refuse to go with you?"

"I can make it easy for you. Just come to the station here in Bondi and we can talk it over tomorrow if you have time. Please check your diary and ask in case someone else to cover your business so we can make time to start a full investigation."

"I will call you tomorrow morning. I don't know if I have a busy day or not. You never know with guests. They can extend or leave earlier than expected so I never know what they have in mind. I'll give you a call."

"Please do so. Because I have a feeling there's more than this simple case that I can't tell you know but I can tell you when we see each other at the station. You have staff, don't you?"

"I used to have, detective." Konrad wanted to smoke but couldn't as the detective might be a non smoker and he had to respect him. "That what makes my case so complicated. He ran away and I don't know where he is. He knows more than he should have and I believe he's behind this case. He knows what's inside that case and for that reason he stole it from me."

"What is his name? Can you give us some more information so we can use it in this case?"

"His name is Paul and he's from England. I sponsored him after his visa expired. Technically I did nothing wrong so you can't sue me but he ran away and planned to rob me. So that's criminal and for that reason you can search him and have him arrested for robbery and being illegal in the country."

"We will leave that to your judges and I don't think it will be your friend. We can't ask help from him but we know others judges who can give us the right permissions for our investigation."

"There's more. There was a woman involved and if I am not mistaken it was Valery Tubbs. You should know her. She's part of our local council and she's the rightful owner of the Lamrock hostel, the shack on the corner of Lamrock and

Jacques Avenue."

"Yes, we know that place. Wasn't that not Robby's place?"

"Yes, it was but she kicked him out. He's no longer part of that hostel but you can find him in the Bondi Lodge. He's one of the receptionists and he works most of the time in the evening. If you want to talk to him see him in the evening. He might be able to help you."

"Anything else?"

"No, that's all I can tell you. What was in that case was very important to me and not to you. In due future I might reveal a bit more but not everything."

"It would help if you can. Only then can we find your burglars and bring them to court. Please help us so we can help you with finding that case and what was inside."

Konrad nodded and sighed after the detective left as one of the last cops his house. Finally, he could have lit a cigarette in his own place. It was his house so he could do whatever he liked to do. He left his Walther P99 in his room in a drawer and locked it. His wife and sister in law had no access to his room but for extra security he locked the door of his room and walked to the kitchen where he made himself a coffee.

In the empty living room, he sat with his coffee alone and thought about the burglary. Why did they pick his house and why on earth did his sister in law who was alone that time of the burglary left a window open while she went out with the dog for a walk? Who were the ones who stole his money and why just now?

He knew the answers but couldn't tell them to the cops. He couldn't reveal to them how much money they stole from him but they made a critical mistake by leaving his expensive laptop untouched in the house. The job was done by people who knew him and the message was clear. You screwed others and we are screwing you. You can't report it to the police who will start a full investigation and will ask you lots of questions how you obtained so much US dollars without reporting it to the right authorities.

Then there was Robby who appeared to be around so early in his neighbourhood. Why on earth was he so early in the morning in the street for what reason? Was he part of the crew or just a coincidence? He had to see him. Hopefully he would be able to answer his questions but then he knew his friend better than anyone else. Robby didn't like questions and always did his best to avoid the right answer. The man was a born liar.

16 Question Time

Robby was alone in the lodge. Julia was for a couple of days again at work in Kirribilli and would be back on Friday night. She would go out after work and would have a couple of drinks in the Marble Bar underneath the Hilton Hotel in the city. He had introduced her to this establishment and nowadays she loved to visit it after her work in Kirribilli. It was ideal on her route back home and she liked the ambiance of the place.

Julia was no ordinary girl but different. She had for instance very short hair what she kept extreme short as it was easier for her while she was very busy in the kitchen in both Bondi as in Kirribilli. She had the looks of a tomboy and wore most of the times jeans but now and then a dress. Julia was a smoker but not as bad as Robby. He was just a chain smoker. He needed his fags and couldn't live without cigarettes. Julia was not addicted to the nicotine and could stop whenever she wanted. Still she liked to smoke and cigarettes were just one thing. Her favourite smokes were cigars what she starts to appreciate when she stayed for nearly two weeks in The Hague. In an expensive four-star hotel, she discovered the fun in Cuban finest cigars and didn't mind they cost more than other cigars.

In Sydney she found a few good cigar shops and smoked them regular. There was still no smoking ban although in Bondi some of the places started to put up signs to all the smokers that they no longer could smoke indoors but outside was still fine. In the city she knew a few good bars where she could enjoy a perfect cigar, a drink and a good book to chill out. Living in Sydney was like a dream that came out and she wanted to have a very good time before the year was over. She wanted to leave the country and city with good spirits.

Robby sighed while he missed her. He knew she liked the job and especially Kirribilli. He knew the place and knew the hostel. He knew Glenda and didn't like her. She was older than him and like him she had years of experience in the field. She lived in the Glenferrie Lodge what she saw as home and wouldn't leave it as she had nowhere to go. The lodge was her home and she was in charge. Konrad walked in the building and saw the tired face of his old friend. He looked bored and was in no good spirits.

"Not now, Konrad. I have no time for you."

"Robby, I need to talk to you. Can I have a word with you in private?"

"No, I am alone and I can't leave the desk because you want to have a chat with me."

Konrad who was still upset with the burglary stared for a moment nasty at his friend. Robby didn't pay any attention to that look. He had seen his friend before when he was in a foul mood and for that reason he didn't give in to him.

"Konrad, I can see in your eyes you had a very rough day but I am not in the mood in hearing your complaints or whatever happened that day. Please, go home and come back when you are in better spirits."

"No, Robby. I am not going. I will ask you plain and simple what were you doing in my street this morning?"

"Excuse me?"

"You heard me. What were you doing in my street early this morning?"

"As far as I know this is a free country and I can walk where I want to walk. The reason I was in your street was because I was hoping to find a cab that could take me to the city."

"Did you find a taxi so early in the morning?"

"As a matter a fact I did. I had an early appointment with my solicitor so for that reason I left early the Lodge and went on searching for a cab."

"You could have called one from your hostel."

"True, but I wanted to stretch my legs for a while and decided to walk towards the beach. I know near my hostel there are plenty of cabs."

Konrad agreed with that. Robby had a plausible explanation but he still wasn't convinced with it. He was a good liar and he had told his friend so many lies that it was hard nowadays to see what was true and what was a lie.

"Where's Julia?"

"She's not here. She's in Kirribilli. You will see

her again on Friday. She's doing some more shifts for our drama queen so he can take his time off while she can work her pretty arse off."

"You like her, don't you?"

"Yes, I do but no we don't have anything in common. I am not her type she told me but we are good friends. At least she helps me with my case."

"Good to hear. I hope she's convinced you can win your case while I have the feeling you're just after her money."

Konrad looked Robby in his eyes. He never looked him back in the eyes what convinced Konrad that he was lying again. Robby lied to everyone and didn't care. "Right, I will ask her a few questions when she's back. All I want to know from you is why you were in my street so early in the morning and please don't lie to me. I know you live on your lies."

"I wasn't lying." Robby defended himself. "I was looking for a cab that could bring me to my solicitor."

"Give me her address or phone number so I can

verify you. It will be between us."

"No, I don't give you her number. Why don't you believe me?"

Konrad stared for a while in the empty eyes of his friend. He was in no good mood to answer Robby's question. He kept on staring till he had enough. Robby wasn't helping him with his investigation and he had to wait till Friday evening before Julia would be back. She was much easier to deal and she would cooperate. He liked her and wished she could work for him but she had made herself clear she wasn't interested in a position in his motel. She was very happy for the moment with her present job and this was only temporary. Sooner or later she would quit before the authorities would discover she was working without the right visa.

Before Konrad left the Bondi Lodge he took a cigarette from Robby's pack on the reception desk and lit it inside the hostel. Robby wanted to shout but he couldn't. He was furious because his friend was once again ignoring the clear signs. He didn't care and he was testing his friend's patience.

"Konrad, please. Smoke outside like anyone else.

There are clear rules inside the hostel and we all should follow them."

"But not all of your staff is following the rules, am I right or not?"

"No comment." Robby answered and sighed. "Please, come back on Friday when Julia is back. She will answer your questions."

"Oh, I will be and she will talk. At least she's always honest what I can't say about you, Robby. Why are you always lying to me?"

"I am not lying." Robby said and got furious. "Look in my eyes. I tell you I have nothing to do with whatever happened to you today. I wasn't there and I can confirm that I was with my solicitor all day. She can confirm it."

"Fine, give me her number so I can call her for the confirmation. If she tells me, you weren't there than you have lied to me."

Konrad left the Lodge and went back home. His wife was upset as he insulted her sister. She was in tears and was still in the house. She felt frightened as he threatened the throw her out because she kept a window open while she took the dog out for a walk. Thanks to her he lost his metal case and with that all his savings.

"Why is your sister still here?"

"Because I told her she can stay. Stay away from her."

"Then you should both go. This is still my house and I don't want you both here. Now get out!"

It was unusual for Konrad to yell at his wife. Normally they could talk things out but lately he was under an enormous pressure since the moment Paul left him. From that moment he suspected the young English lad that he would rob him of the cash money that he claimed from his guests who thought they had to pay an extra tax. His wife knew nothing of his little scheme and was kept in the dark even now he lost it all. He refused to talk to her why he was so upset.

"Konrad, you can't throw me out of this house as it's mine too. And about the motel I own it not you."

"I doubt it. Who signed the papers when we bought it? Is your name on the documents? I don't think so, woman. Get out and don't come back. I say our relationship has come to an end and I don't want you any longer in my house and motel. Goodbye!"

He waited long enough till they both started to pack a few suit cases. He called a cab for them and opened the door as soon as the case were packed and the two sisters stood in front of his house. He took the keys from his wife and her sister and kept them in his pockets of his pants. He closed the door and made himself a drink.

In Kirribilli Julia was busy as hell. Normally Terry left several dishes prepared for Julia but this time there was none. It was the first time she had to start from scratch what she didn't mind. Lydia helped her a bit while she was actually on duty but didn't mind to give her a hand. Glenda sat at the reception while she did some knitting. She worked a few extra hours and wrote the hours down on her time sheets.

"Julia, how's Bondi?"

"Great. I just love it there."

"But don't you want to stay here with us? We do like you and the guys wants you here. We talked about it with Terry and he knows how much you are appreciated by our guests."

"I know, Lydia but I have my space in Bondi. I love the beach and the long walks that I make every day and I will miss my friends I have."

Lydia nodded while she cleaned some carrots that Julia needed for a dish. She took the cleaned carrots and sliced them fast with a sharp cook's knife in thin slices. She was fast with a knife and took care she didn't cut herself.

"Is it true that Robby Henson is working at reception?"

"Yes, he's a star. He collects all the money from our students who owe the hostel a lot of money. Without Robby the managers would never get it out of them. They do nothing and only waste their time when they show up. They know nothing about the business."

"As if you know it better." Lydia replied. "You almost sound like your friend. Are you lovers?"

Lydia looked Julia in the eyes but she didn't look back. She shook her head and continued with her work. "No, Robby and I we're just good friends nothing more. Why does everyone think we have a relationship?"

"I don't know. I was just wondering. You always talk so highly about him and his work. He must be an amazing guy. what I have heard from Glenda is that you should be careful with him. She knows him and she doesn't like him. You can't trust him."

"He's ok. He has lots of stories and every time he talks about his hostel he's over the moon." Julia replied while she defended her friend and room mate.

"Still, be careful. You don't know him and what I have heard from Glenda you have to stay away from him. Don't let him into your life. He's good in trusting but don't believe whatever he will claim. He's full of lies."

"Don't worry, Lydia. He won't get whatever he tries and I don't let him enter my private life. I only tell him what he can hear and the rest is my privacy. I am not afraid of him and don't think he will do me any harm."

Julia went straight back on Friday evening to Bondi. She had a great time again in Kirribilli but for some reasons she knew she had to be in

Bondi. As if she received a message that she was needed there.

Konrad came back that Friday evening and his mood was fouler than the few days before. He knew who stole his money and he wanted everything back. He didn't believe a word of what Robby said that he spent the day with his solicitor. He never gave him her phone number nor the address so he was lying again. Normally he would have done so but not this time. He was hiding things for his friends and it made him very unbelievable. Konrad wondered what Julia thought about him. She lived with him now in the Lodge and they both shared a room together. What did she actually know about him? Did he ever tell her his dark past? Probably not he had too many dark secrets. He was good in telling stories that sounded plausible but in reality there were all lies. He heard most of them and he could tell by the way he talked he was lying to her while she didn't notice it.

Julia wasn't all smiles when she arrived back from Kirribilli. She dropped her bag behind the reception desk and went straight to the kitchen where she made some coffee for the guys. Robby wanted to say hello but she walked straight past him as if she was in a hurry.

"What's with her?"

"I don't know. Hope she will tell what happened. Maybe a guy tried to have fun with her what she doesn't like. I don't know."

Ten minutes later she walked back with three mugs of hot coffee. She gave a mug to the guys and took a seat next of Konrad. "Good evening, Julia. I hope everything is alright with you? You seemed to be in a hurry."

"Oh, I am sorry, Konrad. I thought you needed me here and I know you like a coffee so that's what I made straight away before you ask for a coffee."

"How kind of you."

She smiled and took a sip of her own. It was still very hot but also sweet. "Did anyone call me actually?"

Konrad looked at Robby who looked back at him. They both looked at Julia who stared back at them. "No, I didn't but what makes you so sure you received a call?"

"I don't know. As if I received a message last night saying go back to Bondi. Big trouble ahead."

Robby looked at his friend who sighed and searched for his cigarettes. Luckily Julia was still smoking cigarettes and offered him a fag.

 "Cheers, Julia. That was just what I need." He lit his cigarette inside the reception area and walked slowly outside. Julia followed him as did Robby who took a fag from her pack. She lit his cigarette before she lit her own.

"I have a few questions for you and I know you will tell me the truth."

"Sure, don't worry about me." She replied.

Konrad nodded and looked a short moment to Robby, who said nothing. He was observing his friend and wondered what Konrad wanted from her. She didn't know much about them both so he wondered how she could help him.

"You said you were for the last couple of days cooking in Kirribilli, am I right?"

"Yes, I was." She said. "Call Glenda and she will

confirm. Call Lydia who also works there and she will confirm too."

"I will so don't worry. What time did you leave Bondi if I may ask you?"

"Let me think I left around four in the morning. I was still very sleepy but I wanted to be there early so I could do a proper breakfast without hurrying while the guests queue up for their food. Glenda was waiting for me and she gave me a set of keys; one for a room opposite the kitchen a key for the kitchen and a key for the dining area."

"And what did you do in between cooking? Did you go out or did you stay in the hostel?"

"Don't answer his questions, Julia." Robby suddenly replied. "I don't know what he wants from us but he believes we did something to him and he thinks he's some kind of detective what he isn't."

Konrad looked only a short moment to Robby and returned his attention to Julia. She ran her hand over her short bristles and tried to figure out why he wanted to know what she actually did in Kirribilli.

"Call Glenda and ask her what you want to know about me. She will tell the same what I am telling you. She will confirm that I was there all the time and that I prepared some amazing meals for the guests and the staff."

"Thank you for your cooperation, Julia. You're most kind in answering my questions."

She gave him a smile and finished her cigarette. She dumped the cigarette but in the little bin next of the door and went back inside. Konrad followed her as did Robby who had to when the phone started to ring.

"Your friend doesn't want to answer my questions what's makes him a bit suspicious. I don't know if I can trust him. I know him quite a long time and he was never like that before."

Julia looked Konrad in his blue eyes. They looked so cold and she couldn't look long before she started to feel uncomfortable. "We all have something to hide, Konrad; even you."

Konrad wasn't very pleased with this remark and suddenly he got up and left them. He felt deep insulted by Julia but he couldn't be angry. She was right. They all had something to hide so did he but it was not the right time to explain to them what actually happened. He would tell them when he thought the time was right.

"You will see me back till I have my answers and Julia I will call Glenda to see if you were telling me the truth. You will hear from me."

He got in his Land Cruiser and drove back to his house. He went to his room and laid all night on his bed thinking of the burglary. A few people spooked in his head but he couldn't place names to them but he knew when he woke up the next day who were behind the clever plan.

17 Private Investigations

Paul was left behind in the first barn on a far in
the Hunter Valley. Valery and her lover drove
quickly back to Bondi as they expected a sudden
appearance of Konrad. He had seen her she was
very confident but she never told the guys. She
didn't want to jeopardise the burglary as she
wanted her share. She wouldn't spend a buck in
her dying business. She rather would sell it and
leave Bondi. The sooner she could leave the
better it was for her. Her lover would go back to
New Zealand where Konrad couldn't touch her.

He parked the old Toyota in the barn and took the
heavy metal case out. He carried it to another old
vehicle he kept ready and drove to his other
hiding place. Valery only knew about the first but
not about the second one. He felt more safe and
secure in the second farm. The farmers were kind
people and offered him shelter and lots of dope.

In Singleton he lived in a bigger farm and had a
whole barn all for himself. There was plenty of

wine in bottles and in one of the other barns they grew lots of weed so he could smoke his share as long as he paid them with a part of the loot. He told them he could hold of a lot of money but he never mentioned how much it would be. The farmers got a bit greedy and asked for a few hundred bucks per fortnight what Paul reluctantly agreed.

He opened the box and counted the money he found inside. The banknotes were in diverse nominations but most of the bank notes were $20, $50 and $100 notes. There were some $10 and $5 notes but luckily no $1 notes. Konrad knew exactly what kind of money he wanted to save and had a nice collection of money hidden away from his wife and the Authorities.

Paul was still sober and wrote everything down on a little notebook. He counted the money and recounted what he already had counted so the figures would be all correct. He made little stacks but kept most of the money in a different case that he would burry once he had given the others their share. It would be less than they would have hoped for but they had no idea how much he actually had. Only Paul and Konrad knew the right figures and didn't want to share it with others.

Late in the evening he called her while he opened a bottle of wine and smoked his first spiff in weeks. He wanted to be stoned and enjoyed the moment of being drunk. How much he missed the alcohol and the drugs.

Valery wasn't happy to receive his call so early. She was just back and walked around in the empty old hostel. None of the few remaining guests were around but still she couldn't talk loud to him. She was afraid and expected an unwelcome visit from Konrad any minute. He would show up and ask her lots of questions. He knew she was part of the burglary and he would interrogate her before he would punish her.

"Paul, why are you calling me? Don't you understand it's not wise you call me so soon."

"Val, it's all right. Don't be afraid. I have some good news. This guy was richer than I thought. I have put your share aside together that of your partner. Come and collect it whenever you are around. I'll be waiting for you."

"Make that next month. I am expecting an unpleasant visit from your employer soon so

186

please don't call me again. I will call you. Right?"

"Take it easy, Val. Have a line of coke and chill out. It will be fine. Soon you will be rich I promise you."

He hung up and she threw away her mobile to the old reception desk. Robby used to sit there for days in his little office surrounded by toys and dealing with the problems of his guests. Whatever they said or how they felt about the place he always kept on smiling to them. He never lost his temper what was sometimes very difficult if some guests where arguing over money or lost and stolen things. She knew from the beginning when they started the hostel together he was skimming them. She had seen him doing it but she never said a word. She kept a blind eye on his little money scheme what was quite successful. She knew it was his business and he would go down and not her when he got caught.

Konrad didn't pay her visit although he drove regular next of her business and always looked inside. He never saw any movements so he suspected the place was as dead as he could see it. No backpacker entered the premises looking for a cheap deal but he believed there were still a few poor chaps around the place.

Valery noticed his car when he drove by. Her heart beat went faster and she got a bit nervous. She couldn't move so afraid she was. Her lover was in the house and he observed from the house the car Konrad drove. He sighed when the car passed by. He didn't stop but he drove very slowly passed the old hostel.

Konrad looked at the hostel but decided to give it a miss. He would confront her later but first he wanted to confront Robby. He was not a suspect but Robby knew more about Konrad and the little scheme they had worked out so he wondered how much he would know about his money. Robby made a fortune with only a simple hostel while Konrad owned a motel what was worth more money. His guests weren't poor and didn't mind to pay the extra fake bills and taxes while there was nothing on paper that would prove he was ripping them off.

Robby made some big mistakes and nearly got caught by some guests while Konrad played his game wise. His wife knew nothing and he kept her in the dark. He was afraid she would report him to the cops and take over the business what he didn't want to happen. For that reason, he allowed her only to have a look in the books once in a while after he tampered a bit with them. She never saw him stealing money from his guests and she never saw the big metal case in his office. He kept the case in a cupboard and kept it locked at all times.

Two weeks after the burglary Konrad parked his car far away from the old hostel and walked to the place. Charley Val's lover was alone in the reception and looked up when he saw Konrad. "Hey, what are you doing here? You have no right to come here."

"Is Valery around? I want to talk to her."

"No, she isn't." Charley said while Konrad looked around. "Now, please go."

"No, I am here to see her. Tell her it's important."

Valery came from nowhere and took a seat on the old sofa. It was like the rest of the place worn out and had seen better days. It was still comfortable and she always sat there while she was alone.

"What can I do for you, Konrad?" She asked while she observed him.

"I have a few questions for you and I want straight answers from you."

"Sure, don't we all?" She said while she searched for her fags and a lighter. She found them and lit a cigarette. She never offered one to him. "What do you want to know from me?"

"What were you doing in my street a few weeks back on Wednesday?"

"I can't remember I was there." She replied. "Are you sure it was me and not someone else?"

"No, I recognise you from a distance. I can recognise you from a far distance so I know it was you. Stop lying to me and answer my question."

She took a long drag of her cigarette and inhaled it deep. She slowly blew the smoke into his face when he wanted to lit his own cigarette. "Maybe I was there but what's your business what I was doing there?"

"You're hiding something for me. I can see that

in your cold eyes so why are you lying to me?"

"As if you're always telling the truth, Mr Konrad. Tell me honest how much did you make from your guests what your wife doesn't know about?"

Konrad looked in her eyes and saw how she was playing with fire. She wanted to provoke him but he expected somehow a question from her side. She knew more than she wanted to hide from him.

"I don't know what you're talking about, Val."

"Sure you do, Konrad. We both know that my ex learned you some tricks how to make fast money. We both know that you're running some kind of scheme that's very profitable and that you made around a million all cash and that you're hiding it from your wife and the government."

"Can you prove it?"

"If you think I am bluffing no I am not but yes, I can prove that you are stealing from your guests. I can even prove that my ex was stealing money from his own guests. He was so smart to keep records. Do you keep records of all the money you took from your guests?"

She stood up and walked to her little office. She opened the little safe inside the office and got out a little black notebook. It was Robby's but she remembered Konrad had the same when they started their little scheme.

"This was Robby's. He doesn't know I know more about his little scheme and that he made a nice fortune what he wasted on toys."

"Yes, he should have saved money for later."

"So, how much did you make so far? Are you now close to a million or did you make more than a million?" "None," He replied. "It's none of your business what I did and even if I were doing it how much I was making and what I was doing with my money. You see you think you have me by my balls but you have nothing. Right, I might have been not always fair to people but you're trying to provoke me with some bluff. Congratulations, Val but you have nothing that will say I was stealing from my guests."

She put the book back in the safe and locked her office. No one else had access to the office not even Robby. As soon as he went away for three months she changed all the locks and blocked his accounts plus credit cards so he had nothing. She made some arrangements with the banks so he couldn't reopen his accounts without her permission.

To make it even worse for him she took the remaining cash money what he kept in the safe and used it on her habits. Now there was no more money in the safe except for the little black notebook.

"I know you suspect me because I know you too well so does my ex. He's a suspect of your investigation but I don't think he was part of whatever happened to your place. I know you were robbed. People in the streets talk about it so I will don't deny it. I know what happened and why you came to visit me because you believe I have something to do with it. Have a good evening and stop searching. Leave it to the professionals the cops as it's their job. I have nothing that would make me a criminal but you had something and I believe you keep records don't know where but knowing you there are records of whatever you did all those years. Robby talked a lot about your business when he was still skimming his own guests. He was a fool but he pays the price from the moment I froze his accounts and kicked him out. I hope he learned his lesson from it. It can happen to you. Don't think your wife is stupid. She might know more than you think. After all she's your accountant and they are pretty smart. Good luck, Konrad. Don't get caught and burned."

Konrad left Valery and walked slowly back to his car. He cursed her but he promised her he would be back and demanded answers from her. He got in his car and drove to the Bondi Lodge. He saw Julia and Robby together outside and joined them. "I have nothing to say, Konrad. Mind your own business." "Good evening, Robby. Still upset. You look like your wife. I just paid her a visit." "So, what did she have to say to you? Why are you bothering us? What have we done to deserve all this?"

Julia noticed how upset Robby was. He had changed a bit since Konrad paid him so many visits over the last couple of weeks. Something must have happened around his household but he didn't reveal a thing. He was only asking questions about where they were and promised he would check them out. Julia wasn't so afraid and had nothing to hide while Robby had lots of things to hide. He wasn't so honest as he said he was. She learned he was not completely to be trusted.

"Right, you want to know why I ask you these questions?" They both nodded. "Fine, I got burgled on a Wednesday a few weeks ago and I start my own investigation as I have no trust in the police. They were already interrogating me while I am a victim of burglary. Can you believe it? They think I have engaged this crime so they can blame me. They should know better."

"Oh, sorry to hear, Konrad." Julia replied. "What did they stole from you?"

Robby looked at his friend and read his mind. He knew straight away what got missing. Now he understood why Konrad had so much interest in him as it was he who told him about this little successful scheme. They were both very successful guys but Konrad made more money in the end than Robby who wasted most of the money on collectibles.

"Let's go inside, Konrad. We can talk in the office while Julia can man the desk."

Robby opened the door of the reception and they all went inside. Konrad followed Robby to the little office behind the reception where Felicia and the managers had their office. Robby pointed to a chair and took a seat opposite of his friend.

"Let me guess they stole your money, didn't they?"

"Yes, all of it." Konrad said and sighed. "Every dollar that I made and saved away from my wife and business. I had a nice metal case filled till the top and I was thinking of getting another one. Now I have my doubts if I should get another one. My wife seems to know what I was doing and wants to know more. Then there's her sister whom I can't stand. It's time they both leave the house because it's her fault that I lost my money. The stupid woman kept a window open."

"Does she know what happened?"

"I'm not sure. Maybe she does but she doesn't want to talk to me so she called the cops. They were in my house and torn the whole place down. They see me as a criminal and not as a victim."

Robby wanted to say but Konrad stopped him. "No, Robby. I am not a criminal. I am just a smart crook who runs a successful business and I have a good occupancy rate compare with this dump. If I could get control on this place, I would clean it up and start with several staff members."

"I hope you wouldn't sack me or Julia, would you?"

"No, not you two. You both do a good job but I can't say about the others. Luckily for you I don't own this place so your job is safe. Don't fuck up. Mistakes are easily made but difficult to restore. You should know that."

"So you paid a visit to my wife, huh?"

"Yes, have you seen the place?"

Robby nodded and looked around in the little office. It was very industrial designed. No photos or calendars on the wall. No desk looked personal so it was difficult to imagine which desk was Felicity's.

"I saw your wife that Wednesday. I know she knows that I have her as a suspect. She didn't want to tell me why she was in my street but I believe she's part of the burglars. I know Paul is one of them. He knows what I have and where I do keep it. Val knows my house so the two are my prime suspects."

Robby thought about it. He knew Konrad's house too and been there lots of times. In the past they were very close friends and did some things together but when he got back from his long sailing trip Val had put a lot of bad shit on him and through her he lost everything everyone and was left behind without a single penny in his pockets.

"So you assume she's part of the burglary. How did she take it?"

"She's guilty. I caught her and she knows it. Did you know she had a new lover? He's a Kiwi and he's more muscles than brains. I guess he was the one who got it out of my cupboard as it is very heavy. I don't think Paul can lift it up alone."

Konrad and Robby looked in each others eyes. Robby looked quickly to something else instead of the stone cold stare that Konrad produced.

"Why did you write everything down in a little black notebook? Valery knows what you did how you made your money and she understood I ran the same kind of business back in my motel thanks to you and your little successful scheme."

"Of course she knew. She caught me a few times but I reminded her that I did it as a benefit for both of us. She said she did understand that so she kept quiet. She can't use it to blackmail me."

"Not smart, Robby. Women talk. What would you have done if she would have mentioned this to a copper? What do you think they would do?"

"Konrad, who called the cops? Did you call them? Think about it. You can accuse me. Fine. I made mistakes in the past but I never told anyone else except you about this little scheme and I trained you after I tested it long enough in my hostel."

Julia listened to their conversation from the reception desk. Robby kept on purpose the door open of the office so he could hear the noisy Brazilians who never did a thing than hanging around the desk while he was on reception. They were like always bored and were annoying. He could hear the noise coming from downstairs all the way up to his position in the little office. "One moment, Konrad. Let me deal with these spoiled brats."

Philippo, the biggest and fattest of them all stood in front of the reception desk and made like always a lot of noise. He kept one hand in his baggy trousers and stood in front of Julia who wasn't impressed with them. She was kind and polite but even she had enough of them.

"Hey, Julio when can we have some time together. I mean when are you free?"

"Excuse me?" She replied while he winked with his eyes. He blew a kiss to her direction but she didn't reply.

"You love me, Julio. I know you love me too."

"I don't think she likes you." Robby snapped back when he showed his face from the little office. "Now please, go. Do something. Go out or play table tennis. Please, don't hang around here. I have some important business to deal with and I have no time for guys like you."

"But we feel so bored." He replied. "Why can't we hang around in the lobby of the hostel?"

"Go study or do something else but don't hang around in the lobby. Get a hobby and keep your hand out of your pants."

"I just love it."

Philippo was doing it on purpose and did his best to provoke Robby. Julia noticed what he was doing and looked for a short moment to him. He signed and knew exactly where he kept his hand on. The Brazilian was in that way just a little kid that didn't want to grow up but would love to hang around with young girls so he could show them how he played with his testicles. At least Julia wasn't so impressed with what he was trying.

"Philippo, please. Stop playing with your dick. There are some girls around and you shouldn't do that."

"Oh, sorry, Julio. I didn't mean so but maybe you want to taste mine?"

"No, sorry, mate." She replied while she started to blush a bit. "Get lost, Philippo and play somewhere else with your dick. Stop provoking me and Julia."

Robby got back inside while the Brazilians went back downstairs. They were still making noise but this time it came from downstairs where they occupied the table tennis table in the back of the little courtyard.

"You need to entertain them. That's what's wrong with this hostel." Konrad said. "The old Michael Lenski should have known better when he started this business and he should have told the new owners who as you know are not in control how to run this kind of business. A good hostel owner as you know should know how to make money even when his customers are poor. You know that so do I. Who's leading this business actually?"

"Not me," Robby replied. "I would have thrown them out and keep it only open for backpackers. They are much better and they pay on time. These students are so rude so slack in their payments and when it comes to money they are all suddenly skint while a day later you can see them all hanging around the Bondi Hotel where they spent a fortune on alcohol what they consume in large quantities."

"Can you do something about it? You are working here and the managers should listen to you. At least you have the knowledge in this business and they don't."

"Unfortunately, Konrad. I am just a simple guy and I am glad that I have a job. I wish I could have more power but they don't want to give me that."

Konrad only looked at his friend and remained silent for a short moment. He knew his friend better than anyone else. He knew his friend better than anyone else. "Robby. if you want you still can work for me. I pay you much better and you will get your own room with your own toilet and shower plus my wife will cook your dinner just what she did for that cocksucker who has left me."

"Konrad, thanks for the offer but I stick with these lads. I do have my freedom here and I don't mind working in the evenings."

Konrad checked his watch and made a sudden move. Robby followed him and locked the door of the little office. Julia got up and made space for Robby who took over. She heard some things that she shouldn't hear but she couldn't help it that they were talking so long about the past.

"What you heard tonight please don't ever mention it to someone else. We forgot you could hear us but we are glad it was you and not someone else. "

"No, I won't, Robby. Please, trust me."

They stood for a short while outside and smoked a cigarette. She did her best to stop smoking but it was a mission impossible with Robby who couldn't live without cigarettes. He smoked more than her and was always searching for his fags. Julia smoked only occasionally and always in the presence of others instead of alone.

18 New friends

Through Robby Julia met other guys who had one thing in common. They were all collectors in vintage toys although one of his friends collected more than only toys. He was a collector in old vintage arcade machines and pinball machines. He bought them online through E bay and repaired them before he sold them again on the same site. He made a small fortune with this kind of business and was very technical although he never went to school. He was a self taught kid who was gifted.

Anton was twenty years younger than Robby but he was taller than all of his friends. He carried the nickname Darth Vader as that character in Star Wars is quite tall. Robby and Anton were serious Star Wars collectors and both had big collections over the years.

Julia remembered when the first Star Wars films hit the cinema in the late Seventies. She was still a kid then but had to say she liked the films. She played with toys and not with dolls. Her sister collected Barb dolls and now and then she played with them too but she loved her own toys. Lego was a big hit in the family ass they both played a lot with it.

Julia met Anton in January soon when they both shared a room together in the Bondi lodge soon after Robby managed to get a regular paid job with the hostel and the organisation.

The first two weeks were difficult as they had no privacy. There was already a young Irish kid who never showed his face downstairs and he owed the hostel a lot of money what he didn't have. He didn't even get a job but the simple receptionists never checked him out. It was Robby who discovered he was staying for free in the room and managed to stay in the room for nearly a month. In the end the kid ran away when the managers discovered him during a room check. He made a runner in the evening before Robby and Julia came back from a dinner in Bondi.

For five long months they kept the room for themselves. Robby had the power and the control to block the room so they didn't pay any rent and no one else could book a bed in that room. None of the other receptionists asked him to remove the blocking and let them stay in their shared room.

Robby had a single bed close to a window while

Julia occupied the bunk beds. She used the bed on top of her bed as storage while Robby used the only cupboard in the room for his possessions. He had less clothes than Julia and even less possessions. He lost so much after Valery kicked him out of his apartment and hostel. What he carried were all what he had left. He was hard broken and very bitter by the way Val treated him.

Julia met Anton several times during her year in Australia. The friendship he had with Robby wasn't as good as it used to be. Robby was a hard and sometimes rude man what caused some serious damage to his friendship. He didn't care much about the friendship with him. He used Anton whenever he could.

For a bright young kid with no proper education he was smart and very technical. He even had more knowledge in computing than Robby who wasn't so bad in computing as he had to when he had his own hostel. In the Lodge he knew more about computers than all the other staff members.

Through Anton and Robby Julia started to invest some money in collecting. She did it for fun and not to make money. Robby was in the past a good collector and knew to invest his money well. Anton did it for the money and earned a small fortune what he used to spend it on a house he bought for his parents and redecorated the whole place from top to bottom. He even bought a vintage Rolls Royce convertible so he could take the car out for a drive with his friends. He only had one problem; he couldn't drive a car but luckily some of his good friends weren't bad drivers either.

Over the months during her first six months in Australia Robby introduced Julia to a good friend in Bondi who had his own little collectibles shop. Christakos was a Greek immigrant who ran a small business in collectibles thanks with the help from Robby and another guy who now and then showed up for some more business. The shop was tiny and had all kinds of old toys from early Fifties, Sixties, Seventies and Eighties. All the prices were quoted in US dollars what he accepted for every deal he made with his customers. It was a cash in hand shop.

Robby used to come a lot to this place when he still had his own hostel. From the moment he lost everything it was a while ago that he paid another visit to his old friend, who still did well thanks to another collector who knew a lot of others who liked old vintage toys.

Robby stared at some toys on a shelf and pointed to the toys when Julia looked at it too. "You see that? That used to be mine. I recognised the box as I had one of them too."

"How do you know they were yours?"

Robby took the toy from the shelf and inspected the box. He checked for some marks that he made on them when he owned one of those toys and pointed at it so Julia could see it was his.

"Val must have sold all my stuff to Christakos. I can ask but he will not reveal who sold it to him. He doesn't like to talk about it. I wonder how much he paid for all of it."

"How much is it worth?"

Robby looked at the box. There was no price tag what would ruin the old box but he remembered the catalogue where he saw it years ago when he bought it online.

"I paid somewhere around $600 for this toy. I know it is a lot but there are some other toys who are worth much more."

Julia stared at the toy in the box and put it back on the shelf. Too expensive if she would ever want to start her own collection. She would start simple and not so ridiculous like Robby who didn't mind to waste such amount of money on a toy that he could keep on a shelf in the room.

"You remember the first film Star Wars?"

"Yes, I did. Why?"

"What do you think that made George Lucas rich? The films, oh they did well but it was the toys and all the other things that showed up everywhere when Star Wars was out everywhere. It was the merchandising that made it. And don't forget Star Wars was made only with a twenty-million-dollar budget. Most of the money went into the special effects and they had to create new effects as it was quite unknown then. Nowadays it's computerized stuff but then it was all stop motion effects."

Julia nodded when Robby gave her a lecture. He liked to talk for hours about his favourite films of all times. He knew the lines by heart what was impressive. She knew the films had to say she liked them and she remembered some of the toys back then in the shops.

"So if I want to invest money what would be the best investment and how much we're talking about?"

"You should try to find the classic first twelve figures mint on card if you can get them and we are talking about thousands of dollars. Especially the three figures with the telescope light sabres. They are worth a fortune."

"Hmm, I would start with less then. It's a bit too much for me."

"Trust me Julia, you will find some good bargains. Just look around. You could start with the new toys of the new film that is still in cinema. I guess you have seen the new Star Wars film?"

"You mean The Phantom Menace? Yes, I did in Holland. I saw it in The Hague but I wasn't really impressed with the story."

"So was I but hey it is a new Star Wars film and there are now lots of new toys around what will be soon collectibles. You could start with that.

Have a look around in the city."

"I will see, Robby. I don't think I will start a collection and I will certainly don't want to create a collection like you had in the past. I am not willing to invest too much money in old toys while I could use it for other things."

In the end to please Robby she bought a toy for him what he much appreciated. He thanked her for the little gift and gave it a good place on the second bed in between their beds in their room.

During her stay in Sydney she got much interested in the world of collecting. Robby and Anton were both big collectors although Robby didn't have the money to start a new collection while Anton found a better market for his old pinball machines. In the big basement of his house he had several old pinball machines together with some old arcade machines that needed maintenance.

There was another item in the basement what drew their attention when they paid a visit to his house. Anton managed to buy and repair an old 1970 convertible Rolls Royce Silver Shadow. It was his pride and joy. The only trouble he had was that he had no drivers license but he hoped one day he could take his car out for a nice ride through the city with his friends. Robby still had a driver's license but it was a long time ago he had driven a car.

Through the little toyshop in Bondi Julia met Jonathan who was a part time toy collector and sales man. Together with a good mate he ran a business and bought and sold old and new collections to people who had money and interest in the world of collections.

Jonathan knew Robby and he had seen him at many conventions and Saturday markets in Parramatta. His toy business was just a top up of his income but the Australian market was too small to make a decent buck.

Jonathan was a good looking Aussie. He was a bit chubby and he wore dark clothes. He drove a Hyundai sports car while he worked full time for Audi. He wasn't keen on the car brand but the job paid well and he was able to afford a reasonable car.

Jonathan lived with two other guys in a rented house in Maroubra further south of Bondi close to the beach. One of his house mates was a professional musician while the other house mate was a bump. He never cleaned whatever he was using and he was a pain in the arse to the others. The problem was that the house was in his name and couldn't be thrown out. Jonathan and the musician/ house mate complained nearly everyday to their housemate but he didn't listen and didn't care. They couldn't touch him and he refused to to listen to their complaints. He just couldn't care how he lived. It was his life and his house and he could what ever he liked to do.

19 Leaving Australia (first time)

Paul did his best not to spend much of his part of the stolen money but the farmers were the first who made a mistake by changing American dollars for Aussie bucks. None of them knew that all the bank notes were registered by both Konrad and the police who insisted of a copy of a list of all the bank notes he had in his possession.

The investigation went very slow what annoyed

Konrad. He wanted his money back but now the cops were on it he had to play even with them. He had to answer their questions what he didn't like. He hoped he didn't have to inform the authorities that he was skimming his own guests and that he didn't pay tax over the cash money what he kept well hidden in a cupboard in his house.

His wife and sister in law were still in his house but their marriage was over. He couldn't divorce her as she claimed the motel was hers. He allowed her to do the cleaning but no longer to look at the bookkeeping. He was in charge of the business and knew more about his guests than she did. All she did was cleaning all the spaces and went back to the house where she spent time with her sis who wanted to leave Australia.

The sister in law had a hard time. She didn't like Sydney. The city and the people weren't as friendly as they claimed to be. She missed her own country but as soon as she would fly back to Korea she wouldn't be welcome again in Australia. Konrad was busy in stopping her and wanted her to leave as soon as possible.

In Bondi Robby and Julia got so their own little

problems. They both worked lots of hours for the hostel and dealt with annoying students who didn't care much about rules.

The Brazilians were playing their little game with Robby and were testing his patience. Julia had it easier as she only worked a few days a week in Bondi and a few days in Kirribilli for Glenferrie Lodge where Glenda and Lydia were pleased to see her back. They liked Julia but it was Terry her chef who decided how many days she could work in Kirribilli.

Robby on the other hand had to deal with them nearly every evening and just couldn't stand them. He had enough of them as they never listened to him. Whatever he tried they did it on purpose to annoy him so they hoped to see him getting angry. They loved it when Robby was angry. He shouted a lot what Julia never did. She kept her anger to herself and released it when she went out for her regular walk along the coastline.

A couple of days a week she made these walks and used it to distress herself. Now and then she ran the long distance feeling and hearing the waves of the sea hitting the cliffs of the coast. Only once she walked all the way from North

Bondi to Maroubra Beach further south. It was a long walk and back in Coogee Beach she was so tired that she had to take a bus back to Bondi. Normally she walked all the way to Clovelly or just only Bronte Beach and then through the streets back to the hostel.

Through her regular life what she had thanks to Robby and the Bondi Lodge the time went faster than she could have thought. She earned enough money for her next trip to Southeast Asia but Robby did also his best in asking her for lots of financial favours.

When he first started for some favours she didn't mind and helped him as best as she could but the more he asked the harder it became for her to say no. She liked him and didn't want to see him suffer. She had no idea where it all would lead.

Before she knew it time was flying so fast when she noticed that her first six months were nearly done. She had to leave the country for a short while before she could comeback so she could stay for another six months in the country.

There was one major concern what she couldn't tell the Authorities about her work for the Bondi Lodge. She wasn't allowed to work without the right visa. The managers in the Bondi Lodge never checked her visa status and just signed her pay cheque and paid her every fortnight without thinking they were actually breaking the law.

Julia waited on an evening when Robby was on the desk. It was late and it was very quiet in the hostel. None of the Brazilians were around. None of the other overseas students hung around the reception what was very unusual. Normally they would just hang around to see if there was a call for them from home but the phone remained quiet and Robby had finally some time to deal with other issues.

Robby was the only staff member in the evening and day that took payments. The others were slack in their work or they were too busy with other things. Robby checked every day the balance sheets and made notes of all the names of students who were behind in their payments. None of the managers made any note of late payments. They were just glad when they received their money and they didn't care who took the payments as long as they received it so they could spend it.

"Robby, do you have a minute for me?"

He looked up when he saw her standing on the other side of the desk. Normally she would sit next of him at the desk but not this time. "Sure, what's up, mate?"

"Robby, I have to leave soon because my visa is about to expire."

"Wow, time's flying, isn't it?"

"Yes, it is." She replied. "Then there's this thing. What would happen if immigration discovers I am working here on no working visa?"

"Aren't you sponsored by the managers?" Julia shook her head. She signed and bit on her lip. She ran her hand through her short hair that she kept extreme short because of her job in the kitchen. She didn't mind she wasn't looking very girly. She was a cook and short hair was much easier to keep covered than long hair what she saw as a crime in the kitchen. She was afraid to see her own hair in the food she prepared for others. By keeping it extreme short it was hard to discover in the food but easy to cover with a simple hat.

"When they offered me your position I heard of a contract but I never signed any document nor did I receive one. Maybe you could check it out for me. You know more than I do and perhaps if you see one of the managers ask about my contract. I don't want to get caught and be sent back to Holland and find my name on a black list."

"I will check out for you. Where will you go?"

She had already flight tickets but she wasn't so sure if she wanted to travel to New Zealand. Money was no problem. She earned and saved enough money what she kept on her Commonwealth Bank account so she could use that money when she would travel to Southeast Asia after her year in Australia.

"I was thinking of going to New Zealand. It's further east and what I know it looks like an amazing country to spend at least a week perhaps two weeks."

Robby didn't like the idea of her leave. He hoped she would stay around and not going to countries like New Zealand. There was another reason why he didn't like the country. His ex was now dating a guy from New Zealand so he wasn't very pleased with that either. "Julia, aren't there any other countries you should give a go instead of New Zealand?"

"Why? What's wrong with my planned trip to New Zealand?"

He coughed and looked her in her pretty blue eyes. He liked her although he didn't like her present hairstyle. She had it cut so short that he could see her skin. She had it cut quite often and wondered how far she would go. He remembered her extreme look in January when she had hardly any hair left on her pretty head. She made a little mistake by going to a wrong barber who didn't like to cut women so he gave her a punishment cut and nearly shaved her complete bald.

"Julia. Why don't you fly to Hong Kong? I used to go there often or go to Singapore. Ask Konrad what he thinks of Singapore. These places are much better than New Zealand. What about Fiji or Bali? Lots of Aussies go there and you can afford the flight."

Julia thought for a moment but still wanted to go to New Zealand. At least she had already flight tickets but she could swap them through Cathay Pacific for other flight destinations with the airliner. It wouldn't cost her much so she could give it a go.

"Robby, it's very kind of you to think of my

concern. About my money I can afford all these places and I might go there after my year in Australia. Thank you for being so thoughtful. I do appreciate your concern but this is my trip and I want to go to countries and places that matters me. I don't care what you think of them or what your feelings are but my mind tells me that I should go to New Zealand."

She still had plenty of time before her visa would run out. She left the Bondi Lodge and took a bus to the city. Through the busy streets in the heart of the city she wandered a bit and checked with a few agencies for options.

A short while ago she met in Bondi a collector of vintage toys in a collectible toy shop at the top of Hall Street in Bondi where Robby used to do a lot of business with the shop owner. The guy was from Greece and he spoke both English and Greek. He was a big guy who loved to watch wrestling matches on telly.

Jonathan the collector noticed her in the shop while she looked around and picked up now and then toys she recognised from shops in the past in her own country. When she was young she used to play with toys and not always with dolls.

"Hi, there. Found anything interesting?"

"Hi, I might." She said and smiled to him.

"Where do you stay? I guess you're here on holiday?"

"Yep. I stay in the Bondi Lodge."

He nodded and knew where it was. He lived with two other guys in a big house in Maroubra a bit further south in the eastern suburbs. There was a big beach but he never went to it. He wasn't a beach person.

"Where're you from?"

"From Holland. I'm Julia by the way."

"G'day, mate. Nice to meet ya." He replied with a fake Aussie accent. "I'm Jonathan."

She shook his hand. She liked him. He was a bit shorter than her. His hair was short and he had a beard. He was dressed in black pants and a black shirt. His voice was a bit dark and heavy. She spotted a slight German accent when he introduced himself to her.

"What do you do for a living?"

"I work for Audi." He replied. "I'm dealing with customer service and spare parts of Audi."

"I work for the Bondi Lodge and another hostel in Kirribilli."

"What do you do?"

"I'm a cook." She said with a big smile. "Don't laugh. I am a good cook."

They both spent some time in the shop when Jonathan looked at the time on his watch. He had no business to deal with Costas in his little shop and he wasn't sure if Julia would be interested in his business. Instead he offered her a lift what she immediately accepted.

"How's the food in the Lodge? Do you think I can get a plate?"

"Sure, why not. Just talk with Robby and he might let you eat. He's tonight our receptionist."

Jonathan was thinking. He talked earlier with Costas about a collector who disappeared. for a couple of months and when he came back he was a different man. He forgot to ask him about his name but when he thought a bit longer that

Robby might be that guy who disappeared for a long sailing trip.

"Julia, do you know a guy called Robby Skykiller?"

"Not sure. I know a Robby but he never called himself Skykiller."

Jonathan looked at her while he drove towards the Bondi Lodge. He drove a Hyundai Excel and listened to classic rock music through his sound system. "Why does this guy calls himself Skykiller?"

"Are you familiar with the film Star Wars?" Julia nodded. She loved to watch films and remembered when the first Star Wars films hit the cinema in late 70's and early 80's. She was very young then but she remembered the films.

"Robby calls himself Skykiller as that was the original name and not Skywalker what you should know if you're a big fan. Now Robby is one of the biggest Star Wars fans I know and he had this enormous collection of classic toys from the 70's and 80's when the first three films came out. Now you have this new one "The Phantom Menace" but he's not so keen on it. Yes, it's still a Star Wars film but what I have heard he doesn't want to collect any of the available toys that came with the film. He prefers the old classics and they are worth a fortune."

"You know a lot about it," She answered. "I remember the films and I know my friend Robby claimed he had the biggest toy collection here in Sydney. I first thought he was joking but now you mention it, he might be the one you were talking about."

Jonathan nodded. He looked again at her and showed her a big smile. She smiled back. He touched her hair what was so short he could see her skin.

"Why on earth did you shave your head? Do you want to look like that actress Demi Moore?"

"No, but as a chef it's easier when you don't have much hair than long hair. Besides my hair becomes too greasy while I work in a hot kitchen so for that reason I cut my hair off and keep it as short as possible.

"ha ha, GI Jane the chef."

She laughed about his little joke and stared for a

moment at his beard. It was more a goatee but she didn't mind. He looked cool even with his dark clothes.

"You like dark clothes, don't you?"

"Yes, they refer to my period when I was a big heavy rock fan. I guess you heard the music of Black Sabbath you know Ozzy Ozbourne. That was my kind of music. Still is, cool band."

'Yes, I like rock music. I can't sing or play any instruments but I like to listen to some good music. I listen actually to all kinds of music but rock music will always be my favourite."

"Any favourite band in particular?"

She laughed and nodded. Julia liked rock music. In the kitchen when she was at work she listened to the music of Tom Yorke and his band Radiohead. Then she also listens to some Dutch music from a Cabaret duo Acda en De Munnick. Then there was a disk of Mariah Carey what she played now and then when she was cooking in Kirribilli. Lydia liked her music although she liked the Dutch music too. Jonathan played a CD of Peter Frampton - Frampton comes Alive. She tapped with her hands on her legs while he played loud the hit song 'Show me the way'. He noticed how much she liked the song.

"Some people can't stand him but I say he's cool. This was one of his best albums."

"If I'm not mistaken it's one of the best albums true rock fans should have in their collection." Julia replied.

"True, if you like this you should listen to the album 'Rumours" of Fleetwood Mac. Or what about "Dark side of the Moon" by Pink Floyd."

"Great album. A classic I would say."

He parked his car in front of the door of the Bondi Lodge and opened the door gentle for Julia and followed her. Robby was alone at the desk and was glad to see Julia again. He smiled and stared for a moment to Jonathan. He had seen him before but he couldn't remember.

"Hello, Robby. long time ago we see each other again."

"I'm sorry but who are you?"

Julia and Jonathan looked at each other. She wanted to answer for him but he waved with his hands and stopped her.

"It's ok, Julia. I can talk for myself." He said while he looked straight into Robby's eyes. "Do you remember the Comic Convention two years ago. You were then the biggest collector in Sydney while I was there together with my friend Kevin. We both talked about the rumours of the new Star Wars film when you mentioned to me that you wouldn't invest any money into the toys they would bring out as soon as the film would hit the theatre. Do you remember that day?"

Robby nodded and his mind started to spin. He was then a very rich fellow and owned a successful hostel before he gave it in the hands of his wife and a couple of Israelis. He lost a fortune but most of all he lost his enormous collection what was worth around a million bucks.

"Yes, I remember you. What can I do for you?"

"Julia told me I could have a meal before I would go home if that's ok with you."

"Sure, go ahead. Try it and see for yourself if you like the food here."

Julia and Jonathan went inside the dining room

and joined the queue of hungry students. Like always they filled their plates full and only ate half of their food. The rest would be wasted as most of the time they didn't like what they took.

Jonathan filled his plate and observed Julia who took a little of several dishes. She wasn't so hungry and wasn't so sure if she would like today's food. They found a table and started to eat. Julia made a tea for both of them and tried to enjoy her dinner in peace with her new friend.

"It's not so bad." He said after a few bites. "Why is Robby so hard on everyone?"

"You should ask him. I wonder if he would answer you."

"How much do you know about him?"

"What do you mean?"

Jonathan laughed and looked her in her eyes. She stared back and was silent for a while. She looked around and looked at the guests who had their dinner in the dining room. Most of them were students but there were a bunch of backpackers too. "You think you know him by whatever he's telling you. You'll be surprised how smooth his words are. He's good in it and you aren't the first who would fall for him. There were others before you and they all regretted that they didn't know a thing about him. He hides his past well enough and he gets upset when he knows that you know what he's hiding from you."

Julia lost suddenly her appetite. She dropped her fork and stared for a moment to her new friend. He finished his plate and got some more food. When he got back she looked him again in his face and wanted to know more.

"How long do you know him? When and where did you meet him and how do he approached you?"

"We met here in the street a couple of months ago when I arrived in Bondi. Before Bondi I stayed in the Y in the Park a YWCA hotel but the prices went up around Christmas time so I had to look for a more affordable place and I had to make a choice between this hostel and the one in Kirribilli, the Glenferrie Lodge. I met him a few days later when I came back from the city where he was working for a motel owner."

Robby entered the dining area but he didn't share his food with them. He filled a plate and went back to the reception. He looked only once in Julia's direction but his eyes said enough when they stared for a short moment into each others eyes.

"Anyway I got to know him better with Christmas. He stayed in one of the big dorms and there they had every night a party. He joined the party and thought he was part of the group of Scandinavians. He talked Swedish to them and had lots of fun."

"How was he then? Did he say a lot about his life?"

"We got to know each other just after New Year's Day when we shared a table. We had dinner but we both didn't like the food so he offered me a better option."

"Did you have to pay for it?"

"Yes, I did but then I didn't mind. Now I think he can afford a meal and he still insists that I should pay for all his meals we have together what isn't that much as he works nearly every evening."

Jonathan showed a smile and recognised the signals. He still hadn't changed much and was still behaving like a crook.

"Did he mention his old hostel?"

"Yes, but don't tell me he didn't own one, did he?"

"He actually did own a hostel but I don't know how successful he was. All I know is that he made a nice fortune with a simple and smart way without getting caught."

Julia got curious while she was thinking about Robby's friend Konrad, who had mentioned to her the little scheme he learned from his friend who never talked about it. As if Robby was afraid to get caught while Konrad suffered a terrible loss now he lost his gained fortune through an ex staff member who ran away and robbed him of his illegal gained treasure.

"I don't know how he made his money but he invested most of it in toy collectibles. He built up an enormous collection and it was one of the biggest in Australia. I did some business with him as did Costas the owner of the little collectible shop."

Julia nodded. She remembered him while she

listened to Jonathan's story. He was calm and talked clearly about the man who shared a space with her. She thought she knew him but actually she knew nothing about his past. All she knew what his hostel but nothing about his relationship with his ex wife and how they broke up. Did he have any family and if so where did they live? Did he ever see them? So many questions and she wondered if she would get answers to all her questions or did she have to live with only a few answers. Time would tell and she hoped she would hear more from her friends and from Robby when she would be back from her little break.

20 Return to Hong Kong

Julia left Australia and flew with Qantas to Hong Kong. A couple of days before she decided to go to Hong Kong she booked her flight and hotel with a travel agency in the city. All her new friends told her not to go to New Zealand. She wasn't so happy that she couldn't go there still there were other options where she could spend at least a week before she would return back to Australia for another six months.

Her new friend Jonathan agreed with Robby that she shouldn't go to New Zealand. He wasn't so keen on Kiwis who were in his eyes too laid back and awkward. There was another thing why she should go to Hong Kong as she liked to go shopping. She did a lot of shopping in Sydney and loved to hang around in the two big stores David Jones and Grace Brothers. The latter was her favourite as the first was too expensive. Another reason why she spent a lot of time in downtown Sydney was the big all mall QVB

Queen Victoria Building what was a big mall with a big and affordable food court in the basement. It connected the big department store Grace Bros with other shops where she could spend hours and hours without buying. Hong Kong would be a better option but so was Singapore.

In a travel agency in the basement in between Grace Bros and QVB she checked out cheap flights to a few destinations. The staff gave her some interesting options; Singapore, Hong Kong, Fiji and Bali Indonesia but she rejected the last as she would probably spend enough time in Asia after her next 6 months stay in Australia.

In the end she booked a holiday for 9 days to Hong Kong where she would stay in a 3-star hotel in Hong Kong Island in Wan Chai district. Her hotel was near an MRT station so she could travel to Kowloon by train or catching a ferry from Central. The flight was with the national airline of Australia; Qantas. She got two nights for free what made the deal more acceptable and paid instant cash before she would change her mind. The trip would be great one and a return to Hong Kong where she had a lovely short stopover on her way from Amsterdam to Sydney.

Anton met Julia a few times and liked her. Although he didn't speak a word of Dutch his parents were born and raised in Holland before they immigrated to Australia for a better life. His father was part of the Olympic Comity and he was training young kids for his part of the Opening Ceremony of the Summer Olympics in Sydney 2000.

Anton was very tall and skinny for his age. He was 1,95 and very skinny. He didn't go to school and left it when he was fifteen. He was gifted with electronics and mechanics skills and had his own little online business in repairing and selling old classic pinball machines and old arcade game machines. Robby knew Anton from several conventions and collectors' meetings in Parramatta.

After six months Julia was back on Sir Kingsford Smith Sydney International Airport where she caught a flight with the national airlines of Australia Qantas to Hong Kong. She arrived early as always on the airport and took her time before she checked in her luggage for her flight.

In the morning Robby had a coffee with her at their local coffee bar opposite the Lodge whey they spend a lot of time on coffee reading the paper and for Julia having breakfast and sometimes lunch. The little bar was open 7 days a week and was doing good business. It was a typical local coffee place where locals from across the street would come and have a coffee.

"You should look for some collectibles." Robby told her while they had their coffee outside. "There's the rumour that there's a warehouse somewhere in Hong Kong that has an enormous collection of vintage toys worth a fortune. I don't know where it is but I have heard from others. Ask your friend Jonathan or Anton. They both know the story and will confirm it's true."

"So, how big is this collection and who owns it?"

"That's the question, Julia. I don't know but I know it's true. It's not a lie. If people like Anton and Jonathan tells you it you would believe them, don't you?"

"Not always but yes, I do." She replied.

"See, I am not lying to you. Try to find it and get me some if you can."

"I don't make a promise if I can't keep my word.

I will see."

Julia wandered a bit around on the airport of Sydney before it was time to board the flight. Her flight to Hong Kong was a big Boeing 747 and it was fully booked. The staff on-board was friendly and the flight smooth.

It was her second visit to the International airport of Hong Kong on Chep Lap Kok. This time she didn't need to search for a bus that would bring her to her hotel on Hong Kong Island. As soon as she landed and passed Immigration and customs a man stood with a board in front of him what had her name written. She greeted her pick up and joined some other folks who would stay in the same hotel. He took them to a little bus and helped them with their luggage.

The Hennessey Hotel was a 3-star hotel and was not far away from the night scene at Lockhart Road. There was a Thai seafood restaurant near her hotel and a sports court plus she was close to the nearest MRT station that would bring her to the other side of the Hong Kong to Kowloon.

Two days before Julia flew to Hong Kong Robby managed to get some money out of her for his court case. He needed actually more money but she was willing to loan him a few hundred bucks as long as he promised he would pay her back. She didn't like to be used by him as a walking ATM as she saw herself whenever he asked for money. She wasn't his private banker and didn't like to give him while he earned enough money trough the work he did for the Bondi Lodge.

Robby approached Julia with his court case when he found out she had lots of money. On their first meeting he tested her when he took her to a nice Italian restaurant of one of his friends. In the past he provided the place with staff. His hostel did more for money stripped backpackers than all the others. Robby knew which bar and restaurant needed staff and provided them with only the best. The owners offered him discount or even free meals as long as he could help them with finding good staff.

Robby was a legend in Bondi and many of the local businesses knew him. Till the day he decided to have a long break he was helping others while no one stood up for him when he needed help when he came back from his trip. Robby learned a painful lesson and remembered it.

Julia felt pity when she heard many of his stories. She had a good heart and wanted to help others. Money didn't mean much to her. She was pleased with the fortune that she inherited from her late grand mother but as soon as she would have it on her account it became also a burden.

Robby was still licking his wounds from his previous victim. Only Konrad knew about it and he kept it that way. Some of his friends heard the story but he always denied he had something to do with it. Whatever happened she was no longer in Australia and he had done his best in draining the poor sod empty.

While Julia was in Hong Kong Konrad and Robby were having a private meeting in the little office of the Lodge. It was a quiet night but Robby kept the door open so he could hear the phone or hear guests asking for whatever they needed him.

"Konrad, I want my name wiped out the system of the police."

"I will see what I can do for you, but there's a big chance that I can't do it. I will do my best."

They were quiet for a moment while Konrad tried

to listen to the noise he heard from a group of guys who were playing table tennis in the back of the hostel. Robby opened his briefcase and showed his friend some documents.

"Have a look at this. It's from Julia and it's from her bank in Holland. See how wealthy she is."

"Hmm, that's a lot of money. Are you sure it's not a fake?"

"No, these are other statements she left behind in our room. She should pay a bit more attention to her belongings. She's like all the other guests quite messy. You should know what she does to her underwear."

"Robby, I am not interested in that. I can't believe she's so messy."

Robby smiled and had the attention of his friend. "There's more, Konrad. I asked her for helping supporting me with my court case."

"Yes, I have heard you want to sue the council for neglect. Do you really think you have a chance to beat the council?"

"I have and Julia helps me with my case. A while

ago she took some sharp photos of the hole that is still there next of my old hostel."

"Yes, and was that hole there before?"

Robby shook his head. "No, I should have remembered but I don't so I say that hole was caused by the heavy rainfall we had in April last year when I hurt my back. I nearly broke my leg because that hole was a hazardous threat to my health and the council should have put a cover on it."

"What were you doing that night when we had that hail storm?"

"I was visiting Val. I wanted to know why she froze my accounts and cut my cards in half. I was money stripped and wanted to get some cash from my little box that I always kept in the safe in my old office. The bitch stole my money and refused to help me."

"So, now you want to use Julia as your piggy bank I believe?"

"I don't want to call her a piggy bank but yeah, I might. At least she's wealthier than that other girl who stayed with me in Hornsby. She had money but not as much as Julia has. My only problem is to convince her in helping me."

Konrad had to laugh. Robby thought that Julia was as naive as the previous girl but for some reason she was braver and smarter than the poor girl who nearly found death on her path when Robby got a bit too rough with her. Julia wasn't so easy to persuade and didn't want to waste her money on helping him while he earned his own money. She didn't mind to help him but she was not willing to invest lots of money in a court case versus a council that had better lawyers.

Julia had no idea what Robby was up to behind her back. She had no idea he got some of her latest bank statements and Could from that moment blackmail her. He wanted her money and for some reasons she felt he was after her money. Her friendship with him was quite obvious. Why did he like her? It was not because her looks. She hardly looked feminine and she didn't care. She wasn't a true backpacker but more a flashy traveller with money who did her best to live simple.

Hong Kong was a great place for her to look around and to shop. There were plenty big malls and lots of shops where she spent hours of time without worrying about her time in Australia.

In the evenings she found an English pub called The Old China Hand that was run by a Brit who was born and raised in Hong Kong. The staff of the pub were all Filipinos who did all the work while he sat there every evening and drank his beer. They served food and some Filipinos played cover music to create a nice ambiance.

Julia paid a daily visit to that pub because of one of the guys whom she met in Kirribilli. He had a Filipino girlfriend who worked for that pub. She was beautiful and had very long hair. Julia met the girl on her first night but didn't have a chance to have a chat with her. Her English was good and she did her job perfect so she could receive plenty of tips.

The English owner paid his staff fair. He helped them with the right visa and made sure they all had medical cover. What Julia didn't know but heard from her friend in Kirribilli was that the owner had some intimacy moments with his female staff. The young ones were very easy while the older staff members weren't so keen in having sex with him.

Two weeks before Julia flew to Hong Kong she had a long chat with her friend in Glenferrie Lodge after a long day of work. She drank a beer with the guys while Glenda didn't look. She didn't approve alcohol on the premises but as long as they cleared up their mess they could have a few drinks now and then on the big terrace in the front of the hostel. Nowhere else they weren't allowed to drink and she threatened them by throwing them out if they would break her rules. They all listened to her.

Pete was a nice guy who was only because of a big building job in Sydney. He was actually from the Gold Coast Queensland and was here because of work. The money he earned was good and the place was simple and cheap so he saved himself a lot of money. The moment he met Julia he fell in love with her. It took her a couple of visits before she loved him too.

Robby was a very jealous guy when he heard from Julia she was in love with another guy. He wanted to be her boyfriend but she only wanted to be friends with him nothing more. She liked Robby especially his stories but she didn't feel any compassion for him. No, Pete was more her type and she did her best to start some kind of a relation with him.

The last night they were together at Glenferries he talked a lot about his Filipino girlfriend. He wanted to tell Julia how much he loved her but that his Filipino girlfriend was his Number 1. Julia accepted that she was just a fling nothing more nothing less.

Julia wasn't looking for a man she would start a new relationship. She met guys everywhere and if it clicked she became friends before she wanted to commit herself to someone. For the moment she was travelling and having a serious relationship while travelling wasn't easy. She already broke up with her last boyfriend back home in Holland because he didn't want to travel with her to Australia. If he would have been there in Australia she would never be in Bondi and she wouldn't be working that was for sure.

In Hong Kong she gave herself some time to reflect her life in Australia. First there was Robby who wanted to be serious friends with her. He wanted to have sex with her what she didn't want at all. Friendship ok but sex no that was the last thing she was looking for. There were others whom she liked but sex was of the hook.

Young Anton and Jonathan were guys she truly loved. Anton was a bit too young for her while Jonathan was a serious contender only he was engaged with a Chinese Australian girl Shirley. She was for the moment for a couple of months travelling in Europe leaving her boyfriend alone who was looking for company to fill the empty gap in his heart.

Jonathan liked Julia from the first moment they met in the little toy collectors shop in Bondi. She was so different than his previous loves he had and he wondered what his fiancée would say if they could meet each other. Would Shirley like Julia?

Pete was another contender and she truly loved him although she knew about his relationship with that Filipino girl here in Hong Kong. she met Lisa who was kind and very pretty. She understood why Pete loved her. She was like many other Filipino women very beautiful and fell immediately in love with her.

On her second evening in the Old China Hand she found some time to have a chat with Lisa. It wasn't too busy and the owner gave her some time to talk with his customers.

Julia drank a San Miguel beer while she listened to a Filipino Beatles Cover band. They were pretty good and knew the songs by heart. Julia liked the music and enjoyed her evening in the English pub.

"Hi, Lisa. Can I talk with you for a while?"
"Sure, what do you want to know?"

Julia showed her a photo of Pete together with Julia shot from Glenferrie Lodge a few weeks before she flew to Hong Kong. She noticed how Lisa took the photo and gentle touched it. She smiled when she saw her man on the photo with Julia who was like her all smiles.

"You love him?"

"I do but he loves you too." Julia said. "Don't worry. We have nothing in common although we like each other but he told me you are his Number 1 and I will be forever a fling."

Lisa stared at the photo and nodded. She loved him and missed him dearly. She wished she could live in Australia so she could have a perfect life and have a home for their family. In Hong Kong she didn't have much of a life. She worked every day of the week and did it to support her family back home in the Philippines. They were very poor and she was just very lucky to find a good job outside her country.

"You have kids?" She asked suddenly while she looked Julia in her eyes.

"No, I don't and I don't know if I ever will have one. First I have to find a perfect man who will look after me and support me while I still can have my own life and I am not sure if I want to have children. Maybe 1 or 2 but not more than that."

"I have one baby and she lives in the Philippines. It's not Pete's although he claimed the child. He pays me every month so my baby can go to school when she's old enough and if I save enough money she might can go to university."

"You say it's not Pete's?" Lisa pointed in the direction of her employer. He was flirting

with a new staff member who was just 20 years old and new in the country. An older Filipino woman sat next of her and kept an eye on the two. She knew him too well and did her best to protect the young girl.

"He's not a bad guy he only likes to play a bit too much with us. I worked before for a big office some blocks away and my employers then were terrible. We were second class citizen and in their eyes we had no rights at all. They thought they could do what ever they liked with us and when we complained they would fire us without a pay. I got out on time and found a job as a waitress in this bar and I am still here."

"Does your boss knows you have a child?"

"Yes, he does. I told him when I found out I was pregnant. I couldn't hide it from him and told him it was his child. He acknowledged that he made me pregnant but he couldn't claim the child. You see he has more children with several other women so for that reason he can't support me."

Lisa left Julia for a moment and served a few new guests before she returned to Julia's table with a new beer. Julia took a gulp of her cold beer and smiled.

"I met Pete in this bar and told him I have a baby but I have no one to support me in the future education of my child. He told me he would look after me and my baby and when the time will come he wants to marry me."

"Oh, that's sounds promising."

Lisa took Julia with a few other friends of the pub and went to another pub a few streets away. In the 'From dusk till dawn' pub where a Japanese rock band played covers from some classic rock bands she had a couple of beers and a good night with the Filipinos. They all worked for a long period in Hong Kong and this was one of their favourite spots to hang out. There were lots of Filipinos in that part of Hong Kong where many of them worked as a nanny or a nurse. The money was good and most of the money they earned was send back home to support their families who relied so much on their supports.

Julia had a great time in Hong Kong. She spent some money on new boots she could use for her work in the kitchen. She bought a few films that she could play on her new desktop computer. The films were VCD quality and were very cheap. Her computer back in the hostel was a proper brand and was brand new. She needed a special computer desk for her little room but she could have a look for that when she would be back in Sydney.

Every evening she went to the Old China Hand where she talked with Lisa when she had some time. She drank beer and listen when there was a band to the music. Lisa and her friends took her out to their favourite bars and clubs and gave her a wonderful time.

"You love my boyfriend, don't you?"

"You mean Pete? Yes, he's a wonderful guy. I meet him now and then when I have to work in Kirribilli. He stays in the Glenferrie Lodge and he's a long-term regular. Every time I had to cook there I had some beers with him and his mates on the balcony watching the skyline of Sydney. Cooking for man like Pete are highlights in my life."

"I don't mind you see him but he's mine. We will get married hopefully very soon and I will move to his country. He's working very hard and he will build our dream house overlooking the wonderful views of the countryside."

"How often do you see him?"

"Not often but we do use the internet and we Skype a lot. If you see him say how much I love him."

"I will and I understand. We are only friends and I will not stand in your way my dear."

Julia gave Lisa a warm hug and wished she could love her as she did with her boyfriend. Lisa was a warm and very kind woman.

21 Robby and his Court Case

Julia's big plan was to travel in Southeast Asia for a year or maybe longer. It all depended on her spending. She earned well and saved as much as she could so she could use that money for her future trip but then there was Robby who liked to use her as his private bank and ATM. Quite often he asked her for favours that she couldn't refuse as he promised her so many other things.

Robby started with small amounts but as the time flew by he asked her now and then for some bigger amounts. She wasn't always keen in giving him money but he promised her often that he would pay her back.

Robby was busy with a big court case and he

believed he could win his case. His biggest problem was money. He used to have lots on several accounts but his lovely ex wife froze all his accounts and cut all his cards that he left behind when he went away for three months sailing. She sold his apartment and made him technical homeless. Without a buck in his pockets and no credit card in his wallet he was left stranded. None of his friends wanted to help him so he had to find another way in finding his way back to Bondi.

Julia heard the story a couple of times from the mouth of Robby. He never changed the topic and the story was always the same. He told her his story when they met in the Bondi Lodge. He was looking for a potential victim and found in Julia his ideal prey.

"Do you mind if I join you at this table?"

"No, go ahead." She had said and liked his company. She was alone and didn't know anyone that moment. Robby became after Emily her new friend and she was much interested in his life. He was a good story teller.

"I am Robby and I used to have my own hostel not long ago." He noticed he had her attention.

She showed a smile while she ate her dinner. He ate his but he didn't like the food. Even with the salt he added to get a bit more flavour it still didn't taste good and it was just a waste on his plate. "Do you like steak?"

"Who doesn't?" She replied. He noticed she didn't like her food either but she was too kind to eat as much as she could before she would throw the rest away.

"I know a good place where we can have a good steak and a drink. Do you like to come with me? I can show you a bit of Bondi if you don't mind. You are new here, aren't you?"

Robby showed Julia his Bondi and he showed her his old hostel. He had been so proud of his old hostel what was now a shocking old business in shambles. It was still open but she wondered how many people were staying in that dump. It looked so unsafe but Robby knew there were still some crazy cheap backpackers who didn't mind to live in the old hostel. All the wanted was a cheap bed and no comforts.

"I know what you think when you see my old hostel. Why is the place such a dump while not long ago it was still one of the best running hostels in the country? It was even in the top ten of hostels in Australia. It was the best hostel here in Sydney."

"What happened to it? Why did you loose your business and can you get it back?"

"I wish but that will not be possible. My ex owns the place and see what she has done to my business. She never cared about the place. She only cares about herself and her drugs and booze."

Robby took Julia further into Lamrock Avenue and stopped at the corner between Lamrock and Jacques Avenue. He pointed to a hole in the ground that was quite deep and what wasn't covered what should have been covered. The hole was a hazardous place and a serious threat for pedestrians.

"You see that hole? I fell in it in April last year. We had the worst hailstorm in years and the hailstones were as big as golf balls. If you don't believe me check it in the library. If you look closely around you still can see what it did to the area. You still can see the damage what that hailstorm caused."

"Why isn't that hole covered?"

"Good point. I see you are very sharp what I can't say about the Council. They don't care about these things here."

"What can you do about it?"

"A lot. I want to sue the council for the lack of interest in the environment and for not covering that hole what should have been covered. Do you see anything what should have been to cover it?"

Julia looked around but shook her head. The little bushes were only covered with trash left behind from silly people who were too lazy to throw their trash in the bins anywhere in the streets. There was nothing what should have been put on top of that hole and that caused a serious threat to the people's health.

"Do you have a camera I can borrow so I can take photos of that hole so I can use it in a court case?"

"I do have a camera and if you want I can take some photos for you. I don't want you to borrow my camera but I can take photos for you."

Although Robby was a bit disappointed in her he was glad she was willing to help him. A few days later she took in his presence some clear photos from different angles of the hole and did her best to show how deep the hole actually was. Even without a small ruler and a pencil she still managed to get some clear photos what would show how deep the hole was. Robby used his foot in a few photos to make clear that the hole was a serious threat and that the Council needed to sort out this case asap.

In the city he found a lawyer who was willing to take the case and promised Robby he would sue the Council and was pleased with the photos that Julia took for him.

"Julia, I don't want to ask for more but could you help me again?"

Now that he had a case and a lawyer he needed money to fund his case and there was a serious problem. He still had no access to his old bank accounts and couldn't reopen his own accounts thanks to his ex who froze his accounts and blocked him from any attempt to reopen them.

"I need a few thousand grand for my case but I can't get access to my old accounts. Could you be so kind to help me with donating some money so I start my case?"

Their friendship was still young and fresh. There were no problems and she liked him. She had no idea who he was and how much money she was about to loose when she offered him her help to his so called important court case. If she would have known him better she wouldn't have lent him any money at all but Robby was smart enough to fool her with his smooth talking.

He asked her regular for more money so he could use it for his case. Now and then she asked for some updates what he gave her. When she met Konrad even he learned about his court case and had so his doubts. He knew much more than she did and didn't believe him completely. The hole was genuine and was a serious threat but he wasn't convinced he fell in it on that particular day when Sydney got hit by that dreadful hailstorm in April 1999.

Julia helped Robby as much as she could with his court case and gave him around five thousand dollars over a period of six months. He wanted more but she thought that would be more than enough. He should save money through his new job as receptionist but he came often back to her so he could ask for more money.

First Julia didn't mind to help him but after a while she wondered if she would ever see her money back. He was promising her so much but in the meantime he asked for more and more and more till she had enough of it.

Robby didn't stay long with his first lawyer. He believed in Robby's case but demanded a lot of money up front before he could start to sue Waverley Council where Bondi was part of. Robby explained the thing to Julia who nearly exploded. She didn't want to pay more money for his case while he should work harder and spent more of his earned money into his case.

"Julia, can you please help me. I need more money otherwise I can't sue the Council."

"Is there no other way to sue them? Aren't there better lawyers who offer you better deals who understand that you can't pay upfront but can help you with your case so you can pay them later when you won your case?"

"Yes, there are these lawyers but I am not sure if I should go with one of them. What if they don't believe me and I have to pay thousands of bucks what I don't have if I loose my case?"

"That will be your problem. I won't be here in the next couple of years. I am only here temporary so don't try to use me as your private banker what I am not. So please Robby go out in the city and look around. I am sure you can find a proper lawyer who can help you with your court case. I am sure you can beat them but you have to do it yourself. I can't help you constantly. You have to rely a bit more on your own. You're a big boy so up you go."

Robby showed a smile when she saw him as a big boy. She was absolutely in her right when she complained about the way he was using her as his private banker. She didn't like it and wasn't amused.

"Of course, Julia you are right. You are not my private banker but I do appreciate your help and your concern. Without you I would be still broke and jobless. I owe you so much. How can I ever pay you back?"

"If you can treat me one night special; only one night. Can you do that?"

She nearly thought he would never treat her special but to her surprise he treated her and his friends on a special evening. He owed his friends so much and hoped they all would accept his offer.

Thanks to Julia he found a better lawyer who saw like the previous lawyer so potential in his case. Yes, she could sue the Council on Robby's behalf and understood his financial situation. She asked for a grant up front what he reluctantly paid after he had to beg for the money at Julia.

"Please, Julia, help me. I need that grand otherwise no court case."

"Did you explain to her that you don't have any money?"

"Yes, she heard me and took my case seriously. She wants to see all my documents and photos before she will confront the Council. She thinks I can win the case and I could earn up to half a million bucks."

"How much will she take from you?"

"A third of the total cost. A lot of money but it is better than nothing."

Although she didn't like it she helped him with the grant but she still demanded more updates from him and his case. She even wanted to meet his new lawyer but Robby managed to keep her away. He was afraid she might blow his court case if she would meet her before the case was on and won. She met the previous lawyer and actually liked the guy. He was good and believed in the case but he wanted to see a lot of money before he could start to sue the Council.

Robby took Julia, Anton and Jonathan to the Renaissance hotel down at Circular Quay where they served a buffet. He ordered two plates of rock oysters, a blue swimmer crab and lobster plus he paid for all the drinks. Julia had a white wine, while Anton drank wine and beer, Robby drank only beer and Jonathan drank a beer but not too much as he was driving.

"What are we celebrating, Robby?" Anton asked him while the others looked at him.

"My first success of my court case. I won the first session and received some money from the council." He said and smiled. "You should have seen their faces. They thought they were in their rights but when my lawyer showed them Julia's photos they were all quiet. They all knew they were not in their right so they promised me they will start covering that hole as soon as possible. In the meantime, they offered me a few grant and tonight I want to celebrate it with you."

"You should put the money in your case and not in this dinner." Jonathan replied. "Otherwise, pay Julia a few grant as she helped you with your case. Don't forget she helped you. Without Julia you would be still begging for money on the streets and you would be still broken and homeless."

Julia nodded and agreed with Jonathan. Robby saw how she nodded and agreed with him. He wasn't happy but it didn't spoil the party. They all enjoyed the good food they ate and the drinks they drank but Jonathan was right. Robby should have paid Julia a few grant and the rest of the money should have put into his case. The case wasn't won yet. This was just one part but not the big part.

After the dinner they went out to the Marble Bar

underneath the Hilton hotel. Robby paid again for the drinks and cheered when Julia lit a cigar in front of the guys. Anton joined her and smoked a Cuban Havana cigar while Jonathan wished he could smoke one but he promised his girlfriend he would stop smoking. She didn't like cigarettes and hated guys who smoked so much. It was hard for him but he won her hart anyway and promised her he would stop.

Robby and Julia partied late and went home to Bondi by cab. They had a couple of drinks in the Bondi Hotel before they walked back home. Julia was sick the next morning while Robby was up and never felt so good as he did last night.

22 Return to Sydney

The nine days in Hong Kong went fast and before Julia knew it was time to fly back to Australia. A shuttle bus brought her back to the airport where she checked in as soon as she found the check in desk of Qantas. The Boeing 747 was again full and the flight was smooth. She arrived early in the morning in Sydney where she joined the big queue of arrivals for immigration.

"What's your purpose of this visit to Australia?"

"Travelling." Julia replied when it was her turn at Immigrations. "I'm here to see the country."

"Are you doing any work or studies?"

The officer observed Julia's face but she only

showed the person a smile. She shook her head knowing that she was lying to an immigration officer who could easily stop her if her wanted. "No, I don't. I can't."

"You have enough money to support yourself?" Julia nodded and wished she had the latest statements of her bank account back home with her. She couldn't find them when she was packing her bag and had no idea what had happened with them. She wished they weren't in the hands of Robby as it might be dynamite for him. He would use any excuse to get the money towards him leaving her empty.

"I have, sir but unfortunately I lost my statement from my bank but I can assure you that I have enough money on my account."

The immigration officer checked her passport and stamped it before he gave it back to her.

"Don't try to look for work because we will check on travellers. Don't stay too long in Sydney but you're welcome to enjoy the coming Olympics. Have a nice day."

Julia got her passport with a fresh new stamp and was once again allowed to stay for six months in the country. She collected her luggage and passed customs. This time they didn't check her luggage and let her go. She moved further to arrivals where she looked for a cab. Although it was still very early in the morning it was quite busy on the airport. Luckily for Julia she got a cab when a cab driver noticed her and helped he with her luggage. It was no problem for him to drive to Bondi. She got in and arrived back in Bondi while the breakfast in the Lodge was still going on.

Jock, the messy morning chef was glad to see Julia again. He made her a pancake what was the special of the morning and took a seat opposite of her while she helped herself with a cup of coffee to wake up from her long night flight from Hong Kong.

"Julia, I am glad you're back. I hope you had a good time."

"Yes, I had." She said while she enjoyed her pancake. "So, what's been cooking?"

It was an expressing she got from Konrad. Every time he showed up he mentioned it regular. Robby didn't like the expression but Julia saw the sense of humour in it. As a chef she liked it.

"I know you're just back but I want to ask you for a favour. I know you like to work for the other hostel but is it fine for you to do one morning shift every week so I can have a day off."

Jock never complained although he wasn't glad with Julia's thorough cleaning he had to admit she did a better job in the kitchen than the usual junky Matthew who did half his work and very slow.

"Right, ok. I will have a chat with Robby and Terry and see what they will say. I don't mind although that will mean I can't be doing long day shifts on the Wednesday in Kirribilli what I love to do. It's ok, I'll do it."

Julia thought for a short moment of the words of the immigration officer who nearly caught her. She wanted to admit she was doing some work for a hostel but she lied to the officer. He gave her a clear warning as the Olympics were coming to town so they went to all kinds of venues and businesses where they checked staff records. Everyone caught would be detained and go to prison before they would be deported back to their own country of origin.

Jock tried to read Julia's face when Robby noticed she was back. He just passed the kitchen and saw her sitting at a table together with the breakfast chef. Jock got up and greeted him. "Hey, Julia. You're back."

"Yes, I am." She said with a smile on her face. "How have you been?"

"Busy." He replied. "I had to do your work together with my own shifts so I am glad you're back. I hope you had a great time in Hong Kong? Did you find any interesting shops and stuff?"

Jock went back to the kitchen and made a special pancake for Robby. Normally he didn't eat but he accepted the pancake and enjoyed the hot meal in the morning. Julia made him a coffee while she had a refill.

"Jock wants me to do a shift for him. I said it's ok. I will check with Terry tomorrow when he's doing the Sunday BBQ and see if he agrees."

Robby took a big sip of his coffee and coughed. He smoked too much and he felt it in his lungs. He looked around to make sure there was no one listening to their conversation. He coughed again and looked her in her eyes.

"Julia. I know you don't like it but I have to ask you for a big favour. My lawyer says we have a strong case and believed we can beat the council but I need your help."

Julia wanted to say no. She knew he wanted to ask for more money and she didn't want to help him financially. He should try it from a different approach but he never did.

"Please, Julia. I need your help. Can you help me with a grant?"

She finished her breakfast and drank the last bits of her coffee before she got up and walked in the direction of the kitchen and a small room what was her new room since a young Japanese student couldn't afford to pay the rent of the hostel and was thrown out. Robby kicked the young kid out and offered the room to her. He noticed how she loved to have that space as it was next of the kitchen and soon she would be working regular in the kitchen. He knew something what she soon would find out.

"Robby, I am not a bank and what you ask me is way too much. I don't mind helping you but a grant is way too much money."

He wanted to say something but he couldn't. He followed her and stood in her doorway while she opened her big suitcase and inspected her belongings. The room was small but neat. There was a cupboard where she kept most of her books and her clothes. There was even a small desk and a chair in the room and a brand new Hewlett Packard desktop computer. On the top of he cupboard Robby noticed a life-size foam doll an exact made replica of Yoda the Jedi master from the Star Wars films. She bought it on a comic convention earlier in the year and it was her pride and joy.

"He looks so real." Robby said while he looked at Yoda.

"Sometimes I wish he was real. I wondered what he would say to you, Robby." She replied. "I don't think Master Yoda would agree with your request. Can't it be a bit less?"

This time he couldn't resist himself and got a bit abusive. "Look at you. I know you have money but you don't want to admit, don't you? I ask you only for a favour and what do you do. You reject me straight away and think I will never pay you back."

Julia stared at him but didn't say a word. She only observed his behaviour. She had never seen him before acting like this. He was behaving like a greedy young child who wants more and more till he couldn't get more and then got upset.

"My God. Look at you, Robby. Why are you so upset with me?"

"I only asked you for a small favour and what do you do you reject me. I ask you to help me with my court case. Maybe you forgot that you said that you promised you would help me so I ask you for some help and you refuse to help me by giving me money. Do you really think I am stupid?"

"Robby, I made clear to you that I don't mind helping you but what you ask you should talk to a bank and ask for a loan. Maybe they will give it you as long as you pay back what you have lent. Now you approach me because you know I have money." She looked him in his empty eyes. "I know you have my latest bank statements so you know how much money I have on an account but even I can't always have access and I want to keep it where I have it so I will have some savings for later when I might need them."

"Why is it so hard for you to lend me a few thousand. I promise you I will pay you back."

"When, Robby? Remember I will be only here for another six months and then I will be gone forever. Sorry, no. that's my final answer."

He left her and disappeared for the rest of the day till she saw him again in the evening at the reception. He was still not happy but he knew her answer. He would find another way to approach her.

Konrad showed up that evening and he was glad to see Julia again. During her absence he made some progress in his own case and had a feeling where he could find his ex employee Paul. He couldn't discuss it with Robby as he never listened to what he had to say. He only talked nonsense and only complained about the Lodge and never what he could do.

"Good evening, Julia. Good to see you again. What's been cooking?"

"Lots, Konrad. Lots." She replied and showed a big smile. "How are you? Any news about your burglary case?'

"As a matter of fact, yes. I know where I might find my money. Can you believe it these stupid farmers started to spend some of my hard earned money and changed it to Aussie bucks at a money changer? They always use one money changer and it didn't occur to them that I wrote down the numbers of every bank note and keep a list. As soon as I got burgled I started to contact some banks and gave them my list as I did too with some money changers. One of them is in the Hunter Valley as I believed my ex employee knew some guys who have a big farm and they grow their own weed."

"So you know where they are, don't you?"

"Not precise but I informed the police and they will have a look for me. When I receive their report I will have a look myself but I can use your help if you are interested. It would be a nice way to see a bit of Australia."

"Yes, I will be very interested. Please, keep me updated. I find it actually quite fascinating. I still can't believe what actually happened but I got a feeling you will find and get it all back."

"Thank you for your concern, Julia. Glad

someone wants to support me."

"Yeah, you can support Konrad, but she can't even support me." Robby snapped back. He was still very pissed off that she said no to him.

"Robby, you just want too much money for a case I don't really believe in but I said I will do my best to help you but what you asked me is a bit too much, don't you think?"

"No, I don't. I should as for more and you know that you can pay me. Don't lie to me."

"I never lied to you and never will." She said a bit upset. "I don't know what happened with you but when I met you first you weren't so greedy and look at you know. You earn money and I understand you still have some old debts to pay but if you play it smart you can invest in your own case and if you win your case you can pay off in one go all your debts and you should still have enough to spend it on whatever you want to spend your money."

Konrad noticed how upset they both were. Robby was upset because she caught him what was fair. He wasn't impressed with Robby's move when he showed him a bank statement. He should had asked what he didn't and now he had nothing to say anymore. On the other hand, Julia could have been a bit more honest about her wealth but that was her own choice. He understood why she didn't want to reveal how much she was worth because she would attract people like Robby who were always broke and she had the money they would need to solve their problems (temporary).

"Robby, Julia. Please, stop fighting. You behave like a bunch of children."

"Thank you, Konrad, but this is none of your business." Robby snapped without thinking what he just said to his friend.

"But it is, Robby." He snapped back. "Apologise to her. You are wrong and you shouldn't behave like that to a woman. Now apologise."

Julia looked Robby in his eyes but she didn't trust him. He would go after her money and he would do whatever he could to get access to her account what was almost impossible but then again he would know some guys who might be able to find access to steal money from her account without her knowledge. Konrad didn't stay long as he received a call on his mobile. He still didn't have new staff so he had to work on the craziest hours of the day/ night when guests could call him whenever they liked. He had to deal with the problem before it became a bigger one.

Julia didn't want to fight with Robby and didn't stay long in the lobby of the lodge. She went back to her room where she read a book for a while before she turned of the light and went to bed. Robby sighed and smoked a cigarette with the main door open so he could hear the phone. He was stressed and needed support. Normally Julia would support him but she made clear she had enough of his favours. He never paid her back and she was worried. Would she ever see her money back that he borrowed from her or was he promising her a book full of lies? She didn't know and Robby knew he made a fool of himself in front of Konrad. How could he win her back?

While everyone was asleep in the hostel he entered the little office and made use of the desktop computer of the company accountant Felicity. She left one night her computer on and he discovered her password and lots of interesting files. He used the printer in the office and printed several files and put all the printed copies in his black leather briefcase what he always carried.

He never locked his briefcase what was a stupid mistake but then again he never left it unattended. Wherever he went he carried it with him all the times.

23 Chef absence and replacements

As soon as Julia was back from her little trip to Hong Kong she received some bad news from Terry. Their usual chef of the Bondi Lodge quit suddenly with his job because of illness. He discovered when he went to see his doctor that he had a bad tumour what needed to be removed. Unfortunately for him he had to quit with his job but he was glad to give up his position at the Bondi Lodge. He was already thinking and told Julia that he wouldn't be for long with the hostel. Terry knew nothing then but while she was away he received the bad news.

Before the hostel group could hire another chef Julia became the temporary chef as no one was immediately available. Robby was pleased and supported her. Terry received a lot of positive news about her cooking in Kirribilli and supported her too. She understood her business and was keen to work with him while he continued searching for a new chef.

"Will he make a comeback; do you think?"

"No, he resigned and doesn't want to come back even if he's cleared. He said he had enough of all these students and doesn't feel respected by all the guests. I don't think they would understand what they have done to him."

Julia knew that Lothar was a heavy chain

smoking chef. She always saw him smoking in between the kitchen and the dining room in a little corridor where there was a window.

Felicity was the first who approached Julia when Lothar wouldn't show up for work. She was around and was ready to take over. The managers were around but weren't happy that Julia was so suddenly their new chef. They still had some doubts about her cooking and never thought a woman was capable in cooking for so many people.

"Terry, we have to find a chef asap. I don't think we should offer the service for the moment to her. I don't think a woman should cook and we just wonder if she's capable in cooking food for a hundred or even more hungry students and other guests. We also have our doubts if she's still good while she's cooking under pressure. We can't have a chef that can't coop with heavy pressure. We don't want to see and hear that she flipped because of the work force."

"I have seen her at work in Kirribilli and Glenda is fond of her. She asked me several times to transfer her to Glenferrie Lodge so I could deal with Bondi but I don't want to leave my kitchen.

She's good and fully qualified. She showed me all the papers and knows her stuff. She won't disappoint."

"So glad to see a girl at work." Felicity said when she joined the conversation. "I just saw her in her whites. She looks so professional."

"Oh, she's. I have seen her utensils. She has better knives and is spending lots of money in her own tools. I offered her some service and asked if we could pay for her belongings but she doesn't want. She said she doesn't mind to invest in her job. She's that professional. She only wants the best and she knows how to deal with order lists too."

Terry showed Felicity the latest order list and walked with her to her desk. She wrote the cheques that the managers signed. They checked and double checked with Terry the substance before they agreed. Julia knew about stock and was good in her job. For the moment she could stay till they would find another chef.

"Do you know some chefs who are available?"

"I know plenty of chefs but that doesn't mean they want to work for me. I will call some friends and see who's available. I will let you know. Till then we should give the job to Julia and she can work as a sous chef. She knows our kitchen so it would be wise to use her till we don't need her."

Julia loved to cook and didn't mind to work temporary as a chef. She understood the job was for a short term and that Terry would be her chef. She took care of many things and learned from Terry to make some delicious deserts. She wasn't good in them but the more she worked with him she learned to deal with tasty ones and wanted to stop the enormous food waste.

The first meals were cooked by Terry but she helped with the flavours. He let her do all the veggies and she was good in roasting potatoes and pumpkin. Together they made the meaty dishes while she did all the salads and made sure that the rice didn't taste too much like Terry's oily rice.

Even Matthew didn't mind to work with her and liked her better than Lothar. Julia was kind and helped him with his job. Together they kept the kitchen clean and tidy so he could spend more time on his other cleaning jobs.

Robby showed up now and then in the kitchen

and saw her every time with a big smile and hard at work. There was music from her little mini disk player and some tiny speakers while Terry only listened to some talk radio. Julia liked music and that was what she played every day she was at work.

The Wednesday was a long day for her but she didn't mind. She started with the evening meal somewhere in the morning when all the food was out in the serving area. she cleaned and chopped vegetables so she would have more time for her main dishes and deserts.

Terry only helped her during the first week and let her on her own from the second week. Even the Sundays she dealt with all the cooking and cleaning alone and didn't mind. On Monday she was alone too and worked very hard.

In the evenings she was too tired to hang around in the lobby. Konrad paid now and them a visit and left her alone. She made coffee for the guys but didn't stay too long.

It took Terry two weeks before he found a replacement chef for his usual daily chef. In the meantime, Julia was working 7 days a week without any complaints and kept the kitchen running. She cooked and cleaned and did her job with a big smile on her face.

Matthew her kitchen hand didn't mind to work for her. She kept her place clean and tidy and was a better chef than the others. She was organised but so was Lothar. He was a systematic chef and had so his cooking plan what she just followed. She just copied his plan but changed a bit in the taste of the food. She added more flavour what resulted that the guests actually liked her food compare to the waste during Lothar's reign. She was clearly a better chef who knew and understood the taste of the long-term guests.

Julia was already at work in the kitchen when Terry showed up with another chef. He was a good friend of Terry and needed the extra money as he and his wife just had a baby so they could use some extra money. Unfortunately for Terry he couldn't stay long every day but Julia was around to take over from him and didn't mind to be a sous chef again.

"Hi, Julia. May I introduce you to Marty. He's a good friend of mine and he will be our new chef. I hope you don't mind to work under him so he can take charge of the kitchen."

"No, of course not, Terry. It was a pleasure to work here and I don't mind. I can be around every day and I will assist him with whatever he does."

"Excellent, I knew I could trust you. I hear so many good stories from our guests and even the staff in Glenferrie talk highly about your work. You are a good chef."

"Thank you, Terry. I just do my best and try to understand what the guests like to eat. I do my best to make the food tastier so there will be less waste. It's such a shame how much food is wasted every evening. I was shocked when Lothar was cooking and how bad his food tasted. He smoked too much so he never could taste his food properly. That's why I add a little bit more herbs and spices to make it yummy and Math and I were pleased when we saw less food was wasted."

Marty listened to Julia and looked at her. She looked so masculine with her almost shaved head and was dressed very professional in her whites. He inspected her knives and liked what he saw. None of her knifes were cheap and were all made of quality steel and proper brands. She bought her tools from a shop in George Street close to

Broadway and spent nearly a thousand bucks on her tools.

"Marty, Julia. I guess you will be alright together; don't you think? You don't need my help, do you?"

"No, we will be fine and will have lots of fun together." Julia replied who started with chopping potatoes so the all the chunks were almost the same size before she would put them in the oven for roasting.

"When you are finished with the potatoes can you chop some carrots and zucchini/ courgettes for me while I start with the meat dishes."

Julia went to the big fridge and filled two big metal bowls with the veggies she needed to chop so she could work fast and organised. Marty addressed Terry before he left the kitchen.

"Sorry, Terry, but I work my arse off with the other job so I can only do 4 hours a day extra. I want to see my family and I don't want to work longer than is needed."

"Right, Julia do you mind to help Marty with his extra hours?" "Sure, I can stay and help him if he doesn't mind."

Marty looked at Julia and noticed her professionalism in her uniform. She looked so cool and she was so easy going. It promised to be a good time with her in the kitchen.

"Right, Terry, who's in charge in the kitchen?"

"That will be you and Julia will be your sous chef. She doesn't mind to play the second violin."

"It's ok, Marty. I can work under you. Besides I can help you and take over when you want to go home so I can make sure that there will be enough food in the dining room for all the guests."

"What kind of people are we talking about? What kind of bunch are they?"

Julia had to laugh and tapped him on his shoulders. She knew what the guys were like. She had seen the waste of food every day and she knew how fussy the guys could be with their food.

"Have you ever cooked for fussy folks?"

"Yeah, a lot. I work for airlines. I cook their food. Have you ever tried airline food?"

"A lot. I had some good chances to taste some good and not so good food high in the sky while I was flying from my own country in Europe all the way to Sydney."

"Did you eat all your food or did you waste some of it?"

"I ate my food just out of politeness. I guess I see your point."

"Right, so you will see our guests are like them and they only eat what they like or think it's tasty."

"Do you throw away a lot of food?"

"Before I started to cook, yes but the last couple of weeks not so much."

Terry looked at Julia. In Glenferrie the guests weren't so fussy as here in Bondi but now and then he noticed how full the bins were on particular days. Not every day they liked his food. The guests filled their plates and threw away half their plates instead of finishing their food.

"No, you still can make a tasty dish with your leftover veggies. Serve it as a frittata they will eat it. That's what I make of leftover vegetables."

"Any other kitchen disasters I should be aware of?"

"Not that I can think of," Terry replied. "Julia, have you experienced any disasters while you were working on your own?"

"No, not really. Perhaps burned food what can taste awful. Very annoying but we have to avoid burning food. Nothing taste as horrible as burned food and these guests are the fussiest guests I have ever seen in my life."

"Stir well and use enough oil that wills top the burning flavour." Terry admitted. "Good luck you two. Give me a call if things don't go well in the kitchen but I will hear from you both when I am here again for a meeting very soon. Good luck."

Terry left both Marty and Julia alone in the kitchen and headed straight towards Kirribilli where he was needed to do the cooking for

Glenferrie Lodge. Glenda didn't want to order again for pizzas as she believed cooked food by Terry was still healthier than simple food from a pizzeria.

Julia didn't work long for the Bondi Lodge. In August she gave up her job as she found it too risky now the immigration officers together with the police and the tax office were going almost door to door in Bondi and they were checking every office and business for illegal workers. More and more people got picked up and were locked up before they got deported to their country of origin.

Robby heard the news and rumours too. The police came close to the Bondi Lodge but left the business untouched. It was up to the tax office and immigrations to check that business. As far as they were concerned there was nothing wrong with the Lodge because the managers thanks to Felicity had everything up to date. None of the employees were illegal. Julia didn't even exist in the files although she received every fortnight her pay cheque but as far as the Bondi Lodge were concerned she didn't work for them officially. There was no record that would prove she was an employee but Robby knew better. He had copies of her file that got deleted on orders by the managers as they feared it would open a whole can of worms. They were afraid the authorities would discover more things that shouldn't have happen in this business.

In their new rented apartment Julia made clear to Robby when they were both together that she couldn't work any longer for the hostel. It was too risky. He only nodded and couldn't do much to protect her.

"Sorry, Robby, but I can't do it anymore. I don't want to get caught and end up my year in Australia behind bars before they will deport me back to my country."

"Say that you are just helping a chef?"

"Robby, I cannot lie to the authorities. They already asked me when I arrived back in June if I was planning to do some work. I lied then but I don't want to lie to them again if they would find out what I was doing all the time from the moment I arrived again in Sydney and before I left the country."

Marty didn't stay long either. He didn't like the job and the pay was just a joke. He earned less than he was promised. Terry lied to him but he even he saw his own pay was cut in half. He couldn't complain to the managers as everyone were loosing money.

The food budget went down so Terry couldn't order more fancy stuff for his kitchen in Kirribilli. Instead they had to cook food with less supplies and Marty wasn't good in improvising cooking with less ingredients. Julia was glad she got out on time but she heard all the news from Robby who was pissed off with the managers. They were pissing away money by spending it on stupid things in their spare time and were never around when they should have been. They didn't care much about their own business. They saw it just as a joke and didn't care about the staff and the guests.

Robby smoked more and more cigarettes what he paid with money from the little kitty box in the reception. All the reception staff members were using that little box for their own use and none of them were ever caught by Felicity. She used it herself too for her regular coffee breaks at the little coffee bar Barlevento opposite of the Lodge and just joined the others. She saw how the place was going down by bad management. She complained but they didn't care and didn't even listen to her.

"What's wrong with the Lodge? What are our managers doing to this hostel?" Julia asked Robby who just lit another cigarette. He was smoking almost two packs a day.

"I don't know. I know it wouldn't have happened if I were the manager. You all would still have a job and you would be sponsored by the hostel so immigrations can't touch you. As long as you would stay in Bondi and work regular for the hostel you would be safe."

"Robby, you don't own a hostel anymore but thanks for cheering me up. I can hear in your voice you still miss your place."

"Have you seen what my wife has done to the place? It was a successful business even when I left for my three months sailing trip and in that short period she destroyed my name my business and my life. Now I have to work for a living in this shit hole under some dumb managers who don't have any knowledge in hospitality at all and see I am screwed again. My wife was so kind to freeze my account and I can't reopen it. If I would try she will sue me for whatever she thinks she can hurt me."

"Can you beat her with a case?"

Robby heard her but he shook his head. No there was no chance for him to sue his wife. She had enough proof to sue him and he would loose whatever he had. he remembered when he got back to his hostel straight after his three months of pleasure how hard and cool she reacted when she saw him in his own hostel. She showed him the little black book that contained all the days and amounts he stole from his guests when he ran his money scheme. That was his downfall and for that reason she kicked him out. She didn't want to see it happen again in the hostel. He was a good man but not for his guests. He lied and stole too much money from them.

"No, Julia. I can't. I wish I could but I can't." Robby thought about the good life he had when he was still an owner of a hostel when he was happily married with Valery. She did her best to waste some of his fortune on alcohol and coke and just waited for that moment when asked her for a big break. It was her own opportunity to pay him back and she stabbed him hard in his back by throwing all his belongings on the street, freezing his accounts and changing all the locks on his apartment and hostel while he was away. When he showed up three months later she shuffled him some divorce papers and made clear that the marriage was over and that she would be the sole owner of his former hostel.

24 Fourth meeting

Paul got an unexpected visit from Val who tried
to call him a few times before she drove all the
way to the Hunter Valley. In a small cafe in
Cessnock they met where Paul gave Val her share
of the loot. The money was in a big brown
envelop in a plastic bag and he only gave it when
no one was watching. She put it straight in her
handbag and closed her bag. She never checked
and had no idea how much he actually gave her.
She didn't care as long as she could keep it safe

from Konrad who would love to confiscate it from her if he ever would find it in her old hostel.

"How are you, Val?"

"For the moment, ok but he knows."

"Of course he knows. We both knew what we were doing and we both knew he would go straight of us."

"I don't know if I will ever spend a buck of it as long as he's alive."

"What do you mean?"

He drank a whiskey and it was his second. He ordered another drink while Val drank only a coffee. She ordered a glass of water and went for a moment to the ladies'. When she came back Paul was on his fourth whiskey.

"You should stop drinking. One day will be your last. He's after you and you are no match for him if you continue drinking. Stay away from the booze and the drugs and keep a low profile. He knows you're hiding here in the Valley. He's after you."

"He won't catch me. He first has to enter the farm and the farmers will stop him. He has to face them and they are with more and have more firepower than poor old Konrad."

"Don't underestimate him. He's ex military."

"So are some of these farmers." Paul defended. "Damn, you should see the medals my farmer has. He was with the armed forces when he fought in Vietnam. He was there so he knows and had seen many battles. What does Konrad know about fighting? Nothing. He will loose when it will come to a fire flight."

"You are wanted by the cops. The Feds will start looking for you and they will catch you and you will be deported back to England."

"I won't go back to England. This is my home and I will never go back. I prefer to die than to go back."

Paul paid for the drinks and left while she drank her water. She didn't notice the two guys who were constant sitting in the back and they got up when he got up. They lifted him up and drove him safe and sound back to the farm. Konrad wouldn't have a chance if he would have meet him alone in a bar. He was always surrounded by a bunch of farmers who wanted to keep him alive. They believed Konrad would kill Paul as it was the only way to stop him from spending his stolen money.

The cafe owner accepted the stolen US dollar notes and changed them for Aussie bucks. He gave Paul less than he should but he didn't complain. The owner could keep it and he saw it as his tip. What Paul didn't know was that the owner changed the money at the the money changer the farmers were using. The cashier of the money changer noticed the bank notes and exchanged it for Aussie bucks. He wrote down the numbers and checked them when the guy was gone with a list the received some time ago. The numbers appeared on the list and he made a record of the exchange. He informed his employer who informed the police that again money was changed from US dollars for Aussie bucks.

Valery drove back to her old hostel and hid the envelop in the old safe in the small office. She locked the safe and made sure no one knew the code. She left the office and locked the door. She inspected the building and left the hostel soon after. No guests were left behind in the old hostel. It was now completely empty and wouldn't be occupied by backpackers. They all got the news. The old Lamrock Hostel was closed for ever and would be soon knocked down to make space for a car park.

Valery found a new proprietor who was interested in the ground. The hostel together with the chalet would be both knocked down and he would build a big car park for all the cars that were parked wildly in the streets. There was a desperate need for a big car park and the space was good enough.

Konrad learned from a few local coppers the news that the old Lamrock Hostel was to be demolished. Valery was a rich woman although some of the money went to old bills that still had to be paid and with the new money that problem was to be solved. He stopped when she was alone near her old place. He saw her car and she sat outside smoking a cigarette when he walked towards her.

"Hello, Val. How are you today. What's been cooking?"

"Nothing." She said and wanted him to leave.

"Please, stay. I want to talk to you for a while."

"And I have nothing to say to you."

He noticed she was nervous. He observed her when she tried to lit a new cigarette that was a bit bend. He offered her a cigarette from his own pack but she shook her head. He offered her a light from his lighter what she accepted.

"So, how's Paul doing? Did you see him lately?"

"Why would I want to see him? what have I done what makes you think I have been hiding from you?"

"A lot." He replied. "You know I have people working for me and you don't know them nor do you see them. I have spies everywhere. I know you went to see him so you could collect your share. Where is it?"

"Sorry, Konrad, but I don't have your money. Why would I want your money?"

"Maybe you don't want my money but I have a

strong feeling that you have some part of my money. I can't prove it yet but I know from the bottom of my heart that you have some of my money. You went earlier today to see him so you could collect your share whatever he promised you. I can go inside your hostel and search for it but the chance that I will find it will be zero still I believe it would be the best place to hide it."

"Very clever of you, Konrad, but why do you think I would have your money?"

"I saw you on the day of my burglary and my sister in law told me you spoke to her the day before. She told me everything. Don't lie to me. Just tell me the truth or I might have to hurt you to get the truth out of you."

"Are you threatening me, Konrad? You know I can call the cops right now and have you arrested for threatening a poor woman. You should understand that they will believe me and not you. It is still a serious crime hurting women and it would ruin your life and your career."

Valery stood up and walked to her old hostel Konrad followed her. She let him in and she took a seat on the old leather sofa that was covered in dust. She didn't spend much time in her old place and it was falling apart.

"I heard you sold it. Does Robby know you sold it?"

"Why should I tell him? It is no longer his and I have the rights of the property and not him. He lost it when he went away as he lost everything else."

"Because you threw him out on the streets. I know you did and I don't offend you for what you have done to him. He deserved it."

"What's he doing now? You do see him do you?"

Konrad nodded and took a seat next of her. He put his strong hand on her thin knee and squashed it softly. She didn't stop him while he tried to hurt her. "Tell me, where's my money?"

"I don't have it and even if I should have it I won't tell you." She said calm while she tried to take off his hand of her knee. "And stop hurting me. I can call the cops and have you arrested for molesting a woman."

He took his hand of her knee and looked her in

her dark eyes. "You always have been a good liar like your husband. I see why you liked each other. You both lied to each other for years till you had enough and threw him out while he couldn't defend himself when he went on sailing for a couple of months. Whose idea was the sailing trip actually?"

"It was Robby's. He needed a break so I gave him a chance to get away. I found out what he did in the hostel while he was away and froze his accounts cut his cards in half and sold all his belongings and his apartment. The rest is history."

"Aren't you afraid he might take revenge on you?"

"No, he won't. He knows he can't beat me. He thinks he's tough but he's weak. You know him. You have seen him. He can only beat women who are clearly weak."

Konrad had to think of Julia. She wasn't weak. She was quite strong for a woman and she would be no match for Robby. He wondered how far Robby would go to get access to her money. He would lie and steal from her what he was doing but would she be another Suzie? He didn't think so. What Robby did with that poor young Dutch girl it was awful but he knew if he would try to do the same things with Julia he would certainly kill him. It was the only way to stop Robby from doing crazy stuff.

"So you haven't seen my old employee?"

"No and even if I did I wouldn't tell you. Why should I. You can't hurt me, Konrad. I will report it to the police and then you will face serial problems. They will investigate you and I wonder what they will find. You are just like my ex a man with too many skeletons hiding in his closet."

Konrad got up and left Valery. He didn't want to stay too long. He looked for a very short moment in the direction of the little office but he didn't ask to have a peak inside. He just had a feeling his money was so damn close but no he couldn't get to it.

Valery was glad when he finally left. She rubbed her hurt knee and walked to her little office. She couldn't keep the money in the little old safe. It was the first place where he would look if he would come back. She had to find a better place and thought for a moment. Then suddenly she had an idea. She remembered when Robby talked some time ago about renting a little money box at the bank. She knew that in the city they rented those boxes and she had an account with one of them. It was all too easy. The next day she visited the bank and left her share of the burglary in a money box in a money safe deposit at the bank and left it there till she would ever need it. For the moment no one would know and Konrad had no access to the safe deposit. Her share was safe but how safe was her life actually?

25 House hunting

Konrad received several reports from the money spending done by Paul his ex employee. He was hanging around between Cessnock and Singleton and he lived on a farm. A few coppers went out on a day to check out which farm he was living but they couldn't trace him. The farmers spotted the police car before they could start asking questions to some farmers. None of the farmers wanted to link their fellow farmers to coppers as they didn't like those city slickers.

Konrad received the news from an old friend he knew from his Saturday gun club. The man was a retired copper but he still paid a visit to the station and heard about Konrad's burglary and his investigation. He promised Konrad to stay in touch with the police force and he brought now and then some news about their investigation. The leader of the team wasn't all happy but couldn't stop the old copper from doing his job. They were both members of the exclusive Gun Club where Konrad was a member too.

In the meantime, Robby and Julia got both fed up with living in the Bondi Lodge. They both wanted a place but it was not easy to rent a flat in Bondi. The rent was high what wasn't a problem for Julia but she couldn't rent as she hardly knew people. She had no references what all the real estate agencies were asking for. She could always ask Konrad for being a reference but he would ask her to work for his motel. She didn't want to become too close with him. She had seen the place and didn't want to stay there. The rooms in the Bondi Lodge were smaller and no room really had his own private bathroom with shower and toilet except for two rooms but she didn't want to live under the nose of Konrad. She didn't trust him completely. He was kind but very hard.

In the small cafe opposite the lodge they

discussed the situation with Camilla who lived op top of her little business. She knew how hard it was to rent a place and she was glad she got her own little business. As a foreigner it wasn't easy but she made money and she had her Australian citizenship. Still she was deep in her heart a woman from Puerto Rico and showed it in her bar with a massive flag hanging on the ceiling.

"Rob, have you contacted the woman from five flats down in the street?"

"No, what about?"

"She has a luxurious two flat apartments for rent and she wants new tenants soon. You should check it out before someone else will take it."

"How much does she ask per week?" Julia still had to get used to the fact that every place was per week and not per month. She believed the rent would be high too much for Robby alone but if he wouldn't mind to live with her she was willing to pay her share as long as he wouldn't be unfaithful to her. He had to promise he wouldn't steal from her what would be hard to say it in his face and he had to keep his word.

"Julia, you still want to live in the Lodge?"

"No, I am fed up with that place. Let's rent something together."

Robby and Julia went outside where they had a smoke and drank their coffee. Camilla joined them for a very short moment and pointed to a for Rent sign at one of the flats opposite of the little coffee bar. Robby made some notes and would check the phone numbers once he was again in the city.

"I will give them a call and see how much they charge for the space. I will be soon in the city and might go to their agency. I hope my solicitor can check the address for me out. She's very good, you know."

"So, how's your case going?" Julia did her best to show some interest what Robby didn't mind. He was glad she still supported him although she didn't want to give him constant money. Now and then she gave him some money but he had to promise her to pay it all back as soon as he would be able to win his case before the end of her six months' visa would ran out.

"Julia, how much would you invest in a new

place if I can find one?"

"What do you want me to do? Buy new furniture?"

"No, I can get access to furniture. No, I was more thinking in paying the first couple of months rent plus the bond. That will be a lot of money and I can't afford to pay both the rent and the deposit for our place."

"See what you can find and I will see what I will pay. I can't make you any promises but I will help you that I can promise you."

Robby was glad that Julia wanted to rent a place just like him and she was willing to pay for it too. He wondered how much would she pay and would she give the money to him or would she join him when he would see a real estate agent to sign an agreement and pay the bond plus first month rent.

Julia paid for the coffee while he stopped a cab and went straight to the city to see his solicitor. She saw him later in the evening when he had good news. He found the address of the real estate agent of a flat next door of the lodge and he made an appointment with the woman who wanted to rent her 2-bedroom apartment as soon as possible.

The next morning straight after their little coffee they went to see the place. The apartment was spacious and very clean. Julia didn't mind to live in the space but Robby didn't like the conditions that the woman came up with.

Robby wasn't allowed to smoke what he didn't want to give up. Second was that there was only one original bedroom and a sun room what could be turned into a bedroom but she wanted to know what they both did for work if they would come late and didn't play too loud music. Robby got the feeling that the old lady was a bit too nosy and would disturb their peace with stupid little rules to annoy them and to kick them out if they would break any of her rules.

"What do you think, Julia?" He asked her. "I like the place. It will be a bit hard for both of us but I don't mind the space. We have plenty of space for whatever we bring in but we can't smoke."

Julia already knew that it would be a problem for Robby. She didn't mind. It would be good for her to stop smoking what she tried to do. Robby was in no mood in quitting smoking and not for an old landlord.

"Let's have a look with that real estate agent in Double Bay. If you don't mind I want to pay them a visit and see what they ask and if we can have a look inside before we sign an agreement with them."

Robby arranged a meeting with the agency and a few days later she showed up and showed both Robby and Julia the space. They both liked the place and luckily for Robby he could smoke inside. The rooms were smaller but the rent was also lower and affordable for both of them. Still Robby had to ask for Julia to pay the bond and the first two months of rent if they would agree with the terms of the estate agent.

In the evening Robby had a discussion about how to pay the rent with Julia when Konrad showed up. He had good news and wanted to share it with them. He heard about Robby's news that he wanted to rent a flat so he got interested.

"We found a flat and it's very nearby. We will pay a visit on Saturday to their estate agent and sing the agreement. We both want the place so we have to sign the papers and pay the deposit

318

and the first months of rent."

"Who will pay it?" He asked while he looked a short moment in the direction of Julia. She disappeared to the kitchen and made some coffee for the guys.

"I have to ask Julia to pay for the rent and the bond before we can get access to our new place. She might want to buy some furniture for her room but we both like the space and hope to get in as soon as possible."

"Let me know if you need me for reference or so. I hope this place will not turn into a disaster."

Robby read Konrad's face and nodded. he knew what he meant by that. No, he hoped Julia wouldn't be as bad as the previous young Dutch girl was. She was nice till he stayed for some time together.

"No, Konrad. I know what you were thinking but Julia is no Suzie and I hope it will not go that path as it was a complete nightmare for me."

"I hope so too for you, Robby. I will not help you this time if it would end like the previous time. For me one time is enough and I have my own problems if you understand."

"Any luck with your case?" Konrad nodded when Julia reappeared with three mugs of hot coffee. He held the door for her open of the dining room and she gave him the first mug before she put one on the reception desk and put the third on the little coffee table next of the sofa. She took a seat and gave Konrad some company who sat next of her.

"Yes, as a matter of fact. The police believed to find the farm where my ex employee and thief is living. The stupid dope head is spending some of my money on these wild farmers who also grow dope so he will be probably very stoned."

Robby was looking at his friend and wasn't impressed with the news. He didn't like how Konrad treated his former employee so bad while he did a lot of work for his motel.

"How much have they spent so far?"

"I can't tell and even if I would know I don't want to let you know. That's my concern. All I know is that he lives in Cessnock on a farm but there are some rumours that he also lives in Singleton. He knows a few farmers and they protect him at all costs."

"And I guess you want to find out for yourself, don't you?"

Robby looked quickly at Julia who listened with great care to the story. She wanted to help Konrad and came already with a few ideas what Konrad liked.

"Have you checked out who helped them? How did they have access to your house if you have a dog and an alarm system?"

"So you think one of my house mates was part of it?"

"Your sis in law must know more than she wants to admit and who called the cops? Why did she do it if she could have called you before the police would show up for investigating it."

"How much does she know?" Robby asked who agreed with Julia's opinion.

"Good point, Julia. I have to admit I have a strong feeling that my sis in law is part of the burglary but what part I don't know. I don't think she received money for her job because I would know. She can't spend the money as I wrote down all the numbers on my laptop computer what they didn't take while they had a chance. It would have been too obvious if they would have stolen my computer."

"They didn't, did they?"

"No, but if they had stolen my computer they would have access to lots of important files and all the banknote numbers so it would be easy for them to change it for different currencies. Now I can see where they have gone and to my surprise the farmers if it were them changed their money constant at the same money changer. He contacts the police whenever they want to change dollars for bucks."

Konrad looked at Julia who listened to his story. She would have used different money changers if possible and otherwise go to different places and change the dollars there. It would be harder to chase the numbers and hard to catch if the police ever want to make an arrest.

"Julia, do you fancy a trip to the Hunter Valley with me? I will let you know when we go when I got some more info. I will let you know as soon as possible."

"Sure, I love to."

She had to wait for a couple of days before
Konrad got all the info he needed although the
coppers drew a bad map of where they met the
farmers in the Valley. It was now up to Konrad to
figure out where exactly they would think Paul
was staying. In the meantime, Robby managed to
meet up with the agent from the agency in
Double Bay and they both had a good look in
their new house. It was next door of the hostel
and the room was on the ground floor on the
right. Julia liked the big bedroom and saw herself
living in the place. Robby was happy to have the
small sunroom as his room. He trusted Julia and
offered her the first choice of rooms.

On the Saturday they went to Double Bay to see
the Real Estate Agent to sign the papers and to
pay the bond and the first month rent. Julia joined
Robby as she didn't trust Robby alone with three
thousand bucks in an envelop. He could waste it
on drugs. She believed he was still using although
she couldn't prove it. They had coffee in the
Stamford hotel lobby. It was a sunny day and it
was nice to be in one of the richest parts of

Sydney. They looked at the people who were better dressed then the normal folks they would see wherever they were. Julia was dressed in a dress and she even wore a bit of make up. She didn't like to look feminine and especially not with Robby. He was dressed smart as he was on his way to see his mysterious solicitor. She hadn't seen her so she had no idea how this lady looked like. He didn't tell much about her all he told Julia that she was representing his case and she believed whatever he told her.

"You ok, Julia?"

"Yeah, I'm fine." She replied.

"Shall we see our agent and sign the paper or do you want to wait till I deal with them?"

"No, I can join you." she replied and finished her coffee.

 Robby sighed softly but she heard him. He had hoped she would stay in the hotel or went out shopping while he could deal with the real estate agent. Now she wanted to join him and only pay the money when it was time. Damn. They walked through the streets and had to enter a small alley. On the right they found the small real estate agent. They entered the business and greeted the staff.

"G'day, we're here to sign the papers for the estate on Fletcher Street Bondi."

"G'day, mate. You must be Robby Henson, right?" The agent got from his desk a bunch of documents and joined them on a big table where he showed them all the documents that needed to be signed.

"There's one thing I need from you before we can give you the keys. Do you have a reference letter for us who can guarantee you are truly good people?"

Julia looked at Robby who sighed. No, he didn't have a letter like that on him. He knew a few guys who could stand for him and he would call them as soon as he could leave Double Bay. All the other documents and the money were no problem. Julia paid in cash the bond and signed her part of the agreement but it would be all settled as soon as they would receive a reference letter. They wanted two references what wasn't hard for Robby to come up with. All he had to do was to call a few guys and get them sign such letter so he could give it to the estate agents.

"When do you need those letters?"

"As soon as possible. We will contact them and check with them if they can tell us what we want to hear before we can agree with our deal. We will let you know and give you then the keys. In case things goes wrong what we don't believe it will happen but you never know we will pay you everything back so the money will go straight back to you."

The estate agent was looking at Julia who received a printed pay slip for the payment of the bond and first two months of rent. Robby took the slip from her and kept it in his briefcase what he carried with him. All the documents disappeared inside his case and they both left the agency.

"Can you get such a letter?" Julia asked while they walked away from the real estate agent.

"Yes, one I can get but of a second one I have to ask him friendly. I hope Konrad wants to help us. He can be a hard arse but I guess he will give me a reference. At least I know the guy who helped me with setting up my hostel. He will give me a reference. He knew I had a trustful business and never forget to pay my bills. He will guarantee me that I am a good guy."

They had another coffee and returned back to Bondi. Robby called from the hostel his old friend and business partner. He promised Robby to send him asap a reference to the Bondi Lodge while they now hoped that Konrad would show up. It was Saturday so he was either in his motel or at the Gun Club.

It took a while before Konrad showed up to the Lodge with such a letter. He first didn't want to write a letter but when he confronted Robby in the evening at the reception Julia looked him in the eyes and made clear it was for both of them. Together they would rent a flat not far from the lodge and both of them would live there.

Robby promised Julia the flat would be in both names as they both would be living there. In the end it was actually Julia who moved all her stuff to her bedroom in the flat and was the sole person who lived there. Robby only paid regular visits to his flat but never spent a night in his tiny little sun room what would be his.

26 Old Contacts

Soon after the burglary Konrad contacted an old friend who used to be with the Feds. He learned about the case and knew how Konrad earned his money. It was no longer his business but the cops could pick him up and ask him awkward questions about his motel and the money that got missing. The only thing he did when Konrad approached him was telling him a clear warning. Watch your back. The cops are after you.

In a little but busy Italian restaurant in Bondi Beach the two men had a special meeting and a business dinner. Konrad ordered a bottle of wine with the food and heard from his friend the progress the cops were making in the burglary case. He made no notes but received a big envelop with all the notes from the investigators of the case.

"How did you get this?"

"I talked with the chief and said I know a man who could help them. I never revealed your name and they never asked me any further questions."

"I will read it when I am home."

"You should and there's a map of what might be the location where your former employee has some shelter. It is on a farm but it will be difficult to spot which one as there are many farms in that region. A few coppers paid a visit after we received some serious complaints but they still haven't spotted the guy on any of the farms. It is the best link we have so far."

"So where did they go?" "You have to check a lot of farms in between Cessnock and Singleton. We know he lives on a farm and he has protection. These farmers don't like city dwellers like you and me so don't think they will tell you a thing if you think you can go and have a look. You should watch your back. These guys are armed and we can't stop them so don't start a war as we can't help and protect you."

Konrad nodded and refilled the empty wine glasses. The food was good and simple. The cook was an immigrant who learned to cook Italian food but the owners of the restaurant were true Italians but the staff was all foreigners.

It was a very popular place and they did some awesome pizzas. Robby and Julia knew the place but it was not their favourite restaurant in town. They always went for Italian food at the Grande Cafe.

"So what can you tell me off the hook?"

"We both know your ex employee is behind the burglary. There's no doubt and he had some help from a woman who knows you. What I have learned from your little interview with the cops when they paid a visit at your place straight after the burglary you came with a list of names. Two were confirmed but one name is still a big question mark."

Konrad listened and looked around. He saw a young waitress doing her best in serving other customers when by incident she dropped a plate and spilled some of the food on the customer. She apologised and did her best to clean the area but Konrad was not impressed with the young girl. She was too young and inexperienced for the job. A few years of training was what this girl needed and she shouldn't carry two heavy plates if she wasn't that strong.

"Did you see that? How pathetic. Why do they employ inexperienced youth for these jobs?"

"I don't know. It can happen. She didn't do it on purpose."

"But what if she did? Would you employ such a girl?"

Konrad's friend waved his hand and ignored the inexperienced waitress. "Have you spoken with Valery?"

"Yes, a few times and I know she's lying. She knows she was there. I saw her she knows that too but she still doesn't want to tell me why she hung around in my street on the day of the burglary. She was part of it."

"Yes, the other girl you gave to us we have no information about her. She's not known to us but we keep an eye on her. It looks like she had nothing to do with the whole case."

"She has nothing to do with the case. She wasn't there. She has plenty of witnesses and has a reliable alibi. Robby still hasn't confirmed but I know he was around but even he didn't do it. It's too big and too much for him. I would have known already if he stole my money. He's too stupid and he would spend it on stupid vintage toys."

"I heard he approached you for something else didn't he?"

"Yes, he wants his name cleared from whatever happened a while ago in Hornsby. He says it was an accident and had no intentions in hurting her."

"I will see what I can do for him but for the moment the case stays open. We haven't heard from her since she flew back to Holland but we hope to hear from her soon. We contacted her family but they haven't replied so we keep it open till something else will happen."

"He was such a fool to attack her. I warned him not to harm her but he didn't listen. He called me and asked me to help him with clearing up the evidence."

"Glad you called us. For the moment we keep the case closed but we will reopen it if he does it again. Tell him to be careful. Next time we will arrest him and he can pay for the damages he did to the poor girl."

Konrad looked at a drawn map what was part of the file. He tried to read the map but it was drawn fast and not accurate. He thanked his friend after he paid for the dinner and went straight to the Bondi Lodge where he wanted to meet up with Robby and Julia. This was great news. Finally, some progress.

"No, but I am getting close. I know where my old employee is hiding. Soon I will have him. He can't escape as he has been spotted by the cops. He left a clear trace behind while he is busy in spending my money. He didn't know I have a list of all the bank notes and their numbers. He can't change it at any money changer here in Australia. I gave the list to the cops and they keep an eye on it too. They found out where my old staff member is hiding."

"So what do you want from me?"

"Not much. I don't think you can help me with what I have in mind but if Julia is around I might need her for a favour."

"She will be shortly back. She's in the kitchen but will be soon back."

A few minutes later Julia reappeared with three hot mugs of coffee. She gave Robby and Konrad a mug and took a seat next of Konrad on the sofa. She was like him all smiles.

"I heard your voice. I could hear you have some good news, haven't you?"

"Yes, I do have. Have you ever been to the wine valley just outside of Sydney?"

"No, but I heard about it. They say it's very beautiful but I haven't been there. I haven't seen much of the country expect for a day trip to the Blue Mountains. That was the only day trip I ever made while I am here in Australia. I wanted to go to Melbourne but thanks to Robby I am still here in Sydney."

"As if it was my fault that you stay here all the time." Robby replied. "I never told you to stay here. Put the blame to yourself. It was your decision to stay here and not mine."

"But you asked me to stay for a while and see I am still here. Why?"

Konrad noticed the arguments Julia and Robby had over her stay here in Sydney. He knew how hard Robby cold be. He had done it before with other girls. He was good in manipulating them and he always convinced them that staying a bit longer in Sydney would be good for them but mostly for him. He knew how to get access to their money so they all left him empty handed.

"Robby, Julia. Can I have your attention please?"

"Sorry, Konrad. Sure you can."

"Right, Julia, do you want to go with me for a full day to the Hunter Valley? I need someone who can help me with finding my old employee. I want to find out where he stays so I want to find on which farm he's staying. I don't know how long it will take but I will pay you for the service. You will be rewarded."

"Will it be dangerous?"

"It shouldn't be but we have to be careful. He stays at a farm and these farmers don't like us. I only want to find out where he stays. I can't arrest him I will leave that to the cops. They can deal with the farmers. I only want to find out where he lives." "Wow, I thought you want to get your money back from him what he stole from you."

"I still want my money back but that can wait. In due course I will get my money back and the ones who stole it will pay the price."

Robby and Julia got both fed up with living in the Bondi Lodge. They both wanted a place but it was not easy to rent a flat in Bondi. The rent was high what wasn't a problem for Julia but she couldn't rent as she hardly knew people. She could always ask Konrad for being a reference but he would ask her to work for his motel. She didn't want to become too close with him. She had seen the place and didn't want to stay there. The rooms in the Bondi Lodge were smaller and no room really had his own private bathroom with shower and toilet except for two rooms but she didn't want to live under the nose of Konrad. She didn't trust him completely. He was kind but very hard.

In the small cafe opposite the lodge they discussed the situation with Camilla who lived op top of her little business. She knew how hard it was to rent a place and she was glad she got her own little business. As a foreigner it wasn't easy but she made money and she had her Australian citizenship. Still she was deep in her heart a woman from Puerto Rico and showed it in her bar with a massive flag hanging on the ceiling.

"Rob, have you contacted the woman from five flats down in the street?"

"No, what about?" "She has a luxurious two flat apartments for rent and she wants new tenants soon. You should check it out before someone else will take it." "How much does she ask per week?"

Julia still had to get used to the fact that every place was per week and not per month. She believed the rent would be high too much for Robby alone but if he wouldn't mind to live with her she was willing to pay her share as long as he wouldn't be unfaithful to her. He had to promise he wouldn't steal from her what would be hard to say it in his face and he had to keep his word.

"Julia, you still want to live in the Lodge?"

"No, I am fed up with that place. Let's rent something together."

Robby and Julia went outside where they had a smoke and drank their coffee. Camilla joined them for a very short moment and pointed to a for Rent sign at one of the flats opposite of the little coffee bar. Robby made some notes and would check the phone numbers once he was again in the city.

"I will give them a call and see how much they charge for the space. I will be soon in the city and might go to their agency. I hope my solicitor can check the address for me out. She's very good, you know."

"So, how's your case going?"

Julia did her best to show some interest what Robby didn't mind. He was glad she still supported him although she didn't want to give him constant money. Now and then she gave him some money but he had to promise her to pay it all back as soon as he would win his case. "Julia, how much would you invest in a new place if I can find one?" "What do you want me to do? Buy new furniture?" "No, I can get access to furniture. No, I was more thinking in paying the first couple of months rent plus the bond. That will be a lot and I can't afford to pay both the rent and the deposit for our place." "See what you can find and I will see what I will pay. I can't make you any promises but I will help you I promise you that."

Robby was glad that Julia wanted to rent a place just like him and she was willing to pay for it too. He wondered how much would she pay and would she give the money to him or would she join him when he would see a real estate agent to sign an agreement and pay the bond plus first month rent.

Julia paid for the coffee while he stopped a cab and went straight to the city to see his solicitor. She saw him later in the evening when he had good news. He found the address of the real estate agent of a flat next door of the lodge and he made an appointment with the woman who wanted to rent her 2-bedroom apartment as soon as possible.

The next morning straight after their little coffee they went to see the place. The apartment was spacious and very clean. Julia didn't mind to live in the space but Robby didn't like the conditions that the woman came up with.

Robby wasn't allowed to smoke what he didn't want to give up. Second was that there was only one original bedroom and a sun room what could be turned into a bedroom but she wanted to know what they both did for work if they would come late and didn't play too loud music. Robby got the feeling that the old lady was a bit too nosy and would disturb their peace with stupid little rules to annoy them and to kick them out if they would break any of her rules.

"What do you think, Julia?" He asked her.

"I like the place. It will be a bit hard for both of us but I don't mind the space. We have plenty of space for whatever we bring in but we can't smoke."

Julia already knew that it would be a problem for Robby. She didn't mind. It would be good for her to stop smoking what she tried to do. Robby was in no mood in quitting smoking and not for an old landlord.

"Let's have a look with that real estate agent in Double Bay. If you don't mind I want to pay them a visit and see what they ask and if we can have a look inside before we sign an agreement with them."

Robby arranged a meeting with the agency and a

few days later she showed up and showed both Robby and Julia the space. They both liked the place and luckily for Robby he could smoke inside. The rooms were smaller but the rent was also lower and affordable for both of them. Still Robby had to ask for Julia to pay the bond and the first two months of rent if they would agree with the terms of the estate agent.

In the evening Robby had a discussion about how to pay the rent with Julia when Konrad showed up. He had good news and wanted to share it with them. He heard about Robby's news that he wanted to rent a flat so he got interested.

"We found a flat and it's very nearby. We will pay a visit on Saturday to their estate agent and sing the agreement. We both want the place so we have to sign the papers and pay the deposit and the first months of rent."

"Who will pay it?" He asked while he looked a short moment in the direction of Julia. She disappeared to the kitchen and made some coffee for the guys.

"I have to ask Julia to pay for the rent and the bond before we can get access to our new place.

She might want to buy some furniture for her room but we both like the space and hope to get in as soon as possible."

"Let me know if you need me for reference or so. I hope this place will not turn into a disaster."

Robby read Konrad's face and nodded. he knew what he meant by that. No, he hoped Julia wouldn't be as bad as the previous young Dutch girl was. She was nice till he stayed for some time together.

"No, Konrad. I know what you were thinking but Julia is no Suzie and I hope it will not go that path on again as it was a complete nightmare for me."

"I hope so too for you, Robby. I will not help you this time if it would come to an end like the previous time. For me one time is more than enough and you should know I have so my own problems if you understand."

"Any luck with your case?" Konrad nodded when Julia reappeared with three mugs of hot coffee. He held the door for her open of the dining room and she gave him the first mug before she put one on the reception desk and put the third on the little coffee table next of the sofa. She took a seat and gave Konrad some company who sat next of her.

"Yes, as a matter of fact. The police believed to find the farm where my ex employee and thief is living. The stupid dope head is spending some of my money together with these wild farmers who also grow dope so he's probably very stoned and drunk."

Robby was looking at his friend but wasn't impressed with the news. He didn't like how Konrad treated his former employee so bad while he did a lot of work for his motel.

"How much have they spent so far?"

"I can't tell but even if I would know I don't want to tell you how much is already wasted. That's my concern. All I know is that he lives in Cessnock on a farm but there are some rumours that he also found refuge on another farm somewhere in Singleton. He knows a couple of farmers and they're the ones who protect him at all costs."

"And I guess you want to find out for yourself, don't you?" Robby looked quickly at Julia who listened with great care to the story. She wanted to help Konrad and came already with a few ideas what Konrad liked.

"Have you checked out who helped them? How did they have access to your house if you have a dog and an alarm system?"

"So you think one of my house mates was part of it?"

"Your sister in law must know more than she wants to admit so who called the cops? Why did she do it if she could have called you before the police would show up for investigating it."

"How much does she know?" Robby asked who agreed with Julia's opinion.

"Good point, Julia. I have to admit I have a strong feeling that my sis in law is part of the burglary but what part I don't know. I don't think she received money for her job because I would know. She can't spend the money as I wrote down all the numbers on my laptop computer what they didn't take while they had a chance. It would have been too obvious if they would have stolen my computer."

'They didn't, did they?"

"No, but if they had stolen my computer they would have access to lots of important files and all the banknote numbers so it would be easy for them to change it for different currencies. Now I can see where they have gone and to my surprise the farmers if it were them changed their money constant at the same money changer. He contacts the police whenever they want to change dollars for bucks."

Konrad looked at Julia who listened to his story. She would have used different money changers if possible and otherwise go to different places and change the dollars there. It would be harder to chase the numbers and hard to catch if the police ever want to make an arrest.

"Julia, do you fancy a trip to the Hunter Valley with me? I will let you know when we go when I got some more info. I will let you know as soon as possible."

"Sure, I love to."

She had to wait for a couple of days before Konrad got all the info he needed although the coppers drew a bad map of where they met the farmers in the Valley. It was now up to Konrad to figure out where exactly they would think Paul was staying.

In the meantime, Robby managed to meet up with the agent from the agency in Double Bay and they both had a good look in their new house. It was next door of the hostel and the room was on the ground floor on the right. Julia liked the big bedroom and saw herself living in the place. Robby was happy to have the small sunroom as his room. He trusted Julia and offered her the first choice of rooms.

Julia took the big bedroom and paid a visit to Ikea where she bought a sofa for the living room, a few Ivar cupboards and some other items and asked to deliver them to the new place. In the meantime, she received from Robby a queen-size bed but the quality wasn't as good as it should have been. It was an old bed from the Bondi Lodge what Robby managed to sneak out of the lodge together with two chairs and some other items. He tried to sneak out a little fridge but he didn't manage. Julia was very pleased with her new room. She moved all her belongings from the hostel to the flat and started a complete new life in the new place. She bought a TV and an all-zone DVD player plus a stereo with Dolby surround system so she could watch films as if she would see it in a cinema. Robby liked all her ideas and how she organised the house into a nice place. Jonathan was so kind to offer them a dressing table and his queen size bed. When she received her cupboards and sofa she installed the Ivar cupboards and put her computer on a special shelf so she could use it.

Robby found a perfect printer for her computer while she was away in Hong Kong and she was very pleased with the Canon printer although she actually wanted to buy a Hewlett Packard printer to match up with her Hewlett Packard Pavilion desktop computer. It was a smooth fast running computer and a perfect replacement for the loss of her Compaq laptop what died around New Year's Eve. A stupid Austrian girl stepped on her laptop while it laid next of her bed in the four bed dormitory she shared during Christmas period. The girl never apologised and didn't care that she killed an expensive laptop computer. Now that Julia furnished the place with a sofa, a TV and a stereo system Robby paid for a TV license so she could watch proper TV. He asked a company to install the special decoder in the flat and now and then he found it relaxed to watch TV or a film instead of staying all the time in the Lodge.

Julia was glad to be out of the Bondi Lodge. She liked the place but now she wasn't working for them anymore she wanted to be away from that place. Six to seven months was more than enough and the new place was as cosy as she could get it. The new place was home. She finally had some decent privacy and didn't have to share a bathroom and toilet with others except for Robby who never slept in his own apartment.

27 The Olympic Games

A few weeks after they moved to their apartment Sydney was the centre of the biggest sports event what would be later seen as the best Olympic Summer Games ever. From the moment Julia started to work for the Bondi Lodge it was clear that the Olympics were coming to town. Everywhere she walked through the city she could see banners with the Olympic official and unofficial symbols and mascots.

In the local coffee bar Barlevento she could hear the regular talks about the coming Games and the beach volleyball stadium that was due to be build on Bondi Beach. There were people who weren't happy to see the games so close to them but the majority of the Sydneysiders loved to see the

Games in their popular and favourite city. The weather was predicted to be warm and sunny and slowly many of the sports stars came to test some of the venues before the official day.

Dutch swim sensation Inge de Bruin swam some official games in the Olympic pool and set a new world record on her name. She was one of the many Dutch sport stars that would go for gold. The Aussies were wild on her achievements and saw a future golden champion in her although the competition would come partly from their own swimmers. Both the men and women were qualified for the field hockey and would go for gold. There were chances for the Dutch with cycling and other sports.

Robby wasn't an Olympic fan and didn't want to see anything of the Olympic Games while Anton was very proud for his father who was part of the many volunteers who helped the make the Games the best ever. His father was asked to be part of the opening ceremony.

Most of the sports venues were sold out. Luckily for Julia there was a possible way to see a bit of the road cycling through the eastern suburbs not far away from Bondi. From Hunter Park she could hear during the Games the crowd cheering up for the beach volley players. The stadium was too high so it was impossible to see what was going on but people in Bondi could hear the games.

Julia wanted to see a few games but she didn't have a Visa credit card. Visa was one of the major sponsors of the Olympic Games and forced people who wanted to see the games to use a visa credit card. She only had traveller's cheques and none of them were supporting visa but American Express and MasterCard.

Earlier in the year she wanted to see the Australian Open the first major tennis tournament held in Melbourne Victoria but Robby was afraid she wouldn't come back. He stopped her from leaving Sydney and promised her then golden mountains. She even tried to see the Formula One again at Melbourne at the Australian Grand Prix. Unfortunately, she couldn't even see that. All her hopes were now focused on the Olympic Games but without a credit card it was hard to get tickets to any of the sports evens. Luckily with the new apartment she could see and watch much of the sports at home.

A few days before the Olympics started at the Olympic park in Homebush Bay the Olympic flame made an original entrance to the coast of Sydney. Two days before the Opening of the Summer Games the Olympic flame entered Sydney by boat at Bondi Beach. Some lucky members of the Bondi Life Guards rowed the flame to the famous beach of Sydney where others took over.

In the Bondi Lodge Robby was around and heard like many others the sound of helicopters who flew low over Bondi. Three helicopters tried to catch a clear glimpse of the arrival of the Olympic flame on the beach of Bondi. A massive crowd collected on the beach and in the streets where they supported the celebrities and old sports stars who were selected to bring the flame to the Olympic Stadium.

"What's going on outside?" Robby asked a few others.

"It's the arrival of the Olympic flame."

"Oh, those bloody games." He mumbled and continued smoking his cigarette.

Julia was at Hunter Park and had a good view of

the whole scene. Unfortunately, she forgot her camera and couldn't take any photos of this happening. She was glad to see the Flame reaching the beach where a massive crowd cheered the arrival of the Olympic Flame. She hardly knew any famous Australians so she had no idea who all these Olympic flame bearers were. Channel 7 and the local papers gave updates of the coming Olympics and when the Olympics were on of all the sports and the medal winners.

In the house she watched some of it on her brand new wide screen TV. Robby did his best to annoy her so she missed most of the opening of the Games but she saw how Cathy Freeman got the honour in lightning the Olympic flame. She got soaked that night but she was the absolute star that night and her performance had a golden touch. A week later she won the women's 400 meters and won Gold for Australia and for their indigenous people the aboriginals. She celebrated her winning by showing the aboriginal flag instead of the Australian flag. A week earlier Julia cheered for all the golden moments of the Dutch in the swimming pool. Holland won several medals; gold, silver, bronze and their best swimmers were Peter van de Hoogenband and

Inge de Bruin. The Aussies were the favourites but the crowd cheered all the ones who did their best for their country even if they lost.

The first week of the Games were going well for the Dutch. Julia was a very proud Dutch backpacker/ traveller in Sydney. She read in the papers every morning in Barlevento about the Olympics plus Camilla spent lots of time and hours every day at the Games. She visited the Olympic village where all the sports men were staying and met lots of them. Every morning when she opened up her own cafe she talked about it to her customers when they walked in. Everyone supported the Games even her staff although on of her staff members was still against the beach volleyball on the beach of Bondi. She cheered for all the good results from the Aussies but also of the other countries.

Whenever Julia was in the apartment she watched when she could some of the highlights of the Games. There was no chance to miss a bit of the Olympics. Wherever she went she heard people talking about the Olympics or saw on tellies all over the city.

Jonathan knew some people whom he hadn't seen

for a while and they invited him for a meal at Doyle's fish restaurant at Watson Bay north of Bondi. They knew about his upcoming travel plan so they wanted to see him before he was about to leave Australia.

Julia saw Jonathan a lot and she liked him. He was a good guy and a lover. She knew he was engaged and loved his dear girlfriend but in the meantime he didn't mind the good moments they had together. She was there for him when he missed his girlfriend so much when she was off travelling for a couple of months in Europe.

"Julia. I am invited by a couple of friends. They want to have dinner at Doyles and that is a place you have to see. I guess you love fish, don't you?"

"John, I am from Holland and lived close to the sea. Of course I love fish and yes, I will join you for dinner. Let me know when you come to pick me up. I will make sure I will be ready so I can enjoy the evening with your friends.

He picked her up while she tried to follow the swimming. She turned off the TV and joined Jonathan who drove her up to Watson Bay. His friends were there waiting for him and were glad to meet Julia. They ordered drinks and she ate some delicious grilled fish fresh from the sea.

In between the meal and the drinks, she saw a bit of telly and they showed some swimming rallies but no finals. It was a good evening without any trouble. She was glad Robby wasn't with them. He was as always at work at the reception so he had no time to join her and Jonathan.

The city was one big party venue. The Dutch were very popular because their big beer brewery Heineken sponsored the big tent where all the Dutch athletes and fans met. All the winners showed their medals and got cheered by representatives of the Dutch government as of the sports officials. Even the future Dutch king Willem Alexander was there to join the big party as he was part of the sports officials. The Dutch showed the world how crazy they were when it came to sports. The Holland Heineken House was the place to be for the athletes, sponsors, tourists and locals. They were the talk of the day but they weren't the only one with a special meeting place. The Aussies had so theirs as had the South Africans. The Americans were the best athletes followed by the Chinese but Australia wasn't so bad either. They did well and won many medals.

The Australians showed to the world that they were sports crazy. The Aussies did well but were beaten by the Americans and the Chinese who were still the best sports nations in the world.

After two long weeks of sports Sydney showed the world that they knew how to lit fireworks. Once again Julia saw an impressive firework show when the Olympic Games came to an end. She remembered the opening of the Games when Cathy Freeman got soaked while she lit the Olympic flame. She won gold on the women's 400 meters and celebrated her winning with the Aboriginal flag instead of the national flag of Australia. She was still very proud to be an Aboriginal who won gold for all the Aboriginals in the country. It was a night to remember.

Julia watched the fireworks in Dover Heights just north of North Bondi where on a big hill she had a good view of the city and the famous Harbour Bridge. Again she saw an amazing lightshow and was glad to be in Australia. She couldn't believe how well organised the whole Games were.

When it started there were some problems with the public transport but that was only on Day 1.

After the first day it all went smooth and no incidents disrupted the Games like it happened in 1996 in Atlanta. The Olympic Games in Sydney Australia ended in the books of the Olympic Comity as the best Games ever. Sydney was glad to hear from Antonia Samaranch that they treated the world on the best sports event.

Robby was glad the Games were over. He didn't like it and didn't want to waste his time into it. Konrad was partly satisfied as it meant for him every day full house in his motel. No bed was unoccupied and with the higher price he charged his guests he made some profit. It was only a pity he couldn't set up a new money scheme but still was pleased with the financial results. Unfortunately, he couldn't find a buyer for his motel. He wanted to sell his business so he could spend all his time on hunting his burglars. He knew who done it but they were smart enough not to reveal too much. He knew Paul was the brains and he was hiding in the Hunter Valley while Valery was almost living under his nose and she didn't spend a single dollar on her hostel. She didn't touch her share at all while Paul and Charley were stupid enough to spend some of it. The left traces but not concrete enough so he could follow them and hunt them down.

When time would tell he would find them and take back of what they stole from him. They would pay the highest price for what they had done to him. He was convinced he could find them first before the police could arrest them.

28 Trip to the Hunter Valley

It took a while before Konrad made an appearance at the Lodge. He had been out of action due to an old injury on his leg and needed surgery. Because of the surgery he wasn't allowed to do much so he couldn't work for a while. His wife took over his job and ran the motel on her own as if she had done it for years. She learned a few things from her long-term guests who reminded her on some weird costs they had never head of and paid them always in dollars' cash to her husband. She didn't know but took the money but had no idea she came close to the old scheme that Konrad had learned from Robby. Now she knew about their little game they played with their guests and that made them wealthy. Instead of keeping the money in her own pocket she wrote it down on the system so when Konrad was back in action he could see what he had done over the years with his customers and the authorities. There would be a lot of money to be repaid.

Konrad hadn't changed much while he had been out of action for a month. His mood was still the same or perhaps even worse. He was angry with his wife but now she knew his system he couldn't do much. Time would come soon to end his business and sell it to a rich buyer after the coming Olympics. It was obvious the Olympics were coming in town. Everywhere he went he saw the banners of the Summer Olympics and even in Bondi the protestors gave up their battle over the building of a stadium for the beach volleyball. In a few weeks the flame would arrive in Sydney and that would mean the Games would be on for two long weeks followed by the Paralympics a few weeks later.

Julia was no longer working for the Bondi Lodge and for the first time she could enjoy her time now she didn't have to show up in the kitchen to deal with hungry students and backpackers who where very picky with their food.

Marty was a nice guy and a good chef but the money wasn't as good as he had hoped so he gave up the job. He didn't like the students who were rude and had no respect for his job and his food. He called Terry who got shocked when his friend resigned so soon. It was bad news and it wasn't good for the company. Terry was too busy with the other businesses and had no time to work in Bondi. The company had to come with a better solution or he would fear for more trouble.

Julia was at least honest to say that she had enough of her work. She didn't mind the job but the Olympics were coming near the city and the immigration officers were close on catching illegal workers as she was one of them. If they would have caught her she would have ended in a special deportation centre near the airport where she would probably be deported back to her own country what would mean her long trip would have ended in a terrible disaster. That would have been the last thing she actually wanted to receive on her plate. She had already enough problems with her friend Robby.

Trouble was brewing and the clouds were getting darker by the day what indicated a disaster was near. After eight months of prosperity it was time for trouble. Her lovely time in Bondi would end in a horrible nightmare what she could have prevailed if she would have understood the signals that she received before it all started. The nightmare and all the trouble started when Robby and Julia went on searching for a flat where they both could live. They both needed a place for their own but none of them could get one by themselves. Julia had no references although she knew in half a year time enough people who could act as a reference while Robby had no money. He needed Julia but his court case changed his mind. He got more and more obsessed by money as his new lawyer promised him he could receive a big reward if she was able to win on his behalf his court case.

If Robby would be able to win his case, he could receive around half a million dollars and perhaps more. His injuries on his lower back and legs were serious and very painful. Through some tests she could convince the court that those injuries were caused by that uncovered hole near his old hostel. It should have been covered as the council was still responsible for negligence.

Robby was very jealous on Julia as she had what he wanted to have; money. He had seen some of her bank statements while she was away and it made him almost sick. He wanted it all but she wasn't so easy to give away her wealth. She was happy that she had a lot of money although she did her best not to show to others that she had a nice little fortune on her bank accounts. She protected her own privacy and didn't want to share it with others.

None of her friends were interested in her wealth except for Robby. Even Konrad wasn't interested in her money. It was clear it wasn't his what she had on her accounts. Robby thought and tried to play a dirty game while she was away with his good friend but Konrad never believed she had some shares in the burglary as she didn't know much about him. She got to know him after the burglary when he paid many visits to the Lodge where he asked them many questions while he was busy investing his own investigation. Konrad made his reappearance on an evening straight after a day at work in his motel. Instead of going home he drove straight to the Bondi Lodge and received a cold welcome from his old friend.

"Konrad, what are you doing here? Don't you have your own place to run?"

"I just came from my motel. It's all fine in my place and if something would go wrong my guests know they have to call me on my mobile before I can sort out what is their problem. It's so handy to use a mobile phone nowadays that I don't have to hang around in my motel waiting for problems what actually never occur. All my guests are well behaved men and my place is just running smooth."

"Not what I have heard, my friend." Robby replied and he stared for a moment in his friend's eyes.

"Oh, what have I missed what makes you think my place is not doing well?"

"I can't tell you but you can't use our scheme as

someone discovered what you were doing over the years. You have a lot to answer and the authorities will soon knock on your door."

Konrad looked Robby in his empty eyes and tried to read his mind. "Let them come. I am not afraid of them and I can prove I have done nothing wrong."

"Wrong, you made a nice fortune with our simple money scheme but someone found out and will use it against you. Believe me, it happened to me just before I went away for a couple of months."

"I am not surprised. You made clear to everyone that you were busy in skimming your poor young backpackers who have hardly any money. No wonder someone would have complained but the cops never caught you, didn't they?"

Robby sighed and searched like always for his fags. He found a pack and lit on up right at the reception desk. He couldn't be bothered by telling people off. He had enough of the place and needed a new break what he couldn't afford.

"So who knows about our scheme, Robby? Serious. I want to know who it is so I can have a chat with him."

"You can't use violence on this person. She's a woman and you shouldn't threat her."

Robby tried to smile at his friend but Konrad wasn't impressed. "Oh, so who is it? Is it our lovely friend Julia or someone else we both know?"

Robby didn't want to hear Julia's name but he didn't want his friend know there were some problems within their friendship.

"No, not her. She doesn't know a thing but the longer she stays in Bondi she might hear about it. She's not stupid and she's clearly brighter and smarter than the other blonde girl I had to get rid of."

"You were sloppy and you were nearly caught with your pants down. Don't do it again, Robby. Don't touch Julia. She's not worth it."

Julia showed up with coffee as she heard Konrad. She was by that time chatting with Matthew in the kitchen when he showed up. She made some coffee for the guys and was in good spirits. It was nice to chat with Matthew. She had a good time with him together in the kitchen although he was a lousy kitchen hand. At least he showed up for his work on time and did what was told but not a single thing more. He didn't show any initiative what Julia did. She had keen interest in her job and showed Terry that she was a good cook. She knew her job and was always motivated.

"Did I hear you were talking about me?" She gave the two guys their hot drinks and took a seat next of Konrad. He tapped softly on her leg and thanked her for the coffee. She was at least kind to think of them while Robby would have served him coffee from the coffee vending machine. Konrad didn't like that coffee and preferred coffee from the little coffee bar opposite in the street.

"We were discussing some business but you are free to join us. I don't think there's any topic what you don't know about."

Robby looked from his desk at her. He thanked her while he raised his mug up.

"We were talking about the money that got missing. You know what we are talking about."

"Yes, the missing case that got stolen from your home and you know what I would ask the people who live inside the house as I think they know more but don't want to say a word as they are afraid. You have to look closer to home."

"It can't be my wife, but she learned a few things while I was out for a short while and discovered how I made my fortune. I guess she's the one you were talking about."

Robby didn't answer. He knew that Valery knew more than she should have. She discovered months ago how Robby made his little fortune. She just waited for the right time to throw him out while he was away from her. She froze his account and cut his credit cards that he didn't carry with him during his trip in half and made sure he couldn't get access to his own bank accounts. To hurt him further she wrote everything in her name and erased his name at the bank. She sold all his possessions and his apartment so he had no place to stay. She told some bad rumours about his past to many of his friends so they all turned their backs onto him. There was no one he could ask for help as they all knew what kind of crook he actually was.

"If I were you I should be careful with what you spare with your missus." He said to Konrad. "Before you know it she might throw you out of the house and even take over your motel. Beware of her."

"I am and she will be no serious threat to me. If she wants to try she will end up where she doesn't want to end. I made it clear to her and she knows."

"What if she goes to the cops?"

"She wouldn't but then again she might have gone already. Why did her sister call the cops first before she called me? Thanks for the tip."

Konrad thought of the words what Julia mentioned to him. From day 1 he had a strong belief that his wife and her sister were somehow involved in the burglary. His wife denied and he knew she couldn't be part of it. She was at work in Surrey Hills so she wasn't at home but her sister was. She didn't like Konrad and would do anything to get back to Korea. She didn't like Australia very much and wanted to go home. South Korea was her country and not Australia.

"Oh, by the way, Julia. Do you have anything to do tomorrow? Do you mind to go with me tomorrow to the Hunter Valley?"

"Sure, why not. What will we do there?"

"I want to find out where Paul is staying. I learned from the cops that he is hiding on a farm somewhere between Singleton and Cessnock. They gave me a map but I am not sure if I can use it. I need some help and I know you want to see a bit more of Australia, am I right?"

"Yes, you are. Count me in, please."

"I will pick you up in the morning. Don't stay up late as it will be a long day."

Julia was ready the next morning. She got up at seven and had her breakfast in Barlevento the little coffee bar and waited for a while till Konrad showed up. He stopped in front of the bar and had a coffee before they drove to his house in Francis Street. He picked up some things but he forgot to bring a jerry can with fuel what he normally always carried in his big four-wheel drive. When he got what he needed he drove to his motel where his wife was already at work. She gave them some oranges and water for the long journey and he got some maps that he kept in his office.

"Do you know where he might stay?"

"No, not really. I know he has a few friends in the Valley. His dope dealer comes from the Valley and it is hard to trace the farm. The police can't search all the farms as the farmers don't like city dwellers like us. There's some hostility in the country side and they don't want us to hang out too long. We have to be careful. Paul knows I am after him so he will be protected by his friends who have enough mates so we will be outnumbered if it will come to a fight. Let's hope we can avoid a fight."

Julia went straight into a wild adventure in the countryside. The trip to the Hunter Valley was long but nice. Konrad pointed as they drove through Hornsby to a flat when they were on their way to the valley.

"Your mate Robby did something stupid a while ago and I hope he will never do it to you."

"Oh, what did he do?"

"I can't say. I promised Robby I will not tell you but you will hear it from others. He things that I am the only one who knows the story but I learned there were others who know it too. You see Robby likes to talk to people and sometimes he forgets whom he's talking too. Whatever he did he mentioned it to some guys and they spread the news."

"Did he get caught?"

"By the cops? No but he should have. He called me and asked for my help. I told him that I didn't want to solve all his problems. It's about time he solves his own. I am the one who has to deal with all his fuck ups and believe me he made lots of them."

They passed a few pump stations but Konrad paid no attention to his fuel meter. He also left his spare fuel can back home as he thought it wouldn't be needed together with his NRMA membership card. He was for an organised man very sloppy.

The trip to the Valley was long but not boring. Julia loved the countryside and was glad she accepted Konrad's invitation. He was good company and a very good driver. In the lodge he showed his bad sides while here on the road in the middle of nowhere he was in his true elements. He was quite fond of Julia. She was the kind of woman he wanted so desperately for his motel. She would be great and his guests would love and adore her but she said no several times to all his invitations to work for him. He even promised her a sponsorship.

"I know you mean well, Konrad but I have to say no to you."

"That's ok. You know what you want and I shall not force you to. At least I offered you a proper job although I know you love cooking and I do believe you are a proper chef compare to these clowns these amateurs. I would pay you fair and offer you a nice clean room with all facilities for free. Think about it."

Julia had to laugh and ran her hand through her short bristles. She loved her short look. She looked so different and didn't mind she looked more like a boy than a woman. The cut was so easy and cheap and very suitable for her old job in the kitchen of the two lodges.

"I heard from Robby that you quit?"

"Yes, that's true. I have enough of the job. It was fun but not anymore."

"Why did you stop? Was the pay bad or was the

workforce too much for you?"

Julia kept on smiling while she looked at Konrad. She didn't want to see and consider him as a friend but she felt more secure with him than with Robby. At least he never asked for money. He didn't need to ask for money as he earned his own money through his successful motel.

"Nah, it's the Bondi Lodge. It's the management who knows nothing and don't care about the staff."

"I hear in your voice Robby. He complains a lot about the work. Do you agree with him?"

"About the Bondi Lodge? Yes, he's absolute right. When I heard the news about Lothar the previous cook who quit the job due to his illness I took temporary cover but none of the managers thought I was capable in doing the job. They can't believe that women can do this kind of shit so they told me I wasn't good enough. Luckily Terry backed me up although he had to follow their line so he replaced me soon when he found a good friend to take over my work in the kitchen."

"You could have made clear that you are a

professional. You are a qualified chef, aren't you?"

"Yes, I have all the qualifications but somehow these Dumbo's don't know a thing about cooking and qualifications. They see me as a girl and think gosh she can cook but does that say she can be a chef? You must be joking."

"What was Robby's reaction? He must have said something to you when you quit your job."

"Nothing. All he could do was asking for some more money for his court case. I spent already thousands of dollars and what have I received back from him; nothing, not a single cent."

After a few hours of driving they came close to the farms in Cessnock. Konrad paid close attention to a little piece of paper and a drawn map on it. It was created by some coppers who weren't very good in drawing. He gave the map to Julia who checked it on a bigger map that he took out of his gloves compartment of his car.

"Can you see if that map matches with this big map for me please?"

Julia took her time while Konrad parked his car.

They were on top of a hill overlooking some farms in the distance. He gave Julia a small bottle of water and a few oranges. It tasted refreshing. She gave the map back and followed him when he got out of the car.

"If I am not mistaken that is where he was seen."

Konrad pointed to a few farms and hoped he was still there. Julia looked and used the binocular he gave her so she could look closer. He pointed to a farm in between a few other farms and pointed to a few barns. His ex employee was living there and he wanted him desperately together with his stolen money.

"Do you think you can see anyone at that farm?"

"Nothing." She replied. "Look closer. He must be somewhere."

"Are you sure he lives there and not somewhere else?"

Konrad looked at her and took the binoculars over from her. He looked but couldn't see what he hoped he might see. Bugger, he wasn't there. Maybe she was right.

"What do you want to do?"

"Let me think for a moment." Konrad said and took out of jacket his Walther P99. He aimed his gun on a branch of a tree and fired a few times. The first two bullets hit the branch but the third missed and then the next bullet in his gun got jammed. He was furious and wasn't pleased with that. The bullets were new and weren't proper tested before so he wasn't in a good mood.

"What in the hell was that?" Julia shouted while she covered her ears. The loud bangs did hurt her ears and he should have warned her what he forgot to do what made her furious.

"Sorry, Julia. I should have warned you. Are you ok?"

She shook her head. She had some problems with hearing but he looked in the distance. He saw some dust on the far road coming towards them and yelled at her. "Get in the car. Lock your door and stay there. We got some company."

"Who? What's going on?"

"Do as I say and stay in the car. You will be safe. Just don't say a word even when they ask you questions. I will answer them for both of us."

A couple of four-wheel drive cars showed up and stopped near Konrad's Landcruiser. Several men got out some were armed with sticks others with guns and pointed their firearms at Konrad. "Was that you who shot a firearm?"

"Yes, that was me. Sorry, forgive me please. I forgot the echo in the valley."

"You're damn right. Next time we will fire at you."

"Who are you, what do you want and why don't you go back to that miserable city you are from and stay there."

Konrad stayed calm and looked at the bunch of farmers that surrounded him. Two farmers noticed Julia in the car and wanted her out of the car. Konrad shook his head and tried to protect her while some guns were pointed at him.

"Stay in the car, Julia. You'll be safe there."

"Who's she? Is she your mistress?"

"No, a friend. We are actually looking for a

friend who lives here on a farm. Maybe you know him?"

"Maybe we do maybe we don't. Why don't you leave now before we start shooting at you and your girlfriend?"

Konrad understood what he was up to. He got back in his car started the engine and drove slowly away from the trucks. Then he started to speed up but noticed that some of the trucks followed him. He read in their faces that they were up for some serious trouble.

"What's going on?" Julia asked him while Konrad tried to concentrate on his driving.

"That were the farmers who protect Paul. I am sure they know my ex employee and they promised him they would protect him from me. He knows I would come after him but I will come back and deal with them personally."

He drove fast and paid a lot of attention to his rear window. He could see the dust that was following him. They were still after him till he got out of the Valley. Before Konrad hit the mean road again he stopped for a short moment and threw away the spare bullets of his gun. He kept only two and put them in an old cigarettes pack while he put his empty gun underneath his seat. He couldn't use his gun with bullets that jammed his gun so he was no match for these farmers. He knew they were good shooters. Some of them were ex armed forces and believed that some of them were there in Nam when Australia supported the USA in their fight against the communists in Vietnam.

"I guess we made some progress, don't you think?" Julia only nodded and still pulled a finger in her ear from time to time. It still hurt but slowly she got her hearing back to normal. She paid attention to his fuel meter and noticed how low in fuel they were. Even Konrad looked at it and started to swear.

"Bugger, forgot to tank. Can you help me with finding a pump station on this road?" He pointed on the map again and hoped she would find a pump station.

They drove back towards Sydney but halfway on the highway they had to stop and pulled the car to the side of the road. They passed a few pump stations but none of them were still open after 6pm. Konrad drove as far as he could till he had to stop and park his car at the side of the highway.

"What are we going to do now?"

"Let's hope someone will stop and help us." He replied.

Konrad searched in his glove compartment for his car insurance documents and found some important numbers from the NRMA. He gave them a call but they wanted his card number what he didn't have with him. He tried to explain but the girl on the phone demanded his membership card number. Without his membership card they couldn't help him. In the end they told him a service car was on his way towards them.

During the day it was quite warm but now it was getting dark it started to cool down. Julia was glad she carried a jacket with her and put it on. They still had some oranges and some water in the car so they didn't have to worry about starvation. It was an hour later and already very dark outside the city that a service car from NRMA showed up. He stopped behind Konrad's car but he didn't help them straight away. Konrad was pissed off that the guy refused to help them.

He offered the man from NRMA money but he only wanted to say his membership card what he left at home. It was so stupid from him to leave some important stuff back in his house instead of carrying them in his car what he normally always did. He made that day too many mistakes.

"Will he gives us some petrol or do we have to spend the whole night on this road?"

"No, he will give us but not enough and it will cost me more than a pump station."

In the end the guy took a little spare can out of van and served Konrad with some petrol. It was just enough to reach the outskirts of Sydney where they hoped to find a petrol station so Konrad could fill up his tank till it was full enough.

"Julia, I have to thank you for your support today. I am glad you were with me and appreciated your support today."

"Thank you, Konrad. I was glad to be out with you instead of spending my day in the city or with fighting with Robby."

"He should stop bothering you. Next time

mention it to me so I can have a word with him. He should work harder for his money and not constant begging for money. That's what he did a lot when he had his own hostel. He used plenty of his guests for all kinds of favours and he never paid them back."

"Oh my Lord. Do you really mean that? Is he that kind of guy?"

"You don't know him, I do and I know what he might want to do to you. Be careful and don't lent him any money. He will not pay you back. He can promise you golden mountains but what you will get from him will be a nightmare. Believe me that's how your time in Australia will end."

With the little fuel in the tank they made it till the outskirts of Sydney. They just managed to get into Hornsby where he stopped at a Shell pump station. He filled his tank till the brim while Julia tried to call Robby on her Nokia banana phone. It was a little present from Robby but the quality of the phone was inferior. The battery was weak and died before she even could have a word with him.

"Can I offer you a dinner?" She said to Konrad

when he got back in the car.

"That I should ask you, Julia. Do you fancy a meal on my costs? I mean I will pay you as you helped me what I am very grateful for but I should ask you for this honour."

"Oh, yes, please." She replied and was all smiles.

"Do you like Italian food?"

"Of course, Konrad. Of course."

Robby joined them but he wasn't so enthusiast like Julia. She loved the day trip and was glad to be out again. It was only her second day trip in the countryside and it would be her last. They had dinner at his favourite restaurant in Bondi and drank a good bottle of wine with their food. Konrad gave her under the table her reward what she put straight away in her pockets of her pants. She thanked Konrad who left them soon after the meal and coffee when his phone went.

Robby and Julia went out that night and spent the night in the Bondi Hotel. She ordered a cocktail while Robby had a beer. He smoked a lot that night while she was glad to be back home. She couldn't believe the little adventure she endured in the Valley when those farmers chased them out. She wondered what would have happened if he had no problems with his gun. Would he shoot and kill those farmers while she was in his car or would he leave the area? She didn't know and would never know. She had no idea what the outcome would be in case of fire fight.

Robby was kind to her. He was glad she survived the day but he was furious on the behaviour of his friend. He put Julia's life in danger without consulting her what his plans were for that day. He only asked her to come and to show her where he thought his ex employee might be living. It wasn't still proven that the farm was the right location where he was actually living. Robby had so his strong beliefs that Paul was living somewhere else and only used this farm in Cessnock as a decoy. He knew the farmers and expected a visit from his ex employer sooner or later.

"Julia, tell me. How was Konrad today?"

"Fine. Very kind and friendly."

"Did he talk about me? You know he knows more about me than anyone else."

"He might do but don't worry, Robby. I keep it to myself and I have no intentions in using it against you if that is what you mean."

"It was foolish from him to fire his gun near your ear. He should have warned you in advance. He should never fire it without telling you what his plan was. That was absolute stupid."

"Robby, nothing happened but he knows more through this stupid incident."

"What would have happened if those wild farmers would have start a fight? I mean you are together while they were with how many?"

"I would say ten farmers at least, maybe some more?" She said and read his mind.

"You were close to be beaten to pulp. Those farm boys don't care about us city slickers and don't like us. When it comes to the worse you could have been killed if his gun wouldn't get jammed. He's that stupid in using it with you in his car. Stay away from him. He's trouble and don't listen to him. Don't accept a job offer from him. Look what he did to his old employee. That could happen to you if you would work for him."

"Robby, I am old and wise enough and I won't make such mistake again. I have learned my lesson and I am glad it didn't end in a fire fight or any form of fight. We both got out without a scratch and I experienced a nice little adventure."

Konrad showed up a few days later with an update. He was right that Paul was using one of the farms they visited as a shelter but he wasn't actual living there. The farmers who tried to start a fight with him were the ones who were protecting Paul from him and they promised Paul they would do whatever they could to stop Konrad from paying a visit to their farms. They succeeded and left a clear message behind what was enough proof for Konrad to think they were part of Paul's little protection force. The guy was smarter than he thought he would be but one day he would make a terrible mistake and that would be his downfall.

29 Discoveries

Julia received some bad news from her good friend Jonathan. Over the months they got to know each other and she liked him. He was kind and warm and he was a real man. He had been married before but his first marriage was no long success. He got divorced and was glad his first marriage was over. His new fiancée Shelley was a better girl and came from a good background. Her family liked Jonathan and were proud he wanted to marry their first born child. She had a sister who was a bit younger but she was in love with someone else.

Julia invited Jonathan to the house what she saw most of all as her place. Without her money and her signature Robby had no leg to stand on and couldn't rent a place near the Bondi Lodge. She had the money but he had the references she urgently needed if she wanted to rent a place on her own.

"How often does he come and sleep here?"

"None." She said while she took a seat on her sofa. Most of the furniture were hers. She bought a lot of furniture from IKEA and had it assembled in her own time. The dressing table was a gift from Jonathan as was her big queen size bed. The furniture in the sun room was all from the Bondi Lodge as were the two round chairs and a few coffee tables.

"So, who owns the place?"

"On paper and technically Robby but I am the one who actual lives here. I am here every day of the week and he offered me the big bedroom. He could have taken it for himself but he wanted to be kind to me."

"Do you mind if I have a little look around?"

She let him go and put on a CD in her big sound system. The system together with the TV and the DVD player were hers again. She wanted to watch telly what she paid for. Robby set all the things up but it was her money and her investments in the property that made the flat very cosy.

Jonathan peeked inside the sun room what was Robby's domain. Normally he would keep the door locked but he left it open and even left his dark leather briefcase behind in the room. There were several bin liners on the floor and an old mattress on the floor with some bedding. It was obvious he made the room ready to sleep what he hardly did. Most of the time he stayed awake all night and printed files from the computer of Felicity. He kept the printed files in a big cardboard box what he kept inside his new room. None of the other staff members and the managers had access to this room except for Julia who lived there.

"Hey, Julia. Have you seen these bags and that box?"

"No, what's so special about them?"

"Just have a look inside. Are you sure these are his clothes?"

Jonathan showed her a tank top what looked familiar to Julia. She was missing some clothes and had no idea that her house mate was collecting women's clothes in bin bags.

"Oh, that looks like mine. Where did you find it?"

"Inside that bag. Have a look. Maybe you find more clothes that belong to you."

"Yes, thank you."

Julia stayed five minutes in the room and found items that she was missing. She was furious and wondered why on earth did he keep them hidden from her. She grabbed all the clothes that she found what were hers and put them back in her bedroom. She locked the door of her room and double checked the bags inside Robby's room. Jonathan noticed the black briefcase and wondered what he might find inside. Robby was a very dodgy character and he hoped he could reveal the true face of the man who claimed to be a successful manager of a hostel what was now closed and on the brink of being demolished.

"Do you mind if I look inside his briefcase?"

"Be careful. I don't know where he is and what he will do if he sees you inside his room." She warned him. "He has changed since we have this flat and I have decorated the place. He can't believe what I have bought to make him happy but he is never here."

"Forget him. He's trouble. I will tell you later why."

"Sure. Whenever you have time. I want to hear the story."

"You will and you will be shocked. He's no saint and not a sweet guy either."

Jonathan walked with the black briefcase to the sofa and opened it. He noticed the stacks of documents that were from the Lodge but also a folder that contained letters that were sent to Julia. Furthermore, he found bank statements and a plastic envelop with US dollar notes. He showed some things to Julia who looked surprised.

"Where did you find these?"

"Inside his briefcase. They are yours."

She collected the letters together with the statements when he showed her some US dollars.

"You said you lost some money, didn't you?"

"Yes, don't tell me they're mine."

Jonathan showed a smile and looked further inside the briefcase. He found Robby's passport and had a look inside. He discovered his real name unless he was using a fake passport so he wasn't complete sure. He kept the dollars and wanted to close the briefcase when Robby walked inside the flat.

"What the F**k are you doing with my briefcase? Is nothing safe for me anymore?" He was shouting and took the briefcase from Jonathan. He looked very pissed off and he was absolute furious. "Is nothing holy in this house?"

"Hi, Robby. How are you?" Julia said to calm him down what didn't happen.

"When I walked in I was fine till I saw that swine with my briefcase and the door of my room open. How do you think I feel if I would do that to you?"

"I would be quite upset but I wouldn't shout." She replied.

"I doubt that. I have seen you and heard you yelling whenever you're missing things. Why do you always look at me?"

Julia sighed and wanted to answer but Robby was in no good mood. He searched for his cigarettes and took one from Julia's pack that she left behind on a coffee table.

"I want you out of my house. The place is mine and I don't want you here any longer."

Julia wasn't impressed with the threat when he stared at her and tried to smoke his fag.

"Fine, I can leave but I will take my furniture with me so you will have an empty house."

"No, they stay in the house. They belong to me." He reminded her on the insurance when they went to the bank where they put everything on a file so all the furniture and electronics were insured. Unfortunately for Julia it was all under Robby's name as he changed it a few days later when he went to see his solicitor. He tricked her and robbed her of all her belongings. "You can leave any time you like but you can't take a thing with you. It all belongs to me."

He opened his briefcase and showed her the document. Jonathan took it from her and read it. He nodded and had to confirm the dirty trick he had used on her.

"Whatever you want to say or do it belongs to

me. If I were you I would keep my mouth shut and do what I tell you, ok?"

"Have it your way," She replied and felt insulted. She was furious but she couldn't show her anger towards him.

Jonathan made a signal to her what Robby didn't notice and she only gave a short little nod back as answer. She went to her room took her day bag and locked the door so that Robby couldn't enter her premises. She followed Jonathan who left the flat and walked to his car. Julia followed him.

"Let's go to my place. You can't stay there any longer."

"No, I will be fine. I will do whatever he wants but I will find a way that he will regrets."

"You should be careful with that guy. You don't know him and he will hurt you. I'll tell you leave Bondi leave Sydney and go somewhere else. Forget this place and most of all forget him. He will do his best to hurt you and man he will do you harm. I have seen it before and I don't want to see it again and especially to you."

"I can take care of him. He's no match for me. He

will regret that he wants to fight with me. I shall win in the end and not him."

She got inside Jonathan's car and put on her seatbelt. He got inside and started the engine. He looked at her and then at the flat. He saw Robby standing in front of the main window smoking a cigarette and wondered what went through his mind. Why was the guy so upset? What made him change so rapidly?

"Are you ok?"

"I'm fine." Julia replied and showed a smile. Jonathan nodded and started the engine of his Hyundai and drove to Maroubra to his shared house and let her inside his room. On the way he bought a couple of beers and they had a take away meal from Arnott's what they ate at his place.

"I have to tell you some news that I couldn't say there. That man what you think is a nice guy is a total crook. You won't find any worse than him."

"Nice compliment you give to Robby." She replied while she took a sip of her Heineken beer.

"No, have you heard of a girl named Suzie?"

"No, doesn't ring any bells to me."

"She's like you from Holland and she was here for a year on a working holiday visa. She stayed in his hostel and became friends with him. You know how good he is with you girls."

Julia nodded and was all ear. Jonathan took a big gulp of his beer before he continued his story.

"This girl Suzie pretended she was wealthy. She wasn't and Robby was foolish enough to believe her. He used her and she paid all his bills when they went out and in the meantime he was draining her. She was no match against Robby who only wanted one thing; money. When she didn't have any money but rented an apartment in Hornsby he decided to punish her for all the lies she spread. He tried to kill her but she survived and that's what's following him since. He knows the police found out he was there on the time she laid on the ground pretending to be dead but she was close to death. If the police didn't show up on time she would have died what would make it even worse for him. He would be their prime suspect but he got away. She survived and didn't press any charges against him so the case is disclosed."

"I know he's obsessed with money." Julia had to admit. "Every time he sees me with money I see him smiling. He wants my money but I don't want him to come close to my accounts. Now that I found out he got my latest bank statements I am worried that he might found a way to get access to my accounts in Holland. what if he's transferring money from my account to a secret bank account that even his wife didn't know of?"

"You should call your bank and check it out. Close your account if it is hit by him. It will be the only way to stop him from stealing your money. The downside will be that you will have no longer access to your account and to your money so you have to find a different solution to solve that problem."

Julia was in a foul mood after the story she just heard. She wasn't in the mood for another drink and said no when Jonathan offered her another beer.

"Without me he wouldn't have the flat. I paid for

everything but no he claims it is all his."

"There you can see what kind of crook he is. He doesn't love you he only loves money and as long as you have money on your account he will use you till you're broke. Even then you still have to fear him. He will continue till you die."

"No, I don't believe it. He wouldn't would he?"

"Julia, he would. Believe me he's not the kind of guy as he pretends to be. He's just an ordinary crook who uses young attractive girls as his victims. You are beautiful even without your hair. He likes you and not because you have lots of money but you are an open minded girl. He likes that. He will use you till you tell him off. Then he will show his true face what is not what you hoped you would expect from him."

"How much of the stories he tells me is true?"

"Don't know. All I know he was a big Star Wars toy collector and he had one of the biggest collections here in Australia. He had a hostel and yes it was a successful but that is all I know. The rest is up to you what to believe and not to believe."

Julia was actual quite shocked with all the bad news she received about Robby. She first thought it must have been a joke but when he appeared in the flat shouting at her good friend that was clearly a sign that not everything was as she thought it should be. He slowly revealed his true face. She laid next of Jonathan on his bed. He kissed her lips when she needed comfort and was glad she was in safe hands. She loved him but their friendship couldn't go further. He was engaged with his girlfriend but for the moment she was travelling alone in Europe. He was left behind what was hard for him. He missed her presence.

"You love me, don't you?" She asked him suddenly.

"Yes, Julia. I do. It makes my life very complicated. I truly love you but I do so love my baby who's at the moment in your continent."

"When will she come back?"

"Very soon. She hopes to be back within a month time. I will introduce you to her. She will love you and become close friends hopefully. She's a lovely girl."

She laid for a while in his strong arms before he laid on top of her. She felt his strong and heavy body. Through all the fat he was quite muscular and tasted sweet. She tried to read his mind he did the same with hers. She played with his short hair and kissed him on his big mouth. His beard was tickling her face but she didn't mind. He was so gentle to her and she felt so secure. She wished he could be her bodyguard while Robby was still on the loose but he couldn't be.

"There's something I have to tell you. I might leave by the end of October to the USA. I should have told you before but I just received a few days ago my applied visa for my future stay in America."

"Oh, just when I will need you. I hope to leave in December but I don't know what Robby will do to me between now and December."

"Stay away from Konrad. I don't like him and don't trust the man. He's too close with Robby and I have no idea what he might do if things go wild. Don't forget he helped Robby when he needed help after his fuck up with poor Suzie. He was the one who helped Robby to clear up his mess and don't be surprised if he will ask his friend to clear up your mess what you're causing to him. He will blame all his failures to you and be prepared. It will be very messy."

"How messy, Jonathan?"

"Can't tell you but fear for the worst. He might try to kill you. Just run to the police and report him. He is known to them and they will protect you. You are a woman so you should be safe. You are a foreigner and a woman so they will help you straight away. Don't listen to their crap about the police force how bad they are. They only want to scare you. Don't ever listen to them. All Robby wants from you is your money and he found a way to steal it. Call your bank inform your family because otherwise you mind end up the same way like the other girl who nearly died."

"Robby has never seen me when I am angry. He doesn't know my strength. I can beat him and I know a bit of martial arts."

"Robby is a coward. He might use other guys to do all the beatings so be careful."

They stayed for some time in the house and drank a few beers. Jonathan told a lot about his business partner Kevin who was a manager with a

Commonwealth Bank branch in Parramatta. He was the one who helped Julia with the application for a credit card what she received a short while ago. Robby was jealous that she got a card while his application didn't get approved. His credit history was bad thanks to his ex who still kept his accounts frozen. There was no chance he could get them reopened what annoyed him. He wanted to get access to his old accounts to the money he had but she took it all before she froze his accounts. What she had left were empty accounts where he has no more access and even if he managed to reopen them again he would receive a bad credit history what she just did on purpose. She didn't want to see him succeeding again.

30 Missing money

Jonathan brought Julia back to the Bondi Lodge but her life changed dramatically. Her good friendship with Robby was no longer and she looked at him with a different point of view. He still did his best to be very charming what he was but she didn't trust him.

She didn't work for the lodge and didn't spend much time with the other staff members. Robby was still at work and he only did the late shifts and dealt with outstanding payments. The managers were still in charge but had no idea what Robby was doing with their business. He didn't care and did his best to bring the place down. From the moment she was working for the Lodge there was a constant problem with the cash flow. Money was constant missing but no one knew who was behind it. It started small but over the months the amounts grew steadily larger. Robby was seen as a suspect but it was hard to point a finger towards him. He had a solicitor and didn't like all the accusations and blamed the other staff members who did the reception. None of them had a clean record.

One moment Julia got the blame but she could prove she had nothing to do with the reception. She never worked as a receptionist and never took money from the cash flow. Even when she was for a short while the chef she used her own money and gave the receipts to Felicity who was still around. Julia was honest and had no interest in stealing money from the hostel. Even in Kirribilli there were problems but that were mainly the supplies that Terry ordered. Kirribilli had a healthy cash flow as Glenda was strict and kept a close eye on money payments.

A new receptionist was appointed and he discovered a lot of things when he was alone at the desk. Robby was always around when things disappeared so he started digging in Robby's work sheets. He took lots of payments but when he wanted to check the balance on the computer system he couldn't find the right figures. As if someone tampered a bit with the right figures what made Robby more and more a suspect. Stuart was new in the business but he wasn't a complete rookie. He worked in the weekends as a DJ and dealt a lot with young people. He loved to do his job and was fresh and a friendly face what the guests of the Bondi Lodge liked to see. Most of the guests liked him above Robby. Many of the guests hoped that Robby would soon leave. Plenty of guests complained to the managers about his rudeness and his behaviour. He was not the right man for the business and no one cared about Robby's past. No one knew him well.

Now and then Julia paid a visit to the Lodge when Stuart was at the desk. She liked him. He was friendly and a cute guy. he was the new generation of receptionists who knew to entertain the guests on a friendly and good way. He was never rude to the guests and knew most of their names.

"Hi, Julia. How are you?"

"Good, how's the job."

He was busy with some papers what she recognised. Robby had done a lot of payments lately but none of them appeared on the system and even if they were on the system the figures weren't right.

"Have you seen Robby? I would like to have a chat with him."

"No, I guess he went out to see his solicitor."

"Right, next time you see him he should bring him too. The managers want to have a chat with him and it will not be a friendly one."

"I will remind him when I see him." She said. "Matter of fact I don't talk to him as he wants constant money from me."

"Right, maybe that will explain why we miss so much money lately."

Julia looked up and was surprised. She had no idea that he was stealing money but it wasn't easy to accuse him of theft. You had to come with enough evidence before he would sue you.

"Oh, something wrong, huh?"

"You can say that. I miss a lot of money lately. The managers asked me to check the system and the files of all the guests. They expect a lot of money from our overseas students but it appeared not to be in the books or in the system. Someone played with the computer and wiped out an enormous amount of money that should have been on the system. There's only one person who has access to the system and that must be your friend."

Julia showed a smile but inside she wasn't smiling at all. She didn't want to be reminded as Robby's girlfriend. The friendship was over and what she had learned from her friend Jonathan Robby wasn't the right guy to have as a friend. She heard enough stories and found it hard to believe what she had learned over the last couple of weeks.

"Nice to know you see him as my friend. He isn't."

"Sorry to hear, Julia." he apologised. "But if you see him, tell him to contact his lawyer as he's wanted by the managers. Tell him to pay back the money he took from the Lodge."

"Maybe you should tell it yourself." She replied and left Stuart.

Robby showed up hours later when Stuart confronted him. He hoped he could have a friendly chat while they had coffee. In the meantime, Lonny was at the Lodge and he was running the evening shift. Robby was no longer welcome on the desk till he could explain why money got missing. The managers had enough of the missing money problem and decided it was time to take some serious action.

"Robby, can I have chat with you?"

"Why should I want to talk to you?" He asked Stuart. "Who are you?"

"Just a colleague." Stuart replied. "We have some serious problems and they all point towards your direction."

"Oh, what have I done wrong?" Robby took his coffee and drank it outside in front of Barlevento, the little coffee bar opposite the lodge. Stuart followed him and took a seat next of Robby who lit up a fag.

"You took some payments lately?"

"Yes, I did. Why?"

"How much did you roughly take?"

"Around a thousand bucks."

"When was the last payment you took?"

Robby looked in Stuart's eyes and sensed trouble. He swallowed and signed. He had him caught with his balls in his hands. Now he was in trouble. He had to come with a lie.

"Eh, I took around a few hundred bucks. Why?"

"It's not in the system and I don't think you wrote it down. I guess you took it with you and forgot to write it down, didn't you?"

"Are you accusing me?" Robby got upset and threw his fag away. He wanted to take a sip of his coffee but spilled it on his only clean white shirt. He swore at Stuart who only smiled and remained silent.

"If you think I took money you are wrong. The only ones who take and steal our money is that fat pig at the desk and the managers who don't care what we do with this hostel"

"Right, go on."

"I noticed we are missing a lot of money lately and I wrote a few reports. Did I receive an answer from the managers? No, they never replied to me because that would mean they knew they did something wrong and I can prove it. Where's your proof that shows that I took money from the Lodge?"

"If you come with me I can show you on the system. You made a few mistakes and I caught you. Sorry, Robby."

Robby didn't believe Stuart but he followed Stuart who went back to the Lodge. The managers were there and were glad to see Robby again. It was a while ago they had time to have a chat with him. Robby wasn't impressed with their presence but he was ready for facing them.

'Robby, good to see you. I hope you can explain a few things. It would take long."

They went to the office where they turned on their computer. Robby observed their movements and paid close attention to what they did on their computer. He used it several times and printed lots of files from that computer. He compromised himself and they caught him on stealing files without their permission.

"We know you used our computer lately. We left it on so we could monitor you and your movements. We just want to know why you are so interested in our files."

"Your briefcase looks quite heavy. Do you mind if we have a look inside?"

"Oh, ok."

Robby put his briefcase on the desk and opened it. He always carried it with him and especially after the incident he had lately with Julia and her friend Jonathan. Since that moment he did never leave his briefcase unattended. He always carried it with him. They looked inside and saw a thick folder and a few thin ones. They wanted to see the thick folder but Robby was smart enough to show the top layer what showed the name of his solicitor. He put the folder back inside his briefcase and closed it.

"That my friends is my case against the council in Bondi. I am suing them and I have a good chance to beat them. At least my solicitor believes in my case."

"Our apology." The managers said and saw no reason to ask him more questions. "You have any idea who could have taken the money?"

"Not me. I see my solicitor every day so I don't have time to play around. What about the others who have access to this office?"

They all knew that every receptionist had access to the office as they kept the keys of all the rooms in a special key box next of the door of the little office. There was a drawer where they kept money as there was no real safe. The drawer was never locked as some smart arse lost the keys of the drawer so from that moment they kept it unlocked.

"Right, we have to talk with the other receptionists till we find the thief. He will be fired and we will report it to the police. We take it very serious and we hope Robby that you agree with us."

"Sure, absolutely. I would have done the same if this was my hostel."

They knew his past and knew how good he was when he had his own hostel. Robby was the only receptionist with years of experience but he wasn't the best. Others had more people skills and knew how to deal with difficult customers. Robby was just rude when they didn't want to listen to him. He made clear who was the boss.

31 End of a year in Australia

December came closer and that meant for Julia time to leave Australia. Her year in Australia started well but it ended in a disaster. There was one guy who was responsible for her troubles although she could blame herself too. She met Robby and forgot to check him out. She was too naive when she first met him and thought he's a good guy while he was actually a jerk. She should never tell him she had money as he was too obsessed with money. She remembered when he bought a few lottery tickets. He wanted to win the jackpot while she did it for fun. The same when they went out one night to the Bondi Hotel. Inside is a casino and she played for a couple hours on the pokeys. She was successful and won her money back while he lost all his money. He got angry and asked her regular for drinks. He got so drunk that night so they had to take a cab while normally she would have walked back home to the hostel. The next day he had a bad hangover and was still very grumpy. From that moment she should have paid more attention to his behaviour. He behaved like a spoilt child and now and then he wanted to cry if he couldn't get what he wanted. It was annoying but also very embarrassing for Julia who didn't know what to do so she gave him what he wanted.

Slowly very slowly he got her but she never gives him everything. Now and then she made him clear that he wanted too much and made clear to him she was no bank and didn't want to spend and invest more money in him. He tried but she was not so easy. Robby's behaviour got worse when Jonathan appeared. He knew him and didn't want to come close to him. Jonathan knew Robby better than most other guys. Jonathan had lots of connections in and around Sydney and knew and heard a lot of stories about Robby and what he had done in the past. Not every story that he told Julia was the truth. The guy was a good liar and told her mostly lies what sounded real. It was up to her what to believe but the be extra careful as he was only after her money and not after a love live. He wasn't worth to be a friend but that news reached her too late.

Julia spent most of her time in the city instead of being in Bondi. She hardly saw him and when she saw him she didn't speak to him. All he asked was money and she made clear that she was no bank. If he wanted money, he should work for it instead of asking constant for money.

"I hear you're leaving soon, am I right?"

"Yeah, I fly on the 10th December to KL and from there I want to spend more time in Asia before I fly home. I still want to see parts of Asia as that was the major plan of my big trip. Australia was just one of the many countries I wanted to go but there are other countries I love to go."

"So you booked your flight yet?"

"Yes, yesterday. I fly with Lauda Air; you know the ex Formula One driver Nikki Lauda?"

Camilla showed some interest while Julia had her breakfast coffee in her little coffee bar. She was there every day and the staff made good coffee and delicious food.

"I didn't know he run an airline. So you flying out soon. What did Robby say when he heard the news?"

"He doesn't know it yet and when he does he will flip out. He will do whatever he can to stop me so I can stay illegal in this country and become his slave till I have no more money. That's what he wants to do with me."

"How horrible." Camilla acted. "Why do you think he will do that to you?"

"Because he did this to another Dutch girl. She was unlucky and left Australia broken financially physically and mentally so yeah he will try to do this with me."

"Can you stop him?"

"I don't know." Julia replied and looked outside. She had her coffee inside and saw him leaving the hostel with his briefcase. Like always he was in a hurry and had luckily no time for a coffee. Normally he would walk in and order a coffee what the staff made as long as he paid for his drink.

"Stay inside, girl. You are saver here than outside. I don't want him in my shop but he's still a customer and he pays his bills."

"How? He never has money and he always ask me for more."

Camilla showed Robby's old bill to her and the money he paid her. Julia checked the notes but there was nothing wrong with the money. All she knew the Bondi Lodge lost a lot of money lately but Robby was the only one who knew more but refused to talk to the managers as they suspected he stole money from the hostel.

"When did he pay you that?"

"Last night just before I closed my shop. He walked in and paid his outstanding bill. I never ask questions so I accepted the money and cleared his bill."

"What if that were money from the Lodge? Would you accept stolen money so he could launder it?"

"I don't see how he could access to such amount of money. Does the hostel have a safe or how do they keep their money safe from criminals?"

Julia sighed and looked out again. Robby was gone and the managers arrived at the Lodge. It would be a long day for them to see what Robby had done to them. He was playing dirty tricks and left some nasty surprised behind for everyone who tried to make his life so miserable.

"Glad I am no longer employed there."

"Why? What's going on?"

"From the moment I left the Lodge a lot of things went on. First Robby blamed me but he knew I couldn't have done it as I was only working in the kitchen and not at the reception. A few receptionists left the company when money was missing. Robby accused them but I believe he knew more than he wanted to reveal. If you ask me he stole money from the hostel and put the blame on others and not on himself. He's a coward."

"What would you do if you have to face him and he starts to threaten you? Will you be afraid or do you think you can beat him?"

"I don't know." Julia had to admit. "I truly don't know. I might freak out what would be normal for us but I might stay cool. I am not so scared and the longer I got to know him the more I am aware of what might happen to me. I should stay calm and see what will happen on the day whenever it will happen."

"Be careful. I don't want to loose you. You were a nice customer and you're a good friend."

"Thank you, Camilla. You know I always love to come to your place. I don't do it for the coffee what is awesome but for the company. You girls you rock. You all do."

Julia went back to the apartment and started to clear up the place. She cleared her room and packed whatever she could take with her for her upcoming journey to Asia. A few days earlier she called Kevin and asked if he could come to the house to pick up some stuff. She wanted to make sure that most of her expensive stuff was safe from Robby. He promised her he would keep it safe in his house where he had a special room. All she had to do was to call him when to pick it up and as soon as she was away out of Australia send a message when to send her stuff to her new home in Holland or wherever she wanted to live.

"Kevin, can you come as soon as possible. I don't know what Robby wants to do when he got access to my room. I don't want to loose again my stuff and I want it out as soon as possible."

"I can't come today but I will be there in a few days. I will come in the afternoon so we can load the stuff in my car before he arrives. I will be there, girl. Don't freak out. I will come."

Julia freaked out when she heard suddenly a loud

knock on the door. She first thought it could be Robby but then again he had a key so he didn't need to knock. She got up from her room and checked through the little spy hole in the door who stood in front of that door. There was a moment she thought it could be Konrad. He did it a few times to frighten her but he stopped when she asked him that it wasn't funny. He understood and stopped being so funny. Again she heard a loud knock on the door and she opened it before asking who stood in front of the door.

"Kevin, why do you pretend to be Robby or Konrad. That wasn't funny."

"Sorry, Julia. I didn't know I freaked you out. I didn't know you don't like loud knocks on doors."

"No, not for the moment." She replied. "Thanks to Robby I feel like a freak but I hope to be my normal self when I am out of the country."

"Yeah, the better you're gone the saver you will be. The longer you stay here the bigger the chance that he will do his best to hurt you. He's after your money you know that and if he can't get it he will do whatever he can to destroy you so you can't enjoy your future life."

"Thanks for warning me."

Kevin got inside and followed Julia to her room. She showed him what she already had packed and moved them to his car. He was smart enough to park it near the apartment and put all her stuff in the boot of his car. Before he walked back to the house he locked his car so Robby couldn't steal from him.

"Where's Robby? Any sign of him yet?"

"No, he went early this morning to see his solicitor if she really exists and left before the managers showed up of the hostel to check the books with him. They want to talk with him but he doesn't want to talk to them. I guess he knows he's guilty and they want to prove it in front of him but he runs away constant."

"Let him. He deserves whatever he did and he can't run away from his punishment. He knows he's guilty so he should be smart enough to come with his mysterious solicitor who can help him."

Robby showed up when most of Julia's gear was

already in the boot of Kevin's car. He saw Robby sprinting towards him and wanted to stop him from loading the car. Julia was wise to stay inside the house and saw how Robby attacked Kevin.

"Put it back in the house! It' not yours!"

"Sorry, Robby but Julia asked me to help her."

"She has no rights to move my belongings."

"Your belongings? You say your belongings?" Kevin looked up when Robby mentioned to him that all the stuff in his car were no longer Julia's. He couldn't believe it.

"Yes, my belongings. Like her she belongs to me. I own everything."

"I don't think so, Robby. Let's go inside and ask Julia. If she says no than I suggest you to back up and stay away from her."

"No, you stay away from her and load it all back in the house and leave. You are no longer welcome here."

Julia overheard the conversation and showed her face. She was fuming when Robby mentioned that all her belongings were now his. It was another lie from him. He didn't owe her nor her belongings. He couldn't claim and he had no rights to claim her and her belongings as his.

"Robby, what are you doing? Those are my things and I want them in storage so he can send them to Holland when I am back in my own country."

"Stay out of it, Julia. You have nothing to say anymore. I want you like him out of Bondi at once."

Kevin saw Julia for the first time being very angry. She never showed her anger but what he was doing in front of the house was too much for her. She had enough of his behaviour.

"No, Robby. I don't stay out of it. You know that you couldn't have the apartment without me. I helped you with paying the bond and the first two months of rent."

"Yes, but you didn't pay for the other months so you have nothing to say. You pay me what you owe me and I can let you stay but if you refuse than I ask you to leave at once."

Kevin and Julia looked at each other. she couldn't

believe her ears what he just said to her. Again another lie. She got fed up of all the lies he came up.

"Robby, what did you just say to me?" "You heard me, Julia so please don't pretend to be deaf or dumb. I told you pay me for the months and you can stay but if you don't want to pay good you can leave right now without all your possessions. They are now mine."

Julia returned to the house followed by Kevin while Robby did his best to stop them. Kevin grabbed Robby's hand and squeezed it hard. Robby felt the pain and went down on his knees. He swore a lot while Kevin had Robby finally on his knees.

"Robby, you leave her alone. Let her enjoy her last couple of days in Sydney before she leaves Australia. Don't try to hurt her because I will hurt you. She will call me if you try to come up again with your dirty tricks."

Robby looked at Julia and back again at Kevin. His mind was raging and he was so pissed off. He swore to take revenge on both of them. He wasn't afraid of her but the way how Kevin was hurting his hand.

"Stop bothering her. The next time I will break your hand. And don't try to threat me with court cases. I can assure you that you won't win. You will loose, mate. Let her go. She's not like the other girl who you tried to kill. If you thought no one knows about it, you will be wrong. Too many people heard the story and there are plenty who want to sue you. Get a life, mate. Stop bothering girls or you will regret it for the rest of your life."

Kevin got to his car and drove back to his house near Parramatta with Julia's belongings. They would be safe while she wasn't. Robby tried to follow her but she was faster in the house and went straight to her room. She locked the door of her room and stayed there till he left the apartment again. On her bed she cried for an hour till she had shred enough tears. She got up and went quickly tot he loo before he noticed she wasn't in her room. Like always she kept the door locked as she didn't trust him.

32 Last rough night in Bondi

From the moment she moved her important belongings to Kevin's place her stay in Bondi became very hostile. Robby demanded money every day what she refused to give. She was not his private bank and made clear that he had to stop before she would report him to the cops. She stopped believing in his so called court case and had the feeling he was using her money on drugs and other things.

The apartment looked very empty accept for a sofa two chairs framed from the Lodge a coffee table and a big dressing that Jonathan gave to them. His old stereo was on the big dressing after Julia moved her new stereo to Kevin. He bought all her electronic gear and promised her he would pay her on her credit card every fortnight. She was pleased it was in the hands of someone who could be trusted. She couldn't say that of Robby, who wanted all her stuff.

 "Why don't you sell it to me, bitch? Why did you go to that moron? He will screw you. I know these guys. They pretend to be nice but in the end they screw you."

Julia said nothing. The only thing she did was looking in Robby's eyes. They were so hollow. He never looked you straight in the eye and if he was looking it was more staring. He had a nasty stare what made many people uncomfortable. Julia never looked in his eyes as it would give her a headache.

"You disappoint me, Julia. I thought so great of you when I met you. I thought you wanted to help me but see what you do to me. I feel like being stabbed with a blunt knife in the back."

"Funny that you think that way. I gave you almost a fortune and you still think you can claim more from me. What have I asked you to do for me? Nothing but you ask me nearly everyday for money or for other favours while I ask you nothing."

"Don't lie to me. I helped you with a job. You would have been skint if you didn't accept that job that I was doing."

Julia had to laugh. She didn't need a job and she shouldn't have accepted the job when the managers wanted her in the kitchen. She should have walked away and followed her dreams but she didn't. She felt too much committed in helping Robby, who only became more and more obsessed in her money. She should have never mentioned that she had enough money to travel in style. She should have looked like a poor backpacker so she could have saved some money for her upcoming journey to Southeast Asia. Now she felt she was almost skint although she still had plenty of money on a savings account back home in Holland. Robby had no access to the account but he might try to find a way to get access. He was so good in manipulating people. That's what he had done with the other Dutch girl and he had tried to kill her but she survived. Luckily for him she didn't pressed charges otherwise he would have been in jail for a very long period.

"Robby, you were a nice guy when I met you but look at you now. You have changed and only in the wrong way. I said I wanted to help you and I did. All I hear lately is that you think I haven't done anything for you and you tell so many lies. Please stop with lying. Tell the truth and I might help you."

"Why don't you stop with lying yourself?" He

snapped back. "I thought I could trust you but I can't. I want you out of the house and you pay me what you still owe me."

Again he was threatening her with the flat. She owed him nothing. Without her he would never have a place for his stuff. She paid her share and was promised she could stay till the end of her visa in the flat for free. She paid for more things than he had done. He only stole some old furniture from the hostel while she bought new from IKEA. Even her good friend Jonathan helped them with some furniture what he didn't need as he left the country.

The last week of her stay in Sydney became a complete nightmare. Every day and night she had fights over money with Robby. He didn't want her to leave and hoped she could stay longer in the country and just copy Paul who overstayed too long in Australia.

He was facing a long period behind bars when the cops finally got him. He made a stupid mistake when he tried to change some bucks at a money changer that was known to the police. He called the cops who were in the neighbourhood and arrested him for theft and staying illegal in the country.

Two weeks before she would leave the country she paid her last visit to the city where she bought a new flight ticket to Asia after Robby framed her old flight tickets. She found after searching at several travel agencies a cheap flight to Malaysia although Singapore was another place on her travel list.

Robby overheard her one day in Barlevento when she had her daily caffeine shot while she chatted with CJ one of the girls of the coffee bar. CJ was a wild dark headed girl from Hobart Tasmania and was still a student of the university of Sydney.

"I'm flying soon to Malaysia. God I wish I could go tomorrow."

"Is it that bad, huh?"

"Yes, I can't stand it here. Sorry, but I had a good time till this all happened."

She noticed Robby who hoped he could have a coffee. Camilla barred him as he never paid for his coffee and Julia had enough of paying his drinks. It was time he paid for his own coffee.

"So, you're flying soon to Malaysia? Where will you go? KL, Penang, Malacca or Johor?"

"Sorry, Robby. None of your business." She replied and stopped talking with CJ. She saw the hatred between the two. Eight months earlier they looked so nice to each other and now they couldn't stand each other. How much they both had changed.

Robby left the bar and took a cab to the city. Julia sighed and was glad he was gone. She wondered what he would do now he knew she was leaving so soon. She had to leave Bondi before it would be too late. She didn't want to leave with cuts and bruises. She didn't want to end like the other girl although Robby would need some help to beat her. She was stronger and tougher than the other girl.

"What's on your mind, girl?"

"I don't know what to do, CJ. I like Bondi but I am no longer safe. Robby knows that I am leaving and he will do his best to stop me. I don't know about the others whom I know but I think they will tell me to leave Bondi as soon as possible."

"Why do you keep him as a friend? He looks more like a creep. He's a freak and the only thing he wants to do is making your life miserable. See what he's doing to you. You have enough but you're still here in Bondi while you wanted to see the rest of Australia. Go and leave."

Julia finished her coffee and paid for her drink. She walked to the empty house and picked up a book from her cupboard in her bedroom. She sat comfortably on the coach and read for hours. Later in the day she went to a restaurant and ordered a take away what she ate at home together with a beer and continued reading her book.

The last couple of days in Bondi that became her daily routine. Every day she went to Barlevento for a coffee and some breakfast and then she went back to the house where she read books and ate takeaways. She counted her days and waited till the last day she would leave the country. Robby was observing her and he was making some nasty plans. She was no longer reliable and he didn't trust her. She made clear she would report him to the cops if he would try to hurt her. She wasn't afraid of him but that could change. He knew a guy who was good in freaking young women. He was a scary fellow who liked to hurt people. He wasn't known to the cops as he was not easy to describe. Most girls he had threatened were afraid of him and never reported him.

Two days before she was about to fly to Malaysia Robby decided to stop Julia from leaving the country. He invited a few friends at his place while he knew she was at home. The first person who showed up was Johnny Q, a new guy in the hostel who was like Robby a fuck up and a money spender. Johnny inherited a large sum of money and wasted half of it in only a few days' time in a casino and on drugs. He liked just like Robby cocaine and didn't mind to waste his gained fortune on drugs.

"Hey, Julie, good to see you. Robby told me so many good stories about you."

"Thanks, mate. Nice to meet you."

"He even told me I can stay in his flat so you won't be alone all the time." Julia sighed and only nodded. "Hey, man. I am only sharing the place with you. I have no interest in your personal belongings. You will be safe. I won't bother you."

"Good to hear, mate." She replied. "I like to have my privacy. Welcome on board."

Anton showed up what was a big surprise for her. She liked him and he was good company for her. Whatever he had in mind she had someone who could stand up for her. Konrad showed up together with Robby and another guy. He looked very scary and Julia didn't like to look at his face. He had a nasty stare in his eyes and he stank. He was big bald and definitely trouble. Robby took a seat on the coach next of Anton followed by Konrad who sat on the other side of the coach so Anton was surrounded by Robbie's mates. Mr. Freak stood near her and he was breathing foul air into her neck. Johnny Q sat opposite of her and his eyes were full of joy when he noticed how close Mr Freak came to her.

"Julia, if you want to know why I am here with all these guys is that I want my money and your passport and your flight ticket. If you refuse Mr Freak will hurt you and will only stop till you give me what I want from you."

"And if I refuse?"

She suddenly felt a strong hand grabbing her arm.

He squeezed her arm and did his best to hurt her. She looked up and saw the grim smile on his face. He was enjoying himself while he did his best in hurting her.

"Let me go, you freak."

"He doesn't listen to women. He doesn't like women."

"Well, sorry, Robby but I will not give you whatever you demand from me."

"Hurt her some more."

Mr Freak grabbed Julia by her short hair what was just long enough to get a grip. She felt the pain in her head as he did his best to pull out her hair. Suddenly he pulled a large pluck of hair of her head and threw it towards her. She wanted to cry but she couldn't. As soon as she would show her emotions Robby and Mr Freak would make use of it. She had to be brave and endure the suffering.

"Pull off her shirt. I want to see her tits."

Johnny Q was all smiles so was Robby but not Anton. He wanted to act but Robby stopped him.

He had to sit quiet and enjoy the show Mr Freak was performing. Mr Freak pulled more hair off her head and she felt the pain on her head. He kept on smiling while he wanted to pull down her pants. Julia pulled up her knee and hit him in his crotch. He felt the pain she caused but it was only temporary. He hit her hard in her face.

"Robby, stop with this nonsense. Julia doesn't deserve this kind of treatment from you." Anton shouted when Mr Freak hit Julia hard in her face.

"Keep quiet, Anton. You are here as a witness. I need you hear so it will be her word versus mine."

"You won't break me ever." Julia said and showed a smile on her face. It hurt like hell but she was brave enough to take the hit. Robby remembered when he had his bad fight with the other Dutch girl. By that moment she was screaming and crying like a baby while Julia kept a brave face and stood her ground.

Mr Freak hit her hard in her stomach and saw how she went through her knees. He gave her a hard knee but she bounced back from it. He grabbed her again by her hair and smacked her face once again.

"You will never get my passport or my flight ticket. Never."

"Never say never," Robby said and he got up. "Maybe we need to punish her a bit harder."

He showed a little bottle of Zippo fluid and her zippo lighter. He clicked it open and closed it and repeated several times while he showed her the bottle. Mr Freak took the bottle and the lighter and held it close to her breasts and her bra. He clicked the zippo open and showed her the flame. He came close with the bottle to her face and was ready to leave her some burn marks on her face and body.

"Give me what I want and he will stop this action. If you don't he can give you a special facelift. It's up to you. Give me your passport, the credit card that Jonathan helped you with and the flight ticket and your wallet so you will be free to go."

"Never, Robby! Never!" Julia yelled.

Both Konrad and Johnny Q sat on the edge of

their chair while Anton had enough of the bullshit. He got up and knocked Robby down on the ground. He kicked Mr Freak who looked up when Anton stood in front of him. Anton was taller than him but much thinner than Mr Freak who was big and heavy. Julia saw a small moment and fled quickly to her room. Anton followed her before Mr Freak could hit him. he locked the door as soon as they both were in and sighed. It was the first time he hit Robby and he was nervous.

"Thanks for rescue me." She said while she crawled to bed and crawled up. She wanted to cry but the tears didn't come.

"I don't know what's going on but I had to stop the nonsense."

"He's on drugs." Julia replied. "I noticed when I was looking him in his eyes. He's on a coke trip and so is his friend Johnny Q."

"Do you know him?"

"No, I have seen him a few times in the Bondi Lodge but I don't know a thing about that guy. All I know he's a drug user and a gambler and a perfect friend for Robby. He says he's going to stay here in the flat."

"You should leave, Julia. At once. You can't stay here in Bondi. I can't protect you and the longer you stay the more trouble he will cause to you."

The tears finally came and she sobbed for a while. She looked with her crying face in Anton's eyes who wished he could help her. He was no fighter and wasn't happy with the treatment Robby gave to her.

"Go to the police. Ask for help. They will protect you. You're a woman so they will listen to you. Tell them the truth."

"Oh, I will. Tomorrow morning, I will pay a visit to the police and will report him. I have enough of all the nonsense and hope they can stop him while I can leave the country."

She touched her head and noticed the bald spots on her head. She searched for a small mirror in her luggage and inspected her short hair. The damage on her head was severe but it could have been worse if Anton didn't stop Mr Freak and the Zippo fluid.

"Did you see what he did to me?"

"Yes, how bad is it?" "I don't know yet. I will ask a barber tomorrow and see what he can do. The worst scenario is that I might have to shave my head. No big deal it will grow back but I wanted to grow my hair again but that has to wait."

"How's your face? did he hit you hard with his hand?"

"Yes, but I can handle a punch. I had in the past many fights with my sister and we hit each other a few times hard in the face."

"And your stomach? Glad he didn't burn you. What would you have done if he tried to burn your face and bra?"

"I would have screamed as loud as possible. I would wake up the neighbours who might call the cops."

"Will you tell it to them?"

"Yes, of course. It's an insult what he tried to do to a woman. I hope they can arrest both him as Mr Freak. I don't know where he picked him from but he belongs in jail no where else."

Julia and Anton had to wait till late in the evening when Robby and his friends left the house for a while. She found a moment to run to the loo and was back in her room a few minutes later. Only after midnight she left the house for a long walk to clear her mind. She made these walks before and it always helped. This time it had a nasty surprise when she got back home.

Anton left soon before she made her walk but promised to meet her at the cafe so she could travel together with him to the city. It wasn't wise to stay in the house after what had happened. She would be wise to stay the last night in a hotel in the city where there was security and it was easier to travel to the airport.

Johnny Q was in the house when she got back from her long walk. She noticed her door was open while she locked it before she went out. Strange. So Robby had a key of her room what meant that he could have taken some things again from her. When she opened the door of her room she noticed her two backpacks were no longer next of her bed. She still had her money belt with her passport her flight ticket her credit card and her money but all her travel gear was gone.

"Johnny, did someone went inside my room?"

"Huh? I don't know. I am just here. I'm your new roommate."

"Yes, I know but I want to know did someone come into my room?"

Johnny Q was still doped so he wasn't completely there with his mind. He stared at her while she was angry. There was only one person who could have done something like that and that was Robby. She didn't want to face him. He would demand straight away her passport, her money and her flight ticket so she had to stay illegal in the country.

"Must be Robby. He told me you can get them back if you give him your passport and your flight ticket."

"Is he insane?" She shouted. She was furious but after what he had done to her she was not up to face him again. They would meet each other one more time so she needed all the strength she had to face and deal with him.

"They are not in the house so stop searching. I have nothing to do with it. I am only the messenger boy."

She smiled and nodded. She wasn't upset with Johnny. He was innocent and he had like her a rough night. She returned to her room and went to bed. Luckily she reminded herself that she still had some laundry at the laundrette. She gave it earlier in the day and forgot to pick it up. Glad she still had some clothes but they were not her special travel clothes. All her gear was gone and what she hated the most her day bag was gone with all her letters from her sister and father and her bank statements. He still had no access to her account but he could use it to blackmail her family.

33 Reporting Robby

Julia slept only for a few hours when she woke up early in the morning. She got up and had a shower. She went to Barlevento for her breakfast and a coffee before she would collect her laundry. Camilla was alone and noticed Julia had a fight last night with Robby. She saw the bald spots on her head and one of her eyes was turned black. Normally she was all smiles but not that morning.

"Julia, oh my God. Are you ok?"

"No, Robby beat me last night." She said while she tried to cry. "He paid me a nasty visit last night with a few friends and he beat me up. In the end he stole my travel gear so I have no more backpacks. It's all gone."

"Oh my god. I feel so sorry for you. What are you going to do?"

"I still have some laundry what I will pick up later and then go to the police and report this to them. I want him arrested and locked up. I have enough of all this bullshit from him. I have done so much for him and see what's he doing to me. He beat me up and still demands more. He's a freak a monster."

"I told the girls that they shouldn't serve him. He can try to sue me but it's my bar and I make the decisions and not him. He's no longer welcome."

"You should have barred him long ago. Perhaps it would have helped but I don't know."

Camilla put her hand on Julia's arm and tapped softly on it. "Forget your bill. It's on me. What would you like to have my dear?"

"A latte and some toast."

CJ walked in and gave Julia a warm hug. She took over from Camilla who took a seat next of Julia. She gave Julia a hug and told her that it was on the house. Julia was a regular customer and a friend plus she went through a lot of things lately so she deserved some goodness and friendship from her new friends.

"What happened with your hair? Who did that?"

Julia touched a few bald spots and wanted to cry. It still hurt but it would get over. She had to see a barber but she knew what they would do to her.

Her hair was too short to cover it up so the only thing a barber could do for her was to shave her head bald.

"Thanks to Robby I have to shave my head."

"Ghee, he's a nice guy. So what happened?"

"We had a fight last night and he pulled my hair out and beat me up."

"Have you reported it to the police? You should do so."

"I will." Julia said while she drank some coffee and ate some toast. "I will go straight after my breakfast to the police and report what happened last night. I am expecting a friend who was there and thanks to him I survived."

"Oh my God. Did he try to kill you?"

"Sort off." She replied. "He wanted to burn me with a bottle of Zippo fluid."

"That's cruel. He should be locked up."

Camilla agreed to CJ. "Oh, if Robby walks in don't serve him. Even if he can pay for his coffee. I don't want to serve him anymore. He's no longer welcome."

"After what I just heard I will refuse him. How can you act like that? Why does he want to punish you? What have you done to him?"

"Nothing, absolutely nothing. All I did was helping him with his so called court case but I don't think there's no case. I can't prove it but I guess he was using me so he could take some drugs that he bought and used in the city and not in Bondi. He's always fucked up in the evening so I suspect he's under influence of drugs when he gets back from his daily trip to the city."

"And he claims to be your friend. Nice friends you have, girl." Julia took her time with her breakfast and went afterwards to the laundrette to pick up her clean clothes. Anton showed up and together they walked to the police station in Bondi Beach where Julia asked to speak with a senior officer. She had to wait only a few minutes when two detectives walked inside the building and took her to an interview room. A female copper joined them and gave Julia some company and a cup of tea.

"Good morning, Sheila. How can we help you?"

"I want to report a crime that happened last night to me."

"Yes, I can see you had a bit of a struggle. What happened with your face and your hair?"

"A guy named Robby Henson who was a friend of mine had an argument with me and he wanted money from me and my passport and my flight ticket. As you may know I am leaving Australia tomorrow evening but Robby wants to stop me so for that reason he wants my passport and my flight ticket so I can't leave the country and stay as an illegal in the country."

"Wow, isn't that a bit far fetched?"

"No, not if you know Robby." She replied.

She gave the two detectives her passport together with her flight ticket and noticed how they inspected her documents. One of them left the room and made some copies before he returned.

"What exactly happened and how did it all start? Can you give us some more details?"

"Sure, I met Robby around Christmas time in the Bondi Lodge. He was doing some maintenance work and he stayed during the festivities in the hostel. We met during dinner and we became friends. I had no idea what kind of monster this guy was. I thought he's a nice guy with some interesting stories so I paid only attention to his stories not knowing he was lying to me in my face."

"What kind of stories did he tell you? Who is he where's he from and what did he do?"

"He claimed to be the owner of a hostel here in Bondi but the place looks like a shack. He claimed he was a successful hostel owner of the Lamrock Hostel."

"Yes, I have heard of that place. There were some things going on but we never could prove what happened there as most of the victims were only temporary in the country and none of them had the courage to report it to us. Just a shame. Please go on."

"He, Robby Henson claimed he made money with a simple but efficient money scheme and taught a friend of his one Mr Konrad who if I remember had a hostel nearby. Together they set up this scheme and made lots of money."

"Wow, that's news to us. We will investigate that. Can you tell us a bit more about Konrad? Somehow the name says something."

"You should. A couple of months ago Mr Konrad lost a case with money at his house. He believes his former employee by the name of Polly Boy or something like that was the main suspect. He's now in custody as he's illegal in the country and I heard from Konrad he was picked up by some cops for changing money at a money changer while the notes were marked."

The two detectives looked up and made notes. One of the detectives left the room and went to check some info while the senior detective continued.

"You seem to know quite a lot about that burglary if I may ask. Where were you on that particular date?"

"I was in Kirribilli and I have witnesses who will confirm I was there."

The other detective showed up and whispered

something his his colleague's ear. They both looked at Julia who sat straight up and was very confident while she reported Robby.

"What were you doing in Kirribilli?"

"I was working what I wasn't suppose to do. I am sorry that I broke the law."

The senior detective checked her visa and showed it to her. "You weren't supposed to work but you did anyway. Do you know we have to report you to the right authorities but as you were involved in some serious crimes I might ignore it as long as you are telling the truth to us?"

"I do, sirs." She replied.

"This guy Robby, you say he owns a hostel. What do you know more about him?"

"I heard he tried to kill a girl from my country a while ago but he never got arrested by your colleagues in Hornsby if I am not mistaken."

"Do you know what might have happened? How did you hear that story anyway?"

"I have some other friends who know Robby better and they told me. Even Konrad confirmed it to me. He knows Robby better than anyone else."

"Because he's close to him and learned a trick from Robby. Hmm, interesting story. If you don't mind we want to verify it with some other stations."

They both left for a couple of minutes before they returned with some news. The female copper gave Julia another cup of tea and they continued the interview.

"For the moment you're telling the truth. We have some confirmation about a serious crime that was committed in Hornsby by a man called Robby although it's not for sure it's the same guy. We can find out when we can stop and interview him. It's all up to him for the moment. As for Konrad I think we talk about the same person and we do have in custody his former employee. He will be soon to a detention centre before we can deport him back to England."

"I don't think Konrad will be happy with that news." Julia said while she thought of Konrad. "What I know he wants to kill him what he can't do right now."

"Don't worry, Miss. He's safe in our hands. We don't kill people."

Julia thought of the French guy who got killed by the cops on the beach as he was a threat to the cops as he was high on drugs. She didn't mention it to them.

"Please, continue with your story. How did it happen why he beat you up?" "Robby learned that I have money so he tried to steal it from me. He stole some but not everything. He found a better way to get access to my money by using me. He claims he nearly broke his back through a fall in a hole next of his hostel here in Bondi and claims it's all the fault of the council. They should have covered it but it wasn't so he fell in it. Anyway I helped him with his court case and he begged me for money what I gave him. My mistake."

"Don't think so. You were noble to help him what's not wrong. More a bit naive but you did what you thought was right, right?"

"Yes, that's what I thought so too. I had no idea he wanted to screw me. He used me and when I refused to help him he started to get nasty. He started to threat me but I paid no attention to his threats. They were only words so I though he can't be serious. Then my friends told me the story of this poor Dutch girl and how he tried to kill her after she refused to help him. That was for me the moment that I should have left Bondi but I didn't as I helped him with an apartment what he wanted to rent. He never slept in the apartment but I do. I bought furniture and lived in it. It' both in our names but he changed the insurance in his name while I paid for everything. He got very jealous and he made clear he wouldn't stop till I was ruined like the other girl."

"Why didn't you leave and report all this to us? You could have stopped him by going straight to us. We are no monsters. We are here to protect you."

"I know. I should have done but I didn't, didn't I?"

"Yes, so what happened last night? Was it Robby who did pull your hair out or did someone else did it for him in his name?"

"Someone else." She said and she thought of Mr Freak. It wasn't easy to describe him but she did.

They made notes and discussed things while she tried to explain Mr Freak.

"He's a very scary guy. He's big fat and bald. His face looks East European to me but I could be mistaken."

"Why do you think he's East European?"

"I know Konrad is original from Poland although he was born in Germany but his parents were Polish. I can see it in his face. You can see it when you look him in the eye. It was Mr Freak who did the hard work while Robby kept on pushing me with his crazy demands."

"So it was Mr Freak who did the beating and he pulled your hair out? Right, we will search for him and have him picked up so we can ask him some questions. We can find him as you say through Konrad. Right, you still accuse Robby for some serious things. What has he done to you?"

"He knows I am leaving the country by tomorrow. He knows some people who work on the airport and he will do his best to stop me. All I want is that you can stop him from doing it so I can leave in peace Australia and think back on a far remote place of all the trouble he caused to me. I still have some money and I want to see a bit of Asia before I travel back to Holland. I don't want to end up like the previous girl he nearly killed as she refused to help him. I did more for him than he ever did for me."

The two detectives left the interview room and checked her statement before they returned to her. One of the detectives made some calls to other stations and checked Robby's name on their computer system. They found more info about Konrad and used it as a reference.

When they walked back in the interview room the senior detective showed Julia some photos of the girl who was found a while ago in Hornsby. The photos were shocking and the girl looked more dead than alive. She couldn't see a thing and her head was full of bruises and clearly beaten up by a strong man. Her arms and legs were broken as were several ribs. The damage was severe and enough to put him for a very long time behind bars. Unfortunately, she never made a statement and pressed charges so he was of the hook. Julia's case wasn't strong but with her story of what she knew about the old story of that girl there was a chance they could reopen the case and use it as they had now a new witness and victim who wanted to prosecute him.

"Miss Maier, you said earlier that Robby is blackmailing you and he demands money your passport and your flight ticket so you can't leave the country. He's using a big guy to beat you up so you would give in to his demands but you show to us that you had some courage to refuse him and now you want to sue him, am I correct in that point?"

"Yes, you are."

"You have seen the photos what we just showed to you of the other Dutch girl who wasn't so lucky as you are. Would you sue him on her behalf and use your case as extra evidence to get him convicted?"

"You can't arrest him for what he has done to me?"

"Not for the moment but as soon as he does something stupid like pushing you we might sue him. We have to be careful as he's in the middle of a court case so we have to approach him with some extra care. We don't want to loose our case.

As you mentioned to us he has a solicitor so she might know more and will use her information to protect her client."

Julia had hoped the police would start a full investigation but she didn't have any evidence that Robby did hurt her at all. Mr Freak on the other hand could be arrested for molesting a woman and he would probably end up in jail for a period of time. It wasn't good news for Julia.

"Can you read your statement and sign it. If you want, we can send you a copy to your email account and you can use it later if something might happen to you before you leave."

Julia signed the statement and gave it back to the detectives. They thanked her and let her go. Anton was still around and picked her up. He could see in her eyes she wasn't very happy with the cops.

"So what will happen?"

"Nothing unless he attacks me. Only then they can do something. I need prove evidence that Robby is doing something wrong but I have nothing. I wish I had."

"How about the beating and your hair?"

"That was done by Mr Freak. At least I pressed for charges against him. So if they can spot him anywhere in Sydney he will be taken to a police station and they will interview him. My statement might be enough to send him for some time to prison but I doubt it will ever happen."

Julia sighed and wanted to cry. No tears showed up and she felt so hopeless. She lost her faith in the justice department and wanted to leave Australia as soon as possible.

"I'm sorry, Julia. I wish I could help you but I don't know what to do."

"Can you come with me to the city? I need a place to find where I can stay my last night in Australia. I want someone I can trust and feel safe with so if you don't mind."

"Sure, Julia. Sure."

They left the police station and stopped a taxi when one passed them. She asked the driver to bring them to Hyde Park where she wanted to be for a while. She loved the park and the next one The Domain. From her first day she spent a lot of time and hours and enjoyed the clean and fresh air she smelled while cars passed the parks on the roads. Parks gave her peace in her mind what she just needed.

"What will you do with your hair?"

She smiled while Anton touched a few of the bald spots on her head. It had only been a couple of months that she had her last haircut. Her hair had grown after she had it almost shaved during the Olympic period. It was a crazy moment when she decided to shave it all off. She didn't mind it then but now she thought differently of that extreme look. This time she wasn't ready to go radical but she had to. It was the only thing she could do. This was the moment she wished she had long hair. She would cover her bald spots with her long hair what she had in the past.

"I shall look like Sinead o' Connor, you remember her? On her debut album she had her head shaved and was completely bald. I will do the same and hope my hair will grow back. Otherwise I will keep it shaved."

34 Last fight and humiliation

Julia bought a small backpack for her clothes and new toiletries. She bought some more undies and some proper shoes after she found a place where she could stay for her last night before she would fly out of Sydney. Anton kept her company till he received a call from his father. He had to leave her what they both didn't like. Robby was spotted near his father's house and he was threatening his family. his father didn't like Robby and didn't want to talk to him but only Anton could deal with such situations. He had done it before in the past and it was Anton who stopped him from doing stupid things.

"Sorry, Julia. I have to go. It seems our friend is at my family's house and he's threatening my father."

"Can't he just call the police so he can be picked up?"

"You should have talked to my dad. He might have listened to you but every time I mention it to him he doesn't want to listen to me. I am the only one in the family who can stop him so I have to go home and see what I can do."

"Just call the cops. They can arrest him. He should be locked up and remained behind bars forever."

Julia lost all her interest in the guy she first thought she liked when they met around Christmas time in Bondi. Now they were sworn enemies and he wondered who would be the winner. It looked more like Robby succeeded as she was about to leave the county.

"Can I see you later? Where shall we meet?"

"Meet me at the lobby of the Y in the Park. I will stay my last night in the Y in the Park where I will feel safe. It's a women's hostel and refugee place women with domestic problems. Men are not allowed although there's a floor where men do stay."

"Stay safe, Julia. He's still out there and he will ask me where you are. He might follow me so I would suggest we should meet somewhere else." "No, the hotel will be fine. I will inform the reception. There's security and they will stop him if he tries to enter the place."

Anton left her and took a bus back home. Julia walked with her new possessions and her clean laundry to the Y in the Park. She asked reception if they had a room available for the night and paid cash. She asked for a small safe so she could keep her flight ticket and her passport together with most of her money safe at reception while she would keep only a few bucks in her pockets for whatever she wanted to have in the hotel. She took the elevator to her new room and dropped her stuff in the room.

Again Julia had a room for herself but she still had to share a bathroom and a toilet with other women. There was a little dressing table in the room and coffee and tea facilities in her room plus a little kitchenette on the floor next of the little lounge area where there was a colour TV and some comfortable chairs. No men were allowed on this floor but a few floors below were only for men. She was too close to the men's section of the hotel but it couldn't be helped. It was only for one night and the next day she would be on her way slowly to the airport where she hoped to be safe. Julia changed her clothes and went to the barbers for her dramatic haircut. She didn't want but it was the best thing she could do. There was a barbershop not far away from the hotel and she had been there before when she arrived in Sydney in December 1999. Now she went back again to the same place but this time she would shave her head smooth.

The last couple of days the weather was picking up and it felt warmer than when she arrived a year ago. Dressed in a short dress that she found in a second hand shop in Bondi she walked to the barbershop and looked around while men whistled when they saw her. She looked quite stunning but she wasn't in the mood for being liked. Robby was still out there and who knows. It was busier this time in the big barbershop when she stopped and thought for a moment. She wasn't ready yet but she had to do it. She looked in the glass of the shop window and saw her own image. She touched the bald spots and sighed. It had to be done and she didn't feel any pride in becoming a bald girl. When she arrived a year ago she thought differently about head shaving. Then she actually liked it and thought about it long ago before she had it done. Now she thought differently. She didn't want to loose her hair but there was no option.

"Hi, can I help you, Sheila?"

"Yes, I want a haircut."

It was a different barber who stood in front of the door of the big barbershop. The old man who sat there on his chair wasn't around and it was busy in the shop. She noticed there were even female barbers at work plus even girls in the chairs getting a haircut.

"Sure, we can cut your hair. What happened with it? Who pulled your hair out? Were it you out of frustration?"

"No, someone pulled my hair out when a guy threatened me."

"Did you report it to the police? It looks very serious to me if you ask me."

"I did, thanks."

She walked inside and took a seat on the wooden bench before it was her turn in one of the many barber chairs. She looked around and noticed there were more men than women but it didn't surprise her. It was after all a barbershop and not a hair salon.

Julia thought of Emily who went completely bald. She went to this barbershop and mentioned it to her when they met in the hotel a year ago. She had her short hair shaved to bald and looked ridiculous cool. She looked awesome. Now it was her turn to have her head shaved with a razor. The last cut she had was only clippers and that was during the first week of the Olympics.

"Hello, Sheila. What can I do today with your hair?"

Julia pointed to the bald spot and feared for the worst. He just caped her and combed her short hair.

"You had some trouble with your hair? Some frustration, huh?"

"No, a fight with a big guy who pulled my hair of my head."

"Very nasty. What do you want me to do with your hair?"

"I don't want to think of it but it has to be done. Just shave my head."

"All off and smooth? Can be done."

Julia wanted to cry but the tears didn't want to come. Instead she thought for a while of Robby.

She didn't know why but she felt no sorry for him. First she did but now she had mercy for him. She hoped someone would beat the shit out of him. He deserved a good smack but it wasn't good in thinking so bad about others. She should show some mercy. At least he tried to be nice to her but in the end he screwed her. He screwed everyone. The man was a user.

Robby was out there on the streets. As soon as Anton left Julia he left soon Anton's family's house and went to the city. He believed she would stay for one night either in a hostel or in a hotel. She still had money and she could easily splash out some money with her credit card and stay in some luxurious hotel in downtown city. There were plenty of top hotels where to choose from but then he started thinking. He heard her talking about the YMCA branch and he remembered there was a YWCA on Wentworth Avenue the Y in the Park. He never stayed in that hotel but he remembered Julia mentioned a few times to him that she spent the first couple of nights in that hotel before she moved to Bondi. He met on his way to the Y in the Park a young student who couldn't speak proper English. He pretended to be a cop and let the poor sod pay him all the money he had in his pockets. The kid walked just out of a branch of a bank and had just cashed some traveller's cheques into Aussie dollars. The kid couldn't speak much English and that was all he needed. The kid was afraid of him and gave him whatever he wanted and ran away.

Robby cashed around a thousand bucks and bought some items at Mr Gowings department store. He even had a proper haircut and asked his barber to cut his hair as short as possible. He wanted to look completely different so Julia couldn't recognise him in the streets while he already knew how she would look like. The pulling of her short hair was done on purpose so she had to shave her head. He wanted to see her completely bald as not many women would go so dare. He had no feelings for her and didn't care what would happen to her in the end. All he wanted was her money. Robby went after his new cut to the Y in the Park and asked for a room. He was just very lucky that there was still a room available and like Julia he paid cash for his bed and moved his briefcase and the new things to his room before he went out again. He changed his clothes and looked different. He drank a coffee in the cafeteria and paid attention when he saw a bald woman walking in the lobby. It was Julia and she looked so different. She looked around but didn't recognise Robby.

Julia walked inside the Y in the Park and walked straight to the elevators. She didn't see Robby nor did she pay any attention to a few men who were looking at her. She got in and went to the floor where she had her room. She didn't see Robby but he noticed which floor the elevator stopped. He made a little note on his hand before he got up and walked out.

Anton walked in the lobby when Robby left the hotel. They both looked at each other but he couldn't see Robby's face as he kept it covered with a baseball cap low over his face. He only nodded when he passed his old friend. Robby went to the park in search for another victim. One wasn't enough and he wanted another young and not so smart victim. He found a young Asian girl and managed to steal her wallet out of her handbag that she forgot to close. She carried less money than he had hoped but she had a credit card and the pin number on a little yellow post it in her wallet. He emptied the wallet and threw the rest in the bin when he tested her card at a nearby ATM machine and took out the maximum he could take of her card. Satisfied he lost her card on purpose in another ATM so she would have to call her bank for a new card and had to deal with the losses of money that was withdrawn without her knowledge.

Anton waited for half an hour in the lobby of the hotel when Julia reappeared. She looked so different now she was completely bald. Her skull looked so smooth after the barber shaved her head a few times so she couldn't notice the bald spots. In a couple of months, she would have her hair again but till then she would have to live with her present look. She didn't like it but it was the only solution. She could have kept it covered with a scarf but it was so easy to forget. She could cover her head with a baseball cap but first she needed to buy one what she forgot to do before she went to the barbers. She could have done it afterwards but even then she still forgot to buy a cap.

"What would you do if Robby sees you without your hair?"

"I hope he has money on him so he can pay for the damage."

"You really think he would pay your barber for this cut?"

"He should. Thanks to him I am completely bald. There was no other option than to shave it all off. Now I have to live with this look till my hair grows back on my head. That will take some time before I will have long hair again and I might keep it short as I have done so in the last year."

"Where do you want to eat?"

"I fancy a burger." She said while they walked hand in hand over the pavement towards George Street. "There's a good burger joint next of the cinema. Robby took me a few times to that bar. Let's eat there."

Anton knew the place. It was Robby's favourite burger bar and they made the best burgers in town. Luckily it wasn't so busy so they got a table in the back. Julia sat on purpose with her back to the bar while Anton could see who walked in and out. He tried to spot Robby but he didn't see him. Robby was sitting at the bar but he didn't look up when they walked in. He only checked where they sat and remained on his seat at the bar. He ordered a beer and had his own burger and fries.

"Do you think Robby is here?"

"He might be. This was one of his favourite spots when he is in town. There are a few other places where he might be but he could be back in Bondi but I have so my doubts."

"Why?"

Anton looked in Julia's eyes. Although she was so extreme bald she still looked pretty and he liked her a lot. She smiled back and touched her smooth skull.

"What?'

"Nothing, Julia. I only can say you still are very beautiful."

"Thank you, Anton. Thanks for saying that to me." She started to blush. "I don't know what others might think of me but I don't care. It will grow back again."

"I think Robby is here."

"Why do you think he's here?"

"I think I saw him earlier today but I am not sure. He changed his look like you did so he will be difficult to spot but you look very recognisable.

You have been bald before and he remembered the previous time when you had your head almost shaved."

"Yeah, that was a while ago but I wasn't bald then."

"You were, Julia. You were."

They received their orders and enjoyed a tasty good burger and fries. The food tasted good and it was washed out with a frosty coke. It was the best meal and she would miss this place. She had no idea where she would stay once she arrived in Asia but life would be different. At least there would be no more Robby but it wasn't over yet.

They met Robby when he went to the back for a leek. He looked at her but she couldn't place his face with his new look. He looked so different. She only showed a smile while Anton was thinking. He wasn't so sure if it was Robby or someone else.

Anton paid for the meal and left soon after. Julia followed him. They walked back to Wentworth Avenue where she wished him goodbye. She asked Anton if he could be there on the airport. She would love to see him one more time. The next time would be in her country. She invited Anton long before she would be gone but she hoped one day they could see each other again.

Julia went inside the hotel and went to her room on the sixth floor. Robby followed her from a distance. He carried a newspaper and found out soon which room was hers. She walked out of her room to have a shower. She didn't see him when he hid in the kitchenette when she walked covered with only a towel around her pretty corpse. Robby entered her room. The door was left open so he could sneak in. He searched the place but noticed she didn't have any wallet or money belt in her room. Then he thought of the small safes at the reception. If she kept important belongings like her passport flight ticket and her credit card it must be in one of those safes and he had no access to them. She would know the code and he didn't and he couldn't ask her to give it to him. She might call the night reception for help.

Instead Robby decided to stay in the room and hide behind the long curtains. He hoped she wouldn't open them or the window as he didn't want to stand in the draft of the wind from an open window.

Julia got back in her room and checked the space before she went to bed. She was tired and needed her beauty sleep. The big bed was comfortable and felt warm. She fell asleep pretty fast and didn't pay any attention to the movement from behind the big curtain. She never noticed Robby's presence.

Robby climbed on the bed and laid for a short while next of her. He stared at her body before he grabbed an arm and started to squeeze it hard. He did his best to hurt her so she would wake up. She did and wanted to scream when he covered her mouth with his only free hand.

"You shut up, bitch!"

"Get off me!"

"Give me what I want and I let you go!"

"Never!"

He smacked her face and laughed while she started to cry. He hit her again and again but she didn't crack. He admired her new look and thought of stealing her last remaining clothes so she wouldn't have any clothes to wear. She couldn't run after him if she was stark naked. He hurt her more till she managed to scream very loud. She woke up her neighbours who started to bang loud on their walls.

"I don't know how you got in here but find a way to get out."

"I stay here just like you. I will be fine." He replied back. "My friend should have finished you but he was too sloppy."

"Oh, he did enough damage on me. He's now wanted by the police and if you don't get off me you will be wanted too. I will report you, I promise you."

Robby stood up and gave Julia the hardest punch she ever received in her life. She went down to the ground and felt her head bursting. She tried to stand up but he kicked her hard and kept on kicking till she remained on the floor. He started to laugh while she laid half naked on the floor of her room while he searched her clothes for money and other things. He couldn't find anything as she kept it all in the safe downstairs at the reception.

"I will make sure you won't leave Australia. I will ask a friend to stop you when you think you're safe behind check in. I know enough guys who work there and they can stop anyone. You can run to the cops but hey will not help you. I have no cases running with them so don't try to think you're smarter than me. You can't prove a thing but I can prove what you have caused me. Good luck, bitch and I hope you will rot in hell!"

"The same to you!" Julia replied with a rasp voice. "I surely hope you will have the same."

Robby left quickly before security showed up. She heard some banging on the door and opened. Two security guards stood in front of her followed by her neighbours who had heard enough noise so they complained with downstairs. She let them in and sat on her bed while they looked around.

"So you claim someone entered your room while you had a shower? Didn't you lock your door?" "No, my mistake." She replied. "I left the key card in the socket so the air con would be still working. Besides I don't have a bath robe and no pockets in my top so yeah that's why I kept my door open. There are no valuables left behind in my room so there's nothing interesting to steal really."

"Did you recognise the person? Is it someone you know?"

"Yes, I know him and I reported him earlier today at the police station in Bondi. I will go there tomorrow and report him again as he punched me in my face and he kicked me several times."

One of the security guards gave Julia a glass of water so she could rinse some blood out of her mouth. They saw the damage what Robby had caused and wrote it down.

"Are you ok, Miss? Do you want us to call an ambulance?"

"No, I'm fine. All I want is some sleep. I haven't slept much lately."

"Come tomorrow to reception so we can write a report and give that to the cops. They will be interested in this report and might use it against your friend. Did he say anything else?"

"Yeah, what surprises me he's staying here in this hotel a few floors below me. You should look for the name Robby Henson. That's the guy who did this to me. If he's around have him arrested so I can travel safe and sound out of this country."

"We will check if he's still around. If so we want to have a word with him before we will call the cops. But as you said he hit you and he did his best to hurt you badly the favours will be on you and not to him."

They left and went a few floors below where Robby had his room. They knocked on his door before they opened it. Robby woke up and stared at the two security guards. None of them was armed but they carried smartphones and were connected with their colleagues' downstairs at reception.

"Sorry to wake you up, mate but we have to ask you a few questions."

"Does it have to have to be now? Don't you see I was still asleep?"

"Yes, we know but we want to have a word with you."

Robby got up and got dressed. He took his briefcase with him what he always kept with him as he didn't trust others with his personal belongings. He didn't care about the rest what he left in the room and followed the security guards. They took him to a little office behind the reception and asked him if he knew Julia Meier. Robby didn't deny that he knew her. Yes, she owed him still a couple of thousands of dollars and she never paid him. He admitted he paid a visit to her last night but he never hit her. He lied his way out and walked afterwards free out of the hotel straight in the dark of the night. He didn't want to stay in the hotel and and walked away from the trouble he created.

Julia woke up with a terrible headache and when she looked in the mirror she could see the damage in her face what was caused by the fight she had with Robby. She wondered if he was still in the hotel but then had a horrible feeling he's still out there outside waiting for her. She still wasn't safe and it was her last day in Australia. What could go possibly wrong on her last day in Sydney Australia. She took a quick shower and got dressed. She checked the room before she went for a shower and when she got back she rechecked the room. There was no trace of an intruder so she could dress up for her final day and flight to Southeast Asia.

She took a light breakfast as she still didn't feel fine. She called Anton from the phone booth next of the elevator. It reminded her of Emily who used these phones straight on their arrival a year ago when they both just arrived in Sydney. She called her boyfriend and told her she wanted to meet up with him and his mate. She invited Julia for a couple of pints in the pub what Julia couldn't refuse. She liked the company and actually she liked Emily and her weird friends. They were nice guys from England. She just wondered where they were.

After her light breakfast and the phone call she asked the reception where the nearest police station was. She had a short walk east to Goulburn Street where was the nearest station. She felt disappointed in the Bondi police force who didn't stop Robby while they could have. Now it was the task for the Surrey Hills police force.

35 Leaving Australia

Robby knew a lot of people over the years in Sydney. He had mates everywhere so it wasn't hard for him to meet up with a guy who had a good job on the airport. He still owed Robby a few favours so he was willing to do whatever Robby wanted from him. Robby arrived early in the morning at Sir Kingsford Smith Sydney International Airport and met up with Tony. If there was one guy who could stop Julia from leaving the country Tony was his last hope. He was part of the security team that worked on the airport and his shift was in the late afternoon early evening the right time when Julia was about to leave Sydney.

Tony didn't want to come early to his work but Robby called him and asked him to do him some favours. He couldn't refuse so he showed up. Over a coffee and some donuts Robby explained what he wanted from his friend. He didn't want Julia to leave Australia. The only way he could stop her was to get hold of her flight ticket and passport. It was a dirty trick to stop someone from leaving a country but it was his last resort. If Tony couldn't stop her than all his hope on getting access to her accounts and her credit card would fail dramatically. He wanted her money but she made clear a while ago he had received enough and he should stop begging for more. He was too obsessed with her money and he had done his best to destroy her life in Australia. She had enough of him and wanted to leave Sydney without any further hurdles.

"It won't be easy, mate. Things have changed over the years but I will see what I can do. How can I recognise her? Is there anything special about her so I can pick her up before she slips through your nets?"

"She's bald. Completely bald. I made it happen and her face is somehow bruised. I had to punch her a few times in her face."

"Oh, man that is awful. How can you beat a girl in her face? That's sick, I tell you. You are one sick man."

"Thanks but can you stop her, please?"

"I can't promise you but I will do my best. What

time is her flight?"

Robby signed and wanted to smoke a cigarette. Thanks to the prime minister of New South Wales and the government of Australia he couldn't smoke anymore on the airport. "I don't know. All I know is that she's flying to Malaysia or any other Asian country. I think she's flying with a German airline but I could be mistaken."

Tony checked through a big list of airlines what he carried with him in a little notebook and found a few German speaking airlines. Robby pointed straight away when he saw Lauda Air and mentioned it to his friend.

"Can you stop her from flying with that airline?"

"It will be difficult but I will do my best. I might need to talk with a few employees from that airline and see how I can hold her on the airport. Is there anything else you want me to do?"

"See if you can get access to her luggage. She would be nothing without her luggage, don't you think?"

"Again, not easy to stop someone from travelling but I will see what I can do. I can't make any promises but I will do my best to stop her if I can. If she slips through my fingers than I am sorry but I am no police officer and she's entitled to leave the country. Whatever problem you have with her that's your concern but please don't get me involved in some dirty tricks. I don't want to be part of it."

Tony left Robby and went to see some friends. Robby stayed on the airport and found a perfect spot where he could sit and wait till she would show up.

Julia found the police station and filed another report. The local coppers listened to her and made lots of notes and confirmed her previous statement with the one she signed in Bondi. Her new statement was added and all she could hope now was that the police could stop and arrest Robby for assault and attempt to rape. She had to play a high and dirty game what wasn't her style but she had enough of the guy. The only way to stop him was to come up with these kind of punishments. Assaulting a woman was in a way a serious crime and he would face time if he ever got arrested. She mentioned the other case of what he had done in Hornsby and added that case to her own so he would get convicted if his case ever went to the courts. It would be the end of Robby.

"Thanks for telling this to us. We will use it against him and we will do our best to find him and arrest him as he assaulted you in your room in the Y in the Park. We will consult with the security of the hotel and use their information to build up a case and added to your present case. About the assault in Hornsby we will see what we can do. I would say fingers crossed."

"There's one more thing and it is very important to me. I want to leave this country without any further delay and problems."

"Yes, we do understand. We will inform the airport and put you on a special list so the security on the airport can keep an eye on you so you can travel without any further problems to your next destination."

"That would be most delightful although I still have a bad feeling that Robby might be there on the airport and he will do whatever he can to stop me."

The coppers checked her flight ticket and the time she was supposed to fly out of the country.

One of them called a colleague at the airport and passed her details over to the cops on the airport so she could be leaving the country without any further problems. She was glad she paid another visit to a police station and with this new statement it was now hard for Robby to do any stupid things to her or anyone else. He was now wanted so she felt finally a bit safe. He wasn't arrested yet but the chance would be bigger by the end of the day when she finally was in a plain leaving Australia after a turbulent year. Her trip to Australia was a special journey on his own. She got part in an adventure that no one would ever believe but she was there when it happened.

The last thing Julia did in Sydney was to travel by train to the airport. She could have taken a taxi but she had travelled enough by cab in the city and she didn't mind to travel by train. Thanks to the Olympic Games earlier in the year there was now a better railway link from the city to the international airport just southeast of the city in Mascot. The train was fast and clean and not so crowded.

Anton promised her he would be there for her on the airport but by the time she arrived she couldn't find him. She didn't see Robby but he saw her. He followed her from a safe distance and hoped his friend Tony would do his best to stop her before she would be out of his sight.

Tony saw Julia for the first time and didn't want to help his friend. He didn't like to hurt someone and especially not a woman. He sighed and walked away from his friend. No, it was wrong and he didn't want to loose his job. He didn't and couldn't care about the friendship he had with Robby and took a wise decision. Julia found the check in terminals and searched for her airliner. She read the screens and saw Lauda Air was just open for check in. There was no queue yet so she went straight with all her luggage to the check in counter and showed her passport and her booking with the airliner to the female staff member of the airliner.

"Hello, I have booked a flight with you towards Kuala Lumpur Malaysia."

"Hello, dear. You want a window seat or an aisle seat?" "Window please and how long will it take to board the flight?"

The staff member noticed Julia's hurry. Julia showed the police report to her and explained why she wanted to leave the country so soon. She still feared Robby would do whatever he could to stop her from leaving Australia. He was here he had to be here at the airport and he was probably watching her. She had no idea his new look but didn't care. As soon as she was passed immigration she would be safe. Till then she was still a prey for him.

"Ah, yes. We heard from our superior that you were attacked by a guy who is unfortunately an Aussie. I understand your fear so I suggest go straight to immigration and get checked out. He can't have access to you as long as you are in the duty free zone and when we start boarding the flight. Even if he knows others they wouldn't be so stupid to listen to him. They would loose their jobs and no one wants that to happen."

She gave her big bag as checked in luggage and continued her walk on the airport to customs and immigration. She showed the guys her police report and got cleared in seconds. From that moment she was finally safe from Robby and waited in the duty free zone for her flight to her safety.

Robby saw her leaving and didn't stay much

longer as he couldn't touch her anymore. Julia was gone and escaped from him. She got away and was finally in safety. For him a new chapter started in his miserable life and he had to prepare himself for more trouble from people who used to be his friends. Julia smiled when late in the evening the plane of Lauda Air flew her safe away from what had been an adventurous year in Sydney Australia. Twelve months earlier she hoped she would experience an adventure what would live in her mind forever but she had no idea what would happen. All she wanted to do was to travel for twelve months the six states in Australia and see as much as she could of the big continent what she knew as Down Under. Through her friendship with Robby she had the time of her life in Sydney and from the moment she left Sydney she was glad she met him. Now she was far away and very safe she felt sorry for him and hoped he would pay for all his errors. In a couple of hours time a new life and a new experience was about to start for her....

Epilogue

Robby met Konrad soon after Julia flew away to her destination in Southeast Asia. Konrad was glad she was gone. She had been a wonderful person with a good heart and very helpful to others. Robby missed her not only she helped him with his court case but without her he would be still living on the streets. She gave him hope and helped him with a job but in the end he fucked up as money corrupted his rotten mind.

"She's gone, isn't she?"

"Yes, I saw her on the airport and I wanted to stop her but she was smarter than me."

"She was smarter than both of us. We underestimated her. I hope she's fine and hope she will have a good time in Asia."

Robby nodded and tapped his friend friendly on his back.

"You know, Konrad. She did a lot for me and I was too blind to think of only other things. I didn't pay any attention to her personal feelings. I have hurt them too much, haven't I?"

"A bit late to say it," Konrad replied. "You should have apologised to her before she left the country. She helped me with my personal investigation and without her I would be still guessing who might have done it. Thanks to her I know who were behind I will pay them a visit soon and demand my money back from them."

"What makes you think your money isn't spent?"

"I marked every bill and wrote down on my laptop every serial number so I can see which bank note has been spent and which wasn't. Only around two grand is wasted so not much for the moment but if I don't act fast it might be more."

"And you think you can catch them before the police can stop you?"

"Sure, you will see. I will let you know. In the mean time keep a low profile. The cops are after you and you have a lot to explain to them whatever you did to her. She was never a match for you. Julia was no Suzie and you underestimated her. She beat you and now she's gone. Think of the future and not constant of the past."

Konrad left Robby at the airport. He walked back to his car and drove back to Francis Street. He looked at his empty house and was glad his wife and sister were no longer in his house. They were on their way to Korea and he hoped they would be fine back with their family in Pusan.

Anton wished he could have make it to see Julia off but one pinball machine took too much time to repair and he forgot the time when she was due to fly. By the time he wanted to leave the house it was already evening and Julia was safe and sound in the duty free world where she waited for her flight with Lauda Air to Kuala Lumpur, Malaysia. It landed an hour before it was due to leave and boarding was very fast. Robby saw a glimpse of his friend but couldn't face him. He had done too much damage to all his good friends and he wondered how many true friends did he still have. Konrad was right. Julia was a good girl who did her best to help him with his hard and miserable life. Without he he would be nothing now he was at least a man.

ACKNOWLEDGMENTS

This story is based on my own travel experiences when I travelled to Australia in December 1999 for a year of adventure. I met some awesome people in Sydney Australia and got partly involved in the burglary. Although this story is based on a true event the main of the story is fiction and I hope I did my best not to mention the true names of people I met during my year in Sydney.

www.ingramcontent.com/pod-product-compliance
Lightning Source LLC
Chambersburg PA
CBHW071630260626
47170CB00001B/38